STONESKIN

The Rachel Peng Books

Digital Divide
Maker Space
State Machine
Brute Force

Also by K.B. Spangler

A Girl and Her Fed
Rise Up Swearing
The Russians Came Knocking
Greek Key

STONESKIN

K.B. SPANGLER

A GIRL AND HER FED BOOKS
NORTH CAROLINA

Stoneskin is a work of fiction. Names, characters, places, and events are the creations of the author. Any resemblance to actual persons, living or dead, is entirely coincidental. Additional information can be found at kbspangler.com

Printed by CreateSpace, an Amazon.com Company
Available from Amazon.com and other retail outlets.

For Eli and Mary

In my opinion, the most curious trait about the Deep is its need to communicate. It leaves me little notes throughout the day. I have collected these for the better part of a millennium, even though they are completely unintelligible to me. There may be an order to them, but I cannot see it.

—Williamson, "Notes from the Deep," 16 July 4406 CE

Chapter One

Tembi Moon was eight years old when she fell between the worlds.

This isn't the story of Tembi Moon. This is the story of Tembi Stoneskin, and the story of Tembi Songbird, but it began the day when Tembi Moon fell and woke somewhere…

…else?

There's a universal nature of all alleys, and Tembi Moon had spent enough time in the ones on Adhama to recognize that she was propped up against the wall of an alley the moment she woke. She didn't remember how she got there, or why. There was nothing in her head between waking in her own small bed that morning and finding herself in this…place. (Yes, it was definitely an alley—a thin corridor between two high walls, with piles of what could only be garbage throughout.) But this alley was like nothing Tembi had ever seen, wet and green, a soft carpet of fast-growing plants running across the garbage and up the walls and—

When she looked down, she found they were starting to take her legs.

She gasped and scrambled to her feet. It was slick—everything was *slick!*—and she fell, face-first, into the garbage.

Green tendrils stretched towards her as if to seize her eyes.

This time, she screamed.

Footsteps—she looked up to see wide, thick shoes crashing towards her. Above those, a green-skinned man, whose body was otherwise human until it got to his elbows and then those bent wrong. Tembi tried to find her balance, tried to crawl away, tried to hide under the garbage, but the green man with the huge feet and the wrong kind of elbows caught her up and lifted her out of the muck.

Behind him was a woman, and she was also green and wrong.

Tembi fought him, but the man was strong and it was like punching wood. He spoke in sharp, almost angry tones; then, the woman tried softness, and Tembi recognized a mother's pleading for peace. Tembi searched and, yes, two green children stood behind the green woman, kept from entering the alley by their mother's outstretched hands.

It was the children that did it—Tembi stopped fighting. Their father carried her from the alley and set her down on a flat wooden surface that was mostly clear of the grabbing plants. The mother took out a soft cloth and started to clean the muck from the alley off of Tembi's face, all the while talking to Tembi, smooth and gentle, smooth and gentle.

The green children were younger than Tembi. The larger child made a face at her, his long fingers pricking up to mimic Tembi's own ears. She giggled at the boy; his mother smiled at them both.

They had drawn something of a crowd, green faces with their earthy eyes, all of them staring down at her. Tembi couldn't bear to look at them, so she tried to take in the facts of the street, with the buildings and shops that were so close to those of home, but also not. The doors opened the right way; the windows didn't. There was no metal or stone anywhere she could see, only wood and green-colored plass, and all of this slightly soggy from the damp air. The plants that ran rampant in the alley were trying to eat the street; down the road, two men with long wooden blades were slicing and scraping the plants from the buildings.

*Wooden buildings? Wooden **streets?*** She kept checking the sky to make sure it stayed clear—a single storm would bring every scrap of this town tumbling to the ground.

The mother chased the crowd away with hand claps and gestures that made the boy laugh. Tembi told them her name: she repeated sounds when prompted, and the delight on the little girl's face made Tembi think she had said the child's name correctly. But there was no way to tell them who she was, or where she was from, or how badly she wanted her own mother, not this strange woman whose arms bent the wrong way and who smelled too much like a vegetable.

The green man knelt beside the woman. There was some discussion; the woman inspected Tembi's right hand, then asked Tembi something using s l o w   w o r d s that still had no meaning. The man held up his own hand and tapped his wrist; his children did the same.

Tembi felt as if she was failing, and began to cry again.

More green men arrived. She was transferred from the family's care to theirs: the father took the children and left; the mother rooted herself beside Tembi, and held her hand while she cried.

"Witch," said one of the men. It was one word nearly lost among others, but Tembi's head whipped towards the familiar. He repeated himself; all she recognized was "Witch."

Another green-skinned woman arrived.

No—she *appeared.* Even through her tears, Tembi had been watching the sky, and this new woman was tall enough to be caught in the edges of that. One moment the street around them was clear, and then she...*appeared*...in a cloud of white-and-silver robes.

She has money, was Tembi's first thought at seeing her. Then: *She's a Witch!*

Tembi had never met a Witch, but she had seen plenty of them on the channels. They always dressed like money wasn't real. Some, like this one, had a patch of painted skin twisting from their ear to their collarbone. The paint on this Witch was done up in tree branches, bare winter branches, black skeletons that were stark against her left cheek. These vanished beneath the folds of a white-and-silver scarf the Witch wore loose around her shoulders.

And the Witch herself? She looked angry. Furious. An ageless face with tight eyes. The green-skinned men stepped away; the mother tried to put herself between the Witch and Tembi.

No. That couldn't happen. The Witch was her way home.

Tembi pulled away from the mother, from the men.

The Witch saw her, and the fury that had pulled her eyes tight disappeared. "Hello," she said to Tembi, in Tembi's own language. "I'm pleased to meet you, Tembi Moon. May we take you home?"

Those who were near enough to hear the Witch froze at the sound of her multilayered voice. The Witch was not alone in her body.

But…home.

"How do you know me?" she asked, as she took another cautious step towards the Witch and her unseen rider. "Did you bring me here?"

"Oh." The Witch saw all of Tembi for the first time. "Oh, you poor thing."

Tembi clenched her fists; she was a mess, she knew that. The Witch didn't have to point it out in front of everyone.

"Let's get you some food," the Witch said. The vibrato had left her voice; she spoke gently but with the confidence of someone who expected to be obeyed. She knelt and extended her long-fingered hand.

"Did you bring me here?!" Tembi insisted.

"Me? No," the Witch said. She had an accent now, as if Tembi's language were suddenly awkward in her mouth. "But I will bring you home."

"Promise?"

The Witch almost smiled. "Promise."

That was that. Tembi took the Witch's hand, and, green skin against Tembi's own brown, they walked into the strange city together.

Right before they turned a too-round corner, Tembi glanced over her shoulder. The kind mother from the alley had both of her hands pressed hard against her mouth, as if keeping herself from calling out. Then, the Witch took her down another street of plass and wood and green growing plants, and the woman was gone.

The Witch took her through a door and into a single large

room which smelled of fresh bread. There were many people in the room, eating and drinking all manner of things, and they smiled at the Witch as the two of them passed. Griddle cakes came next. Or, the Witch said they were griddle cakes, and they had the appearance of griddle cakes, but no griddle cake on Tembi's world had ever tasted like straw. Her mother would have slapped her for turning down food, so Tembi ate every bite and ignored how her stomach twisted.

Tembi stared at the empty plate in front of her, and then at the Witch, and then at the room. It was a large room, bigger even than her school back home, with green-skinned people eating at row after row of long wooden tables. Only she and the Witch sat alone; the green-skinned woman who had led them to a smaller private table came by with a pitcher of liquid whenever the Witch's glass ran dry, but otherwise they had eaten in silence.

"Where are we?" she asked the Witch.

"This is Miha'ana," the Witch replied. "The eighty-third planet in Perseus."

Tembi shook her head. "Why do you keep your food here?"

The Witch took a quick breath and asked Tembi if she had ever been to a restaurant before.

Tembi pricked her ears up, holding them as high as she could make them go. "Yes," she said. "Of course I have! It's different on my world, that's all."

"Of course," the Witch said, as the corners of her mouth crept up. "Well, on Miha'ana, we want to make our guests welcome. Would you like to come shopping with me before I take you home? I need new shoes, and I know where we could find some in your size."

Shoes. Tembi hiked up her legs and sat cross-legged on the wooden bench to hide her bare feet. "No, thank you," she said.

"Then will you walk with us, just for a little while?" The Witch was speaking in that melodic two-toned voice again. The sound of it cut straight through the quiet noise: the others in the room fell silent; a couple at the rear of the restaurant jumped up to leave, throwing ceramic chits across the long tables on their way out the door. "We want to talk to you."

Tembi didn't like that, no, not at all. The Witch seemed nice enough, but she wasn't just a Witch, no, not now. What if Tembi said the wrong thing? There was no one else who could take her home, not unless she found a ship and she had no idea how to do that. Ships might as well be the stuff of stories, ideas that only existed in words and images on the channels. Besides, wouldn't a ship need a Witch anyhow?

She suddenly wished she had paid more attention in school.

"I want to go home," Tembi said, and remembered to add: "Thank you."

"Then we will take you home," the Witch said. She stood and placed some of those chits on the edge of the wooden table. "We will take you straight to Adhama, straight to your neighborhood. Right to your doorstep, if you wish it."

Oh. Oh dear. Tembi hadn't considered that. What would happen if she were to appear out of thin air? With a *Witch?!* Old Kayode had nothing to do except watch the streets and gossip. He would never—

"Or," the Witch added, unfolding the white-and-silver scarf as she spoke, "we could arrive somewhere quiet, somewhere just a little ways away from your home, if you don't mind the walk." The scarf went over and around the Witch's head, hiding the painted branches. With her face in shadows, the Witch was also not so…so *green.*

Yes, good—Tembi nodded as quickly as she dared.

"But we've promised to see you home safely, so we will walk with you," the Witch said. "Promise you won't run off and leave us after we've jumped?"

Tembi's own eyes narrowed at the Witch.

The Witch winked at her, and held out her hands.

The girl hopped down from the bench. "Does it hurt?" she asked.

"It's like dreaming," the Witch replied, as she folded her wrong-jointed arms around Tembi.

The galaxy bent around them.

---

they come
mother father
far
far
they come

Excerpt from "Notes from the Deep," 16 July 3616 CE

Chapter Two

Riding the Rails was very much like a dream, if a dream were made of nothing but song and colors and teeth and razor-sharp wings, but Tembi knew what the Witch meant: like a dream, it moved without moving.

This is the Deep, Tembi realized, as ideas pulsed along with her heartbeat. *I didn't think it'd be so pretty.*

"Thank you," the Witch replied in her two-toned voice. "That's very kind of you."

And then Tembi was home.

She knew the scent of her city as soon as the Witch opened her arms and let her go. Dry, almost musty, stone and metal slicing into each other. They had come out of the Deep in another alley, but this one was spotless (as alleys went). The buildings on either side were solid, with strong roofs and shutters open to expose the plass windows. The sun was bright; some of the windows were open—

No. There were too many open windows. Too many shutters for one person to close if a storm rolled in without warning. The people on the street were dressed in robes much like Tembi's, but these were made from thick cloth in bold patterns. Tembi took a few steps from the mouth of the alley and saw the ground was paved in straight lines of gray, but she didn't recognize—

A thick stripe of gold cut through the gray.

Oh, gods! Yes, she *did* know where they were!

"We have to go!" Tembi clutched at the Witch's sleeve. "We can't be here!"

"Tembi?" The Witch sounded amused.

"They'll pop us," she said, as she tried to pull the woman back into the safety of the alley. "We can't be in the gold! We need to hide!"

"Tembi," the Witch said as she knelt so she could meet the girl's eyes. "What's wrong?"

"We can't be in the gold!" Tembi knew she was shaking; she couldn't seem to stop. Her ears had flattened against her head so tightly she could barely hear. "They'll *pop* us," she insisted. "Take us somewhere else! Take me home! Take me home right now! I don't care what Old Kayode thinks!"

The Witch stood and walked out of the alley, straight into the center of the gold stripe.

Tembi nearly screamed.

"Come," the Witch said. "I promised to take you home, and I will. But you promised to walk with me to your house."

"I didn't promise anything," Tembi said. With her ears pressed back along the sides of her head, she couldn't help but hear the whine in her voice.

The Witch raised an eyebrow, and started walking.

Oh, *gods!*

Tembi darted out of the alley, determined to try one last time. "Please, *please* get off the gold stripe—"

Too late.

A lawman, short and round, his long silver popstick slung over his shoulder on a thick leather strap. The law in this part of town wore blue robes over gold; the lawman moved towards the Witch so quickly that the thick fabric churned behind him.

Tembi decided the Witch was on her own. She darted back into the alley, searching for a place to hide. There was...

This alley is too clean!

...there was nothing to hide behind! Which, in Tembi's experience, never happened. Not in an alley! She said the kind of words that would make her own mother cringe as she grabbed a slick metal pipe and climbed as high as she could, just to make it harder for the lawman when he came to pop her.

She clung to the pipe and shivered and looked towards the bright mouth of the alley and—

Nothing happened.

No, wait. Conversation happened.

Tembi forced her ears forward to take in the sounds of the Witch and the lawman. They were speaking too quietly for her to hear their words, but the popstick was still in its sling. Maybe the Witch had agreed to leave? Sometimes the law let you off with a warning if they didn't realize your pockets were full.

"Tembi?" The Witch had returned to the mouth of the alley. The lawman was beside her; he had gathered the bottom of his robes around his boots in a gesture of penance. "You can come out now."

"Why?"

The Witch followed Tembi's voice up the side of the building. "Oh!" she said, as she pressed a long-fingered hand against her lips. Tembi had the sneaking suspicion the Witch was trying not to laugh. "Come down, then. The lawman would like to say something to you."

"Msichana, I apologize." The lawman had rolls of fat beneath his chin, and these bobbled as he spoke. "I didn't mean to give you a scare."

Tembi stared at the lawman. He didn't sound sorry, but lawmen never did.

"The lawman is busy, Tembi." It was the note of irritation in the Witch's tone, soft and subtle but nonetheless there, that got Tembi moving. She slid down the pipe and joined the Witch.

This close, Tembi could see the lawman's skin was smooth from easy living. In her part of the city, the law had skin as thick as tanned hide and twice as rough. She wondered if this round little man had ever been in a fight, or a chase, or anything more difficult than walking up and down a gold stripe along the road.

The lawman watched Tembi with dark eyes. His own ears were tipped backwards, as if a storm were coming in and he knew the dust was about to roll over him. "Where do you live, msichana? In the Stripes?"

"No. In Tuff," she replied.

He nodded, and turned his attention away from her, back to the Witch.

Good. The lawman had been right: she didn't live in Tuff; she lived down in the Stripes, in the neighborhood of Marumaru. No thin-skinned lawman from Gold needed to know that.

There was more discussion between the two adults. Tembi didn't join in, but she drank in their conversation like water on a dry day. The lawman was all but bowing to this green alien woman and...

...Tembi couldn't be sure, but the Witch still had her head covered by that scarf, and...

...yes!

The lawman didn't know the Witch was a Witch!

How? If the Witch had thrown back her scarf and shown off those painted winter branches, then yes, of course the lawman would bow. The law would scrape along on the ground for a Witch. But this?

No.

This made no sense to her. None at all. When the Witch and the lawman parted ways, Tembi followed her. The Witch was walking in the general direction of Marumaru, not even caring if her feet touched upon the gold stripe running along the road.

After some time in silence, the Witch glanced down at Tembi. "They have this on other worlds, did you know?" She pointed towards the gold stripe, and then held up her right hand. "If you have an Identchip under your skin, it tells the officers you're someone who belongs, not someone who should be... What did you call it? Popped?"

Tembi nodded.

"Have you ever been popped?"

Tembi touched a spot on her left shoulder. It was covered by her robes, but the skin was still thick from where a lawwoman had set her stick. Tembi had been caught picking pockets; she could still remember the shame of lying in a pool of her own urine, unable to move until the effects of the popstick wore off.

"No," she told the Witch, her chin and ears high.

"I was born in a place very much like this." The Witch sighed as she gestured to the too-tidy buildings around them. "My parents named me Pihikan, their oldworld way of saying I was a baby girl who would grow to become a soft, gentle delight.

"When I was taken from my home and put in school, I chose the name Matindi," she said. "You can call me that instead."

Tembi didn't much enjoy this new knowledge that the Witch had a name. It was like bumping into your teacher when you were both on your way to the public water supply—maybe you knew, deep down, they were just like you, but the reminder set your teeth on edge.

(Besides, at the heart of it, the name Matindi sounded very much like the name Tembi, with lots of sharp short vowels piled on top of each other, and there was a question rolling around in that comparison which the girl wasn't ready to ask.)

They walked along the gold stripe until it was joined by first a red stripe, then a blue one, then that shade of disgusting crimson that the Witch—Matindi—called maroon. The buildings grew shorter and rougher, and Tembi began to recognize landmarks here and there along the roads. Her steps grew eager; Matindi's slowed.

"I can find my own way home from here," Tembi promised the Witch. The green-skinned woman was drawing more attention the deeper they went into the Stripes. She was not talking half as much as before, but when she did, she seemed to be arguing quietly with herself in that two-toned voice. It was beginning to chew on Tembi's nerves.

"One last favor," Matindi said in something of a rush. "Do you have frozen cream on this world?"

"Don't you know?" Tembi was surprised. She had decided the Witch knew everything about everything. She had made the lawman step down, even!

"The Deep doesn't have any need for food," Matindi said. "So while it might not care about sweets, I certainly do. I try them on each world I visit. Would you share some with me?"

Tembi's stomach turned over in its need to cleanse itself of those false pancakes. "Well…"

"You could show me your favorite restaurant." The Witch was

staring at the sky. "I would pick up the cost, of course. To thank you for such an interesting day."

Well. That was different! Of course Tembi knew a place to buy frozen cream! It was a quick run back the way they had come, and a couple sharp turns up the blue stripe. The frozen cream parlor was a blaze of pink and purple in the middle of a row of shops, and children running wild with distraction within.

Another group of children sat on the curb outside the shop. They were younger than Tembi, and watched those who went in and out with too much hope on their faces. There were almost enough of them to call the law down for a fast chase-off; Tembi hoped they knew better than to stick around.

The shop was cool, with fans spinning the hot air up through glossy black vents. When she and Matindi entered, the adults turned to watch the green-skinned woman with her enormous feet and her white-and-silver clothes. Some of them, the ones who looked like they did business up in the gold, nodded to her.

The children in the shop noticed Tembi. Some of them laughed.

Tembi memorized their faces. She knew where they played after school; their too-soft skin needed some pounding. She tipped her chin and ears up again, and walked straight to the counter, ignoring the queue. "You want mango," she told the Witch. "We eat mango here. And chocolate. And vanilla. But not together. Ackee and salt—*those* go together!"

The Witch ordered ten different flavors.

(When Tembi asked how she had paid, the Witch explained she had swiped the Identchip in her wrist across the counter so the clerks could take credit from her account. Tembi had stared at her until the frozen cream had arrived, her mind blown apart at learning about the existence of this...this *magic!*)

The servers brought their orders to the table, smiling at the green-skinned woman, and even nodded politely to Tembi! As they sat at a shiny metal table in the center of the restaurant, surrounded by scoops of frozen cream on cold stone tiles, Tembi didn't mind at all that the children were still watching her.

Tembi tried every flavor. Most of them twice. The mango and the vanilla, those she ate until the spoon scraped across the tile.

Matindi tried most of them too, but kept returning to the ackee. It was different, she said, and that was rare enough in the galaxy for a Witch. She was still very quiet, but at least she had stopped muttering to herself—when Tembi asked what was wrong, she said she was enjoying the experience.

As Tembi put her spoon down, full to bursting, she heard Matindi mutter, "I'm getting to it!"

"What?"

"How old are you, Tembi?" the Witch asked quickly.

"Eight," she replied. "My birthday was last month."

"Oh, you are out of your mind!" Fury, almost as fierce as when she had first appeared in the street back on Miha'ana, snapped Matindi's eyes tight once more.

Tembi jumped down from her chair, ready to run.

"No, Tembi, stop!" The Witch dropped her head into her hands. "I'm not angry with you, no. Gods, no! This is…

"Come," the Witch said, standing. She left the store, her robes snapping as she moved past the children still gathered on the curb.

Tembi followed. She wasn't sure why. She caught up with Matindi at the first corner, and the Witch paused to allow the girl to fall into step with her.

"I'm sorry, Tembi Moon. I don't know how to talk to you about this," Matindi said. "Do you know what a Witch does?"

"You make the Deep take you anywhere you want to go," Tembi said.

Matindi made a pained face. "Yes," she said. "I suppose… Yes, that's one way to look at it. And do you know why Witches are important?"

"Because you talk to the Deep," Tembi said. "I just said that."

"Do you know what a supply chain is?"

The girl's first thought was that the Witch wanted to know where to buy jewelry, but that made no sense, so she stared at her own feet and didn't say a word.

"You don't choose to become a Witch," Matindi said. "The Deep chooses you. And the Deep doesn't choose many people to become Witches.

"Once I was just a normal girl," Matindi continued. "Just like you. The Deep found me, and it wanted to be my friend."

No. Oh no, oh *no*, Tembi didn't like this conversation *at all!* She began to kick an empty carton down the road. It bumped across the marbled white stripe that marked the boundary of Marumaru.

"I had to go to a special school for many years." The Witch was still talking. "I had to train my mind to understand how to talk to the Deep. And there's much—*so* much!—a Witch needs to know about how the galaxy works, and—

"Tembi." Matindi dropped to her knees in a swirl of white-and-silver cloth. "I was older than you—I was fourteen years older than you when the Deep chose me! I had the chance to be a child, and…and…"

Tembi began to cry.

"I can't do this," the Witch said softly.

There was a quick rush of air.

When Tembi looked up, Matindi was gone.

---

choice away
choice fight

Excerpt from "Notes from the Deep," 9 March 3294 CE

Chapter Three

The homes in Marumaru were boxes, metal containers that had begun their lives on starships. Once emptied, these were moved from the docks to the edges of the city, then piled on top of each other and bolted together to form a stack, five, six, sometimes seven units high. The Moon family lived at the top of a stack: their unit had a small weather cage over a garden on the roof, and a window that faced the city below. Tembi ran up the street, raced to the top of the stack, threw open her door, and found...nothing.

She had expected...something. It shouldn't be possible to disappear and reappear across the galaxy—twice!—without... something. But even though Tembi waited patiently on her doorstep for her family to find her, her mother got home from work as she usually did, and then her sisters got home from work as they usually did, and Tembi realized it had all happened within the space of an afternoon and she hadn't been missed at all.

Had it happened? She had nothing to prove that she had gone to Miha'ana or met a Witch or eaten straw-flavored griddle cakes. There was a paper napkin from the store where Matindi had bought frozen cream, but Tembi had picked up enough of those from the streets without any involvement from a Witch. She kept working up the courage to go back and ask if a green-skinned woman had come in with a little girl, and kept turning away when she caught sight of the other children begging in the street.

It didn't take too much for Tembi to convince herself it had all been a dream. In fact, when she went to bed at nights, she felt as if she were still dreaming: the Deep, all of its beautiful multicolored self, came and sang to her. She never saw more than a small part of the Deep at once—it was too vast, and her mind couldn't catch the whole of it. It was never more than a leg, or a wing, or a wide, broad back, and never ever any part of its face. But its songs? Those were always complete and clear. It sang her stories about faraway places, with heroes who fought battles, and heroes who kept battles from being fought.

(The Deep kept insisting the latter were the more important of the two, but they made for dull dreams.)

Weeks passed. Tembi went to school when it was in session, and ran in the streets with her friends when it wasn't. They rolled marks and picked pockets, and sold what they stole to Mad Ysabet behind the markets. And sometimes, when her frustration about the Witch and the trip to Miha'ana became too much for her to bear, she would go out and fight with anyone who made the mistake of thinking a skinny little girl would be an easy toss.

When the storms beat down and the channels stopped working, Tembi would hide at home and reread the old book with glossy paper pages, the one with the images of the planets in the Orion Arm. She always stopped on the page with the planet carved from unmistakable greens and blues.

Earth.

It had been renamed Earth Prime, and then Old Earth, and then a mess of complicated designations as its children tried to puzzle out the new shapes of their galaxy. But, inevitably, it shrugged off the cumbersome names and went back to its roots. It was, and would always be, Earth.

At night, in her dreams, the Deep showed her every planet except Earth.

There was a library in the Stripes. Not the nicest place, to be sure, but one of her sisters worked nearby and knew some of the local law enough to ask them to keep an eye on her. Tembi started reading what she could about Earth, and the other worlds down in Orion. After that, she found Perseus, and then located Miha'ana. The library had a rickety old public information 'bot, and it helped her turn the leagues between Miha'ana and her own home planet into numbers she could understand. That night, she climbed through the window and lay on her back in the family garden, trying to see the stars.

There was no way of knowing where that path would have led, as Tembi went to school the next morning and found that her teacher had been replaced by a green-skinned Witch.

Matindi walked into the classroom with Tembi's old teacher in tow. She was wearing another scarf over and across her head, this one in dull reds and browns. The painted branches had been scrubbed away. Her robes were red and local, and she wore no shoes on her too-large feet. She stood beside the old teacher and smiled at Tembi, as she did the other students. As if the girl was just another body in a seat. As if she hadn't brought Tembi sixteen thousand lightyears—

The Witch winked at Tembi.

Oh!

Tembi sat a little taller and listened to her old teacher talk about unforgettable opportunities in other cities, and cultural exchange programs, and the problems of finding local (Emphasis on *local*—please *please* **please** tell your parents this is only a temporary arrangement!) replacements this late in the term. Then, Tembi's old teacher went to sit in the back of the classroom to make sure this strange creature wouldn't devour his former students on her first day.

"Well," Matindi said, and pushed up the sleeves of her robes to show her wrong-jointed elbows. "Let's get this out of the way."

The Witch put her arms behind her back, then swung them up and over her head in an impossible motion which set the students to squealing. Then, she placed one of her bare feet on the teacher's desk. "Why am I green?" she asked. "And why are my feet so big?"

The class giggled.

"One word," Matindi said. "I know you know it. It's in all the fictions on the channels."

Isaac, a boy who made nothing but trouble and bruises for Tembi, shouted: "Terraforming!"

"Very near," the Witch said. "First comes terraforming, then comes bioforming." She pointed to the display screen at the front of the classroom. A planet appeared, mostly browns and blues. "This is my world, Miha'ana, when humans found it."

The image of the planet shifted to green with dense streaks of blue. "This is what it looks like now," she continued. "Terraforming can bring a planet very close to Earth-normal, but it's nearly impossible to get it exact. There will always be something about a planet that makes it uncomfortable for an Earth-normal person to live there.

"Once terraforming is done, you bridge that distance with bioforming. An Earth-normal human body is changed just enough to make it so we can live comfortably on an alien planet."

She bent her arms over her head again, and the class squealed anew.

"Sometimes it takes a lot of work to live on a new world," she said. "What do you think Miha'ana is like?"

"Green!"

"Weird!" That was Isaac again; the other children giggled.

Tembi remembered those moments of panic when she slid around the quick-growing plants in the alley. "Wet?"

"Yes!" Matindi pointed to Tembi, the briefest acknowledgment, then moved her attention across the classroom again. "Miha'ana had more deep underground water stores than expected. When terraforming brought that water to the surface, the local vegetation had new opportunities to grow. It became aggressive—so aggressive that the settlers who paid to have the planet terraformed decided to sell it instead of moving there.

"My ancestors couldn't afford a planet that was closer to Earth-normal. They bought Miha'ana and paid to have their genes bioformed instead. They allowed themselves to be changed to give their children a chance at a better life."

"Are you a plant?" Not Isaac this time, but one of his friends.

The Witch took the boy's question with levity. "Our green pigmentation began to emerge several generations after my people moved to Miha'ana, so no, I am not a plant," she replied. "I do have some biomarkers to warn the plants on Miha'ana that I'm dangerous to them, and that's how our green pigmentation emerged, but it's a little too early in the day for the lesson on allelopathy. Instead, why don't you tell me about your world?"

The students were happy to talk about their home world. Adhama, beautiful Adhama, at turns dry and rainy in their proper seasons, with windstorms that ripped across the planet. When those storms passed through, it was time to *hide!* They showed their new teacher how they could move their long ears to protect their hearing in case of blowing dust, and how their skin could harden in response to threats. Isaac tried to drop a chair on his hand to prove it; their old teacher, who knew something like that was coming, intervened.

And then they were learning about the distance between their two worlds, and lightyears, and the distance between each of their worlds and Earth, and only Tembi—who had done this on her own as a form of curious self-defense—realized that this strange green woman had gotten them excited about maths!

The next day, their old teacher showed up with two of the children's parents.

The day after that, Matindi had the school to herself.

Schools in the Stripes were slapdash creations. Up in the gold section of the city, schools had entire buildings to themselves, and classrooms with a teacher in each. There were grades and designations and classes set aside for art and (Tembi had heard, but she could not believe) *music!* In the Stripes, schools were started when there was a critical mass of demand and available space. Tembi's old teacher had taught three dozen students, some younger than Tembi, some nearly old enough to set off for whatever work that would have them. Their classroom was two units wide, with the joining wall cut out to form an awkward rectangle. There were windows, because a long-forgotten somebody had added them, but their old teacher had kept them sealed with their shiny metal shutters, because he was lazy.

Their strange green teacher never insisted, never demanded.

All she was, at first, was different, and she knew how to push back when Isaac and his friends went to work. She didn't insist on changes to her classroom, but they seemed to happen in spite of that. The windows were opened to let in the air; the previous day's best two students were appointed storm watchers, and they were awarded the seats nearest the windows to keep an eye on the sky. The display screen finally died; somehow, there was money to replace it with a newer holoscreen. The holes in the roof that had been covered over with layers of patching gel were repaired with heavy metal plates. A weather cage was built around a small patch of bare earth just outside the door; the ground beneath it was tilled up and fertilized, and the students planted an ackee sapling bred to thrive on Adhama.

It was a lovely time in Tembi's life.

Matindi taught them what she could, when she could. Meditation, history, and art joined the practical skills of reading, languages, and arithmetic. There were trips up and down the Stripes, and the older students found employment, apprenticeships...

Tembi never spoke to her new teacher about Witches, or past adventures. Not at school, where everyone could hear. But at night, in her dreams, they spoke about everything.

"At some point," Matindi told her late one night, as the Deep sang to them and moved their minds across the galaxy, "you'll have to go to Lancaster."

The Deep's singing stopped.

"She will," the Witch said with a sigh. "You know that. She'll hit adolescence and know everything about everything, and then there'll be no keeping this a secret any longer."

"I'm sitting right here, Matindi. What's Lancaster?"

"It's where Witches go to train," the green woman replied.

Tembi thrilled to that idea. Her fear that she would become (or already was? Matindi could be frustratingly short with the details) a Witch had bled away through these dream-discussions, replaced with eagerness to learn all she could about this strange new life of hers. A school for Witches! A real school!

Blue sorrow from the Deep; cold emotion from Matindi.

"It sounds wonderful, I know, but it's not what you think," Matindi said. "They take young people and train them to hear the Deep, yes, but they're trained to hear the Deep in a very specific way. And the other Witches… Tembi, you don't want to go to Lancaster. Not now. Not until you know your own self well enough to fight back. If you can't—" The Witch made a noise that was very unWitchlike and flopped backwards to rest against an especially comfortable shade of gray. "I am *so* bad at this!"

They had, through trial and error, learned that Tembi could remember what the Deep said in the dreams if Matindi spoke for it. The Deep's two-toned voice flowed from Matindi in layers of sadness, and the colors around them turned a deep violet. "I brought her to you," the Deep said through its Witch. "Don't make her go."

"You're too much, beautiful beast," Matindi replied in her own voice. "I can keep her safe until she's older, but can't give her what she needs to take you on. Not alone. Lancaster will help her learn how to talk to you.

"You know that," Matindi repeated, as if talking to a child much younger than Tembi.

More sorrow from the Deep, with a note of oh-so-petulant acceptance.

Usually, Tembi loved to watch Matindi and the Deep bicker. It reminded her of how she and her sisters shared space within their small unit, pushing against each other with words instead of fists. This time, though? The Deep kept swinging itself around and around, as if unable to rest. As the two of them were riding in the Deep while it was also riding along them in their minds, this was rather unnerving.

"Stop it," Matindi said, swatting the air around them. Colors blurred into feathers around her hands, and the Witch mimicked scratching a cat behind its ear. The Deep rolled over and quelled. "Quit making new problems."

The Deep used Matindi to say something quite foul; the

woman slapped her hands over her own mouth, her brown eyes wide. Tembi tumbled through the colors, laughing.

"Enough, enough!" Matindi used her teacher's voice, which was very different than anything the Deep could muster. The Deep curled up around Tembi, bleeding silver and soft contentment. "Lessons, my dear little problem-makers. Lessons. More meditation, I think—we all need to know how to stay calm within the storm."

It was a lovely time in Tembi's life; she liked to think it was for Matindi, too.

It lasted three years.

When she turned eleven, the Deep betrayed them both.

mother father
come
come
help me
help you

Excerpt from "Notes from the Deep," 28 September 4181 CE

Chapter Four

The end of that lovely time began with a trip to the docks.

Adhama had one moon, but it was a crumbling mess good for nothing but keeping the tides on schedule. Instead of investing in its stability, or building an orbiting platform around it, the local governing councils had decided to build planetside docks. One of these wasn't too far from Tembi's city, just a short flight away by hopper.

Most of the students hadn't been on a hopper before. They took a beat-up bug that shook a little too much in midair. The plass windows were scratched so badly that no amount of polish would bring them back to clear, and the seats smelled of... feet.

Still.

Tembi and her classmates zoomed about the hopper. The parents who had come along as chaperones would try to impose some semblance of order, shouting or waving their hands, sometimes bobbing in their own seats.

Matindi, who never raised her voice unless accidental death was imminent, merely watched the ruckus and sipped tea from an old metal bottle with a little smile on her lips.

The hopper flew through a weather cage and landed on a dock sized for a vessel many times larger than itself. It was a wide open space within three walls, with the missing wall protected by a weather field so shipping and fishing vessels could come inside the safety of the human-made harbor. The students leapt out and spilled across the room like ball bearings, followed by the chaperones, and several commuters unlucky enough to catch an earlier flight. Matindi brought up the rear, her brown robes swirling in the air cast by the anti-grav lifts around the landing platform.

"All right, your attention, please," she said, clapping her hands. The students fell into rough order. "We are guests and are here to learn. Anyone who does not act like a guest *and* a student will spend the rest of the day in a bathroom, where your time will be at least somewhat productive." Only the chaperones laughed; the students knew it wasn't an idle threat. "Stay with your assigned chaperones. No one is to get lost or ship themselves across space."

Tembi snuck over to her chaperone, a harried man whose son was named Escher. Escher was two years younger than Tembi and prone to daydreams: Tembi was sure she had been assigned to this group because Escher's father would spend most of the day making sure that his son didn't fall into heavy machinery.

"Watch," Matindi had told her in last night's dream. "Tomorrow, watch everything, no matter how inconsequential it seems. This is what you need to know—the hands-on part of working with the Deep."

Dream-Tembi had nodded, eager. Around her, the Deep fluffed itself in a rainbow of excited noise.

"Remember the rules," Matindi had said. "Don't talk to anybody outside of the class. Don't say anything aloud, unless you have a question that any student would ask. And if you see another Witch?"

"I put on my 'kit and pretend to sing along."

(Tembi both loved and hated her soundkit. It was secondhand, and the earcuffs were designed for Earth-normal humans: if she moved her ears too much, they fell off and bounced away. But it had been a gift from her mother and sisters, and it gave her music!)

"Good. Why?"

"Because young Witches are taken to Lancaster as soon as they're found."

They had talked about this. They had talked about this a *lot*. Lancaster was an inevitability, yes, but they had decided that Tembi should go when she was fifteen. That would make her the youngest Witch at the school, but not too young to begin the next phase of her life learning the skills she needed to work with the Deep.

Now," Matindi had said, "I know bribery is a terrible teaching tool, but I'm going to use it anyhow." She held up a sound chip. There were no markings on it; Matindi had not bothered adding those details to the dream, but her intention was there regardless. "You get through the day without calling attention to yourself, and this is yours."

"Who is it?" Tembi asked, trying to catch any sign of what might be on the disk.

"A talentless shrieking pretty person," Matindi sighed. "One of your favorites. It's a live performance, too, so—"

The Deep had thrown irritation into their minds, and its song took on another chord.

"Yes, yes, you're the prettiest singer of them all," the Witch said. "But I'm trying to bribe Tembi into good behavior here!"

The girl had grinned at her teacher and rolled onto her chest. The Deep appeared beneath her in clouds of rainbow feathers, and she tickled its sides until it wiggled and its song rang out as a cascade of chimes.

Now, this morning at the docks, Tembi still felt the Deep around her. It was harder to feel its presence in the waking world than in the dreams, but Matindi had said its attention would be concentrated at the docks as it worked with the local Witches. Tembi wished she could reach out and pet it, maybe tell it how happy she was to be here—

—a nudge at her back from something unseen—

—a flutter of color at the edge of her senses—

Tembi kept the grin from touching her face, and followed Escher's father and the rest of her class into a large room. The plass windows were opaqued and there was nowhere to sit; the students ran about in the darkened room, wild creatures in a cage.

(Tembi made sure to follow Matindi's directions and act exactly like her classmates so as not to arouse suspicion, and anyhow Isaac had tried to punch her and she was not about to let him get away with *that*.)

A man entered through an opposite door. He was older, with a dusting of white hair against his brown scalp, and was wearing a Spacers' uniform of a heavy black jacket over black pants. The grounding plates in his boots rang against the metal floor with each step, and the…the…*authority!* of that sound quieted the students almost immediately.

"Welcome, welcome," he muttered, both hands lost inside a satchel that was slung across his shoulders. He found what he was looking for: a gray tab, thin as paper, which he flipped around in his hands until it beeped awake. "Okay, ah… Madam…Green?" He looked up and noticed Matindi for the first time.

"My surname does not move easily from the tongue," the Witch said demurely.

"Ah, yes, very good," the Spacer said, as if a green woman with a false name was an everyday occurrence. And perhaps it was, even this far off the Earthbound shipping lanes. "Welcome, everyone. First time here?"

The class bleated a yes.

"Good, good, I remember taking this tour when I was your age. Wouldn't it be something if you ended up working here?"

The students giggled. Work was for *old people*. You didn't begin working until you were a *teenager!*

The Spacer shared a glance with Matindi and the chaperones. "I know," he said. "But maybe it'll be an option someday. So…" He pressed a button on his tab, and the plass windows shimmered to let in the view of the docks below. They were built on the same model as the dock on which the commuter hopper had landed: the enormous room had three walls, with the fourth open to the ocean but protected by a weather cage. "We're not the biggest or the busiest dock on Adhama, but we get the most diverse traffic. There's a big demand for shaa fish on most worlds, and the rich folks from hundreds of planets'll pay plenty to get it fresh. We get small ships in and out all day."

As if to prove the Spacer right, the open air above the dock was instantly filled by a grayish craft. The plass windows rattled from the sudden air displacement, and the children squealed.

Tembi realized that outside of the channels, she had never seen a real spacecraft. It was flatter than she would had expected, and hung like a thick saucer in the air. With a rush of its jets, it lowered itself to the platform below. As soon as it landed, a series of doors along its edge opened, and Spacers and dock-hands began to exchange cargo.

"As you can see, we're all about efficiency here," the Spacer said. "This is a cruiser-to-ground transport. We load the imports off, then we load the exports on, and we get the ship back into space. Everything has a place, and if part of the system breaks down, it causes problems down the line."

The Spacer talked them through the loading process, which sounded especially dry despite its reliance on the ocean around them. Tembi watched the dance of machines and workers on the dock below, and tried to feign disinterest.

It was easier than she had thought it would be. These were just…*things*. Boring, irrelevant *things*. In spite of Matindi's warnings, Tembi had wanted to see another Witch. Not that she would have said anything! She would have just…watched. Like Matindi had said to do.

"C'mon, this way," the Spacer said, and led them out the side entrance to the shipping platform below.

The workers had filled the docks with a frighteningly massive quantity of shaa fish, each of the fish in different shades of bright red with four eyes on the very top of its head. The fish had been packed in stasis fields contained in cubical frames, with three centimeters between each fish to keep them from damaging each other during their journey. Tembi thought the cubes looked like militarized aquariums.

"Why do people want *those*?" Isaac asked, quite loudly. "They taste like mud."

The Spacer ignored him.

The class stayed behind a yellow line painted across the edge of the loading dock. It was hard to see what was happening;

they had had a better view of the action from the observation room above. The noise of the place was deafening; Tembi and her classmates flattened their ears, and Matindi pressed her hands against the sides of her head.

It was also slippery; the weather shield serving as the room's fourth wall kept out the worst of the wind and the flying debris, but air and mist could pass. The ocean was happy to oblige, and the floor and walls were damp. The Spacer was the only one in their group who could walk without his arms outstretched, as the grounding plates in the soles of his boots grabbed the floor with each step.

Well, not just the Spacer. Matindi looked very much at home, dancing along the slick floors on her oversized feet.

"Grace is where you find yourself," their teacher said to no one in particular.

They paused so the Spacer could yell at them about shipping lanes. Tembi's attention shot away and landed on the cube full of fish beside her, four hundred empty red eyes staring at her. She poked the cube—honestly, she couldn't *not* poke it—but while her fingertip broke the surface of the stasis field, nothing happened to either her finger or the fish inside. She snuck a glance at Escher's father to make sure he was preoccupied with his son, and then stuck her entire hand into the field.

It was cold inside the cube. Tembi had thought the stasis field would feel like water, or at least be as damp as the loading dock itself. The weather cage around the family garden was a type of stasis field, but the temperature inside the cage was always the same as the outside environment. In the cube, it just felt…cold.

She touched the nearest fish. It bobbled around a little, then came back to center.

"Kid."

Tembi looked up to find a dock worker glaring at her. She yanked her hand out of the stasis cube. "I wasn't doing any—"

The worker hoisted the cube onto an anti-grav lift cart and moved it away without another word.

Tembi rejoined her classmates, brushing away the cold of the cube on her robes.

"All of this is thanks to the Deep," the Spacer was saying. "Do you know what the Deep is?"

"Energy," said one of her classmates.

"Sentient energy," the Spacer clarified. "It's found in the inter-planetary and interstellar medium, and doesn't go beyond the edge of the Milky Way. So while we can use the Deep to travel across the galaxy, we can't use it to move beyond that point."

One of the chaperones asked, "How does that work? If it's sentient, where does it keep its brain? Does...does it have a brain?"

If a brain can be an entire galaxy, Tembi thought, and knew the Deep was laughing just beyond the range of her senses.

"Some scientists think the Witches are its brain," the Spacer said.

Tembi couldn't hear the Deep huff its annoyance, but when she looked at Matindi, her teacher was hiding her smile in the folds of her headscarf.

The Deep.

It wasn't human—it wasn't anything close to human. Tembi had figured that out for herself years ago. And Matindi said that most fully trained Witches didn't spend time with the Deep in their dreams. Instead, the Deep and the Witch shared space in the Witch's mind, which (Matindi said) made the Deep seem more human.

More manageable.

Yes, the Spacer might think of the Deep as part of a Witch. That made sense. He could talk to a Witch—he couldn't talk to energy.

(He couldn't tickle it until it turned itself into bubbles and drowned you in laughter.)

(He couldn't see its ideas of planets yet unknown, or unborn.)

(He couldn't sing along with it until the sun came up.)

Tembi felt very sad for this man who thought he knew how things worked.

"The Deep has always been there," the Spacer said. "A long

time ago, scientists from Earth discovered patterns in deep-space waveforms. They thought this might be a signal from an alien civilization, but it turned out to be a part of space itself. They started talking to it, and they learned it could be used to transport people and ships all over the galaxy."

"Why?" asked one of the students.

"Once an object goes into the Deep, it no longer exists in normal space-time. It can enter at one point in the galaxy and exit at another."

That's not what she asked, Tembi thought to herself. *She asked why, not how.*

(Not that the Spacer would have had an answer. It was a question which Tembi had asked the Deep herself in a dream—*Why do you do this for us?*—after Matindi had described how an entire process of galactic colonization had sprung up around its generosity. The Deep hadn't used Matindi to answer in words Tembi could hear. Instead, it wrapped itself around Tembi in soft emotions and sang to her in feelings of endless lonely time and space, and she had pressed her face against its colors and wept.)

"Where are the Witches?" Isaac asked.

This time, the Spacer answered him. "Around," he said, as he led them into a hallway. It was quieter here; Tembi and her classmates let their ears return to normal. "They're busy and don't have time to talk to us. This building is built like a wheel, with seven more docks like the one you just saw. Every ship that comes through here needs to be coordinated by a Witch.

"This facility is small, like I said," the Spacer continued. "So we only have five Witches working here at all times. Some of the larger facilities on this planet need up to twenty."

Five Witches! Tembi's head whipped around, as if hoping a strange Witch might appear in the hallway with them. *Five!*

The Spacer took them to a large lift. "This is the center of the wheel," he said. "All of the control operations happen here."

The lift started at the docks with walls of metal, but these turned to clear plass as they went up. As they rose through the complex, each floor seemed more brightly painted than the one below. When the lift stopped, the Spacer pressed another button on his tab, and a gray cloud of nanobots dropped from the ceiling and descended on the lift's occupants.

"Cleaners," he said. "Not the prettiest 'bots, but they're efficient. The folks on this level don't like visitors who smell of fish."

The students squealed; some started to thrash. Tembi stared at the gray film made from mote-sized robots crawling across her body and reminded herself they *weren't* insects, that *everyone* outside the Stripes used cleaner 'bots, that it was just part of normal life and *not creepy at all—*

And then the cloud lifted back into the ceiling and was gone, just like that.

The students looked at each other and started to giggle.

Tembi's skin was slightly sore, as if she had scratched herself a little too hard. She checked her robes; the dust that always collected around the hem was gone, although the tiny stain left over from a tomato sandwich was still there.

"Don't worry about your makeup," the Spacer said to one of the chaperones. "They're murder on hair products and cosmetics, so they've been set to ignore those.

"Ready?" he asked the students, and then opened the doors to the lift.

They stepped out onto another platform. Beneath them was a room filled with people on comkits, all of them talking (or shouting), and interacting with various displays and holo-projections.

Tembi had never seen an office before. It looked like a wildlife documentary straight out of one of the nature channels: she was sure someone was about to die, probably while being eaten.

Her classmates started to mutter and point. There were off-worlders in that mix, some of them as far from Earth-normal as Matindi. One of them, a man easily nine feet tall, stood in the middle of the chaos, his holos clustered around his upper body. Two women with bald heads and too-thin bodies were sitting on a wire ledge suspended from the ceiling: as Tembi watched, one of the women unfolded a set of bony skin-thin wings and glided down to the floor.

In her dreams, the Deep had shown Tembi people like these. But to see—really see!—that woman with wings...

She looked at Matindi for confirmation, and found her teacher smiling. Not at Tembi or the other students, but at the madness playing out before her. It was a sad smile, the kind her mother got when she talked about Tembi's father, and Tembi realized she had never asked what Matindi had done before she had come to Adhama. Or what she had given up to take on her new life as Tembi's teacher.

The Spacer answered questions, and then moved them back into the lift. Tembi thought the tour was over, but instead they kept going up.

At the top of the lift was sunlight. Sunlight all around; the top level of the docks was clear plass, with a view of the ocean, and the moving ships both above and below. A weather cage protected a balcony adjacent to the lift, and the Spacer moved them onto this.

The children (and the chaperones) stared at the ocean below, then at the circular room, eyes wide. There were five desks stationed around the room, four of which were empty. The fifth had a heavyset man sitting at it. His ears perked up first, before he took notice of the class and gave them a little wave.

"I was wrong," the Spacer said. "You do get to see a Witch today."

Tembi stared, her soundkit forgotten. That was okay; all of her classmates were staring. The Witch was roundish and buried in a mountain of paperwork and holo-projections. His ears were long and tapered to points, and there was a band of fish painted against the left side of his face.

Those are shaa fish, Tembi realized. The Witch was from Adhama.

Her heart fell a little. Paperwork and...and fish?

She found herself at the edge of the balcony, pretending to look down.

Somehow...

...somehow, when she had thought about her future as a Witch, paperwork and fish hadn't been on her mind at all.

Or sharing an office with four other people just like her.

Or staying on this planet on the edge of nowhere, forever.

Or...

...or...

...below, a flicker of silver—two ships, moving straight at each other, about to collide.

Tembi gasped and panicked; the Deep heard her. The two ships blurred and reappeared several meters apart.

She realized her mistake a moment too late: the ships had been nowhere near each other. It had been a trick of perspective; the larger ship was nearly on top of the ocean, with the smaller ship flying safely above it. If she had been paying attention—if she hadn't been worried about *fish!*—she would have known that!

Stupid *stupid **stupid!***

She slunk away from the edge of the balcony and rejoined her classmates. Matindi hadn't seemed to notice.

Let's not tell her, Tembi thought at the Deep. *Not even in dreams, okay?*

The lift went down with Tembi and the others aboard, and no one saw how the round Witch with the painted fish watched them leave.

choice run
choice fight

Excerpt from "Notes from the Deep," 14 July 3828 CE

Chapter Five

On the day when Tembi's life broke into a million pieces, the Deep had surprised her with a creature made almost entirely of eyes, bones, and teeth. This was nothing new. Matindi had told Tembi that since the Deep had a personality, they should think of it as a person. Which was all fine and good, except the Deep most certainly did not have a human personality.

For example, it found nightmares to be *hilarious.*

It was especially fond of putting monsters in Tembi's head right before she awoke. Matindi would end the night's lessons a few hours before dawn so the two of them could get some real sleep; Tembi would tip from the teaching dream into her own natural sleep cycle, and would usually awake refreshed and ready to take on the day.

Except, of course, when the Deep was in the mood to play its version of a practical joke. Tembi had learned early on that the Deep might not have much in the way of an imagination, but that meant nothing when it had an entire galaxy of horrors at its disposal. She woke up screaming at least two or three days a month, hands flailing at the image of whatever multi-mouthed spider demon the Deep had found on a remote planet to slide into her subconscious.

She would go to school, furious, and Matindi would notice and give the class a pop quiz to keep them busy while she told the Deep—again—that Monsters Are Not Playthings.

At the edges of Tembi's mind, the Deep laughed and *laughed* and ***laughed!***

Tembi had decided the problem was that the Deep had no body. It witnessed the birth and death of humans and knew what a monster could do to the flesh, so it treated bodies as if they were made of spun sugar.

But dreams? Dreams were of the mind and spirit, both of which the Deep had in abundance. And dreams were still the only place where it could interact with Tembi.

"Just you wait until you've been trained and can carry this *ulol* beast in your own mind," Matindi had told her one night, as the Deep spun around them in a chiming-colored laugh. "It'll stop playing jokes in your dreams and start messing with you in reality. Like hiding the notes you needed for a class presentation on…where was it? One of the moons of Ellis-3?"

Tembi was not *quite* looking forward to *that*.

The creature of eyes, bones, and teeth had been one of the Deep's better monsters. The image of it racing towards her, mouths wide open, was still seared into her brain as she trudged towards the schoolhouse. The air was heavy, and sand was beginning to kick up into clouds along the road.

A storm was coming—a bad one. Everyone on the roads had their heads down and their ears flattened back. Some had pulled scarves over their hair. Tembi had, of course, forgotten her scarf in her haste to get to school before the storm hit. There would be dust in her hair the whole day, maybe longer if the storm lasted into the evening.

The school would be open, there was no doubt of that. It was a designated shelter; on storm days, the door was kept open and the building shielded by a weather cage. If you needed shelter, you were welcome. Tembi loved storm days, as Matindi would ask those seeking shelter to tell the best story they knew, and everyone had at least one good story.

(The school had become something of a community event during storms. For the stories, yes, but also because the supply closet was always full of the kinds of rib-sticking foods the human body craved during times of stress. Tembi was sure that Matindi was using the Deep to do grocery runs.)

And then, after the stories (and the food), they would sing. Songs from across Adhama. Sometimes, songs from across the galaxy, or Earth songs that were simple but were as old as time.

…*twinkle twinkle little star*…

Tembi had her soundkit on and the volume as high as it could go. She had finally gotten so fed up with the ill-fitting earcuffs that she had asked one of her sisters to ice and pierce her ears, and she had threaded a wire between her new piercing and the cuffs to hold them in place. It wasn't a perfect solution: when she had first modified them, the wires pinched enough to break the skin when she folded her ears back. But her skin was starting to harden as it adjusted, and the cuffs were much less likely to fall off of her ears and bounce across the floor.

She was tired. She was distracted.

She was not expecting the man with black hair and boxy blocks of yellow paint on the left side of his face to appear in front of her.

Tembi, like everyone else on the streets, had her head down, and she plowed straight into him. The man staggered backwards, but not too far; Tembi didn't have enough mass to knock him down.

"I'm sorry!" she shouted.

The man pulled himself tall and said something which got lost within her soundkit.

"Very sorry!" Tembi said again, and sidestepped him with the dexterity of a street urchin used to evading the law. "You better get home before the storm hits!"

She kept walking.

He appeared in front of her again, and this time, she realized he was a Witch.

Matindi had made her practice what she should do if she was ever caught alone with a Witch. Head down. Pretend to be lost in her music. Walk away.

Tembi did all of this again, but this time it was intentional; a cold sweat was starting to catch against her back.

He appeared in front of her a third time.

She made a production of turning down the volume on her soundkit, and then began shouting at him. "I said I was sorry! What is your *problem?!*"

The school was just a block away.

Matindi was just a block away.

He knelt in the street before her. "Tembi," he said in a two-toned voice. "It's time to leave this world."

The Deep was talking through him.

—*the Deep!*—

If the Deep was in on this, then the Witch was going to take her away—

No.

No!

She might not be a Witch yet, but she had been born and bred in the Stripes, and she had handled men like this before. This was her home, and no Witch was going to come into her home and yank her offworld!

"Why are you doing this?" she yelled. "Help! This man is not my father!"

The man with the boxy yellow paint blinked.

"Stranger!" Tembi shouted. "Stranger! Help! *Stranger!*"

He stood and took a step away. "Wait," he said, hands up, pleading, looking around as if the residents of the Stripes were about to descend upon him.

A quick rush of air, and Tembi turned up to see a bald woman in a Spacers' uniform step into the street. Her skin was almost pure white, and she had black paint in five-spotted patterns running across her head. "What's the delay?" the bald woman asked the man.

"Strangers!" Tembi shouted again. "Help!"

Storm or no storm, they had managed to attract a crowd. The male Witch didn't look too different from the locals, but the bald woman had appeared out of thin air and she had pale skin and ice-blue eyes. The residents of the Stripes were starting to get loud.

"Just grab the kid and jump," the woman said.

The man started moving again. He was bigger and faster than she was; if he managed to get his hands on her...

Tembi hauled back and hit the male Witch as hard as she could in his genitals.

(She would have gone for his feet; there was nothing as satisfying as the feeling of a pervert's toe breaking beneath her heel. But Witches seemed to have a strange fondness for shoes.)

The male Witch's eyes went wide, and he slowly lowered himself to the ground, saying, very quietly, "......ohhhh."

The bald woman gasped, then started *laughing!*

Tembi took a step away from the Witches, and then another, and she was running before she knew it, racing down the street as fast as she could. The storm was almost upon them; sand and dirt and stray pieces of trash were flying through the air. If she didn't find cover soon, the Witches would be the least of her—

And then the man with the boxy paint was in front of her again, still sitting on the ground but able to move. He grabbed at her; she was moving too fast to turn, so she jumped over him, one foot hitting him in his face as she went.

This time, Tembi felt something break.

He shouted after her, but it sounded muffled and she couldn't make out the words.

She didn't look back. The school was right ahead of her, door wide open.

"Matindi!" she shouted, and hoped her voice wasn't torn apart by the wind. *"Matindi!"*

Something seized her arm; Tembi's feet shot out from under her and she hit the ground. The bald woman had grabbed a handful of her robes, and she was still laughing. "Oh, kid," she said, wiping tears from her eyes with her free hand. "Thanks. That was a good one."

"Tembi!" Matindi was there, blue robes crackling with static as she appeared in the air above the bald woman. She landed on the woman with her full weight, and brought the bald woman to the ground. Matindi spun around, robes flying, and used one of her enormous feet to kick the bald woman in her face.

As the bald woman fell, Matindi grabbed Tembi around her waist. "Hold on!"

Tembi shut her eyes, waiting for the rush of the Deep—

Nothing.

Tembi opened her eyes. The expression on her teacher's face had gone cold with anger, the corners of her mouth twitching ever so slightly as she argued with the Deep in her mind.

"Looks like someone's been forgotten," the man said. He had both hands pressed against his nose, blood slowly dripping from between his fingertips.

That's not true, Tembi thought to herself. *Matindi used the Deep just a second ago.*

"Give us the kid." The bald woman this time, bruises already forming on her too-pale face. "Give us the kid, and we won't haul you in, too."

Matindi pulled Tembi away from the other Witches.

"Fine," the man said, and laid his hand on Matindi's shoulder. "We'll take both of you."

Again, Tembi closed her eyes against the jump; this time, she was crying…

…but nothing happened.

The man stopped and glanced up in the way Matindi did when she was talking to the Deep, but the bald woman? Oh, the look on the bald woman's face was half-mad with anger. "Why can't I jump?" she snarled at Matindi, hands curling like claws. "What have you *done?!*"

Matindi stood and pushed back her scarves to show the black-painted winter branches against the green of her face. "I promised not to warn them," she said, the Deep riding her words. "Or let them jump. But they are not yours to take."

The bald woman couldn't tear her eyes away from those painted branches. She said something in an unfamiliar language; Matindi nodded once, sharp as a knife, and the bald woman knelt before her. She gestured and whispered, "Down, idiot!" and the man knelt (unsteadily) beside her.

"Come," Matindi said in her own voice, as if commanding a disobedient pet. She took Tembi's hand and walked towards the school.

After a moment, the strange Witches followed them.

They entered the school as the storm touched down. The

weather cage did its best, but the building rattled and the atmosphere in the schoolroom dipped as some of the air was sucked outside.

The male Witch stumbled and turned, and stared through the open doorway. "Is that—" he gasped, dropping his hand away from his broken nose. "That's a tornado!"

"You should know what a world has to offer before walking into it," Matindi said, as she settled herself on the edge of her desk. "Now. Talk."

Tembi was torn between curiosity and self-preservation: she could either listen to the Witches, or drop back into the crowd of her whispering classmates and pretend this madness had nothing at all to do with her. Self-preservation won. She worked her way towards her seat, but her classmates were there, armed with questions and, in one case, a cheese sandwich.

"What happened?"

"—saw them try to grab you—"

"Is Madam Green a *Witch?!*"

Tembi seized on that last question. "I think she is!" she said, her own eyes wide. She was not a good liar at the best of times, but she could twist the truth until it wept. "She… She just appeared in the air! And she's got those branches painted on her, and—"

"Tembi?" Clay, one of her friends, was staring at her. "Your… what's wrong with your face?"

"What?" Tembi asked.

Her classmates began to edge away from her. Worse, some of the adults who were taking shelter from the storm were now beginning to stare at her instead of the three Witches.

"What?!" Tembi asked again, slightly panicked. She touched her face. Her skin was a little rougher than normal from exposure to the wind, but it was already starting to smooth itself. There was nothing to explain why the other children were backing away from her, mouths open and staring.

"Tembi." Matindi's voice was a summons. Tembi took a breath, and moved from the safety of the other students to the front of the room.

The green woman looked different. The bare branches on her face were now bending beneath the painted outlines of spring-green leaves. The decorations weren't tattoos: they were just pigment, and if Matindi gave her face a good scrubbing they vanished in trails of black down the drain. But she had assumed Matindi woke up, drew the same branches on her face every morning, and then went to start her day.

Not so. Unless Matindi had been busy with a cosmetics brush in the last three minutes, someone had painted her face for her.

Her teacher stared down at her. She sat a little taller than usual, and the little pale green lines that crinkled at the corners of her eyes were gone. "You didn't tell me the Deep listened to you when we visited the docks," she said. "I think you've realized that was a mistake."

Tembi nodded, chin and ears high, seeing nothing. She was unsure where the mistake lay—was it talking to the Deep, or not telling Matindi, or both?—but she was *not* going to cry. Not now. Not with three Witches and her classmates and a dozen strangers taking shelter from the storm, all of them watching her.

Matindi relented. "The birds suit you," she said, her smile touching her eyes again. "Take your seat. We'll leave for Lancaster when the storm is over."

Dismissed, Tembi walked to the rear of the classroom, holding herself as straight and as steady as she could manage.

Lancaster.

—supposed to go years from now, they won't let me see Mom, they won't let me listen to music, they won't let me come home—

She was numb. Nothing felt real, not even her classmates hurrying away from her as she passed, not even their whispers of Witch, *Witch,* **Witch!**

Her desk was beside a window. She had been one of the class's storm watchers for most of this week, and sitting there was still something of an honor even though the metal shutters had been locked and shielded. Her reflection stared back at her from the polished steel, and she was not at all surprised to find that the left side of her face had been painted with a rising cloud of golden birds.

human
human nature
FIGHT

Excerpt from "Notes from the Deep," 3 November 3364 CE

Chapter Six

Her second ride through the Deep was dark and silent, and she couldn't shake the notion that the Deep was…sad? Hurt?

Hurt. Yes.

The bald woman with the painted spots held her hand as they moved through a world of color and song. It was different than when Matindi had brought her to Adhama; the Deep's colors were muted, its song less vibrant.

She could feel Matindi behind them. The green-skinned Witch hadn't been allowed to travel alone: the man held her by a wrist, as if to keep her from stepping off the Rails and vanishing forever. Tembi felt deep satisfaction at having broken his nose.

"How do you keep a Witch in one place?" she whispered to herself.

"You make the Deep promise to ignore her requests." Matindi's voice cut through the colors, and the feeling of—*hurt*—grew deeper.

Neither of the two other Witches spoke.

It was a shorter trip than the jump between Miha'ana and Adhama. One moment, they stood in the street, watching Tembi's classmates walk home in the aftermath of the storm. The next, they were sliding across the Rails. And the moment after that, they were walking across ground as soft as a green cloud.

Tembi gasped and tried to find firm ground. There were plants *everywhere*, growing all around her, just like in the alley on Miha'ana, but their blades were *pointed* like *spears*—

The bald woman laughed. "If you're scared of grass, kid, this place'll kill you within a week."

Matindi raised an eyebrow at her. The bald woman turned red beneath her painted spots, and dropped her eyes to the ground.

"It's safe, Tembi," her teacher said, as she set off across the… grass? "The plants are used for decoration and rainfall control."

Oh. Practical plants. Tembi followed, cautiously; the grass seemed harmless enough, and was very pleasant between her toes. But there was pavement not too far away, a slab of white cutting through the green, and she moved onto that as quickly as she could. Once she was safely on solid ground, she looked up.

And up.

And *up!*

"Welcome to Lancaster Tower," the man said.

The Tower was a shell! A shell cut in half to show off a perfect spiral of whites and creams, plucked straight from the ocean and dropped within this sea of green. It was dotted with shining stripes of pale golden plass, all of it with the appearance of being as fragile as a wish. Paths radiated from it in slow, sweeping curves, and the main door was an archway of spun crystals, the entrance protected by a weather cage and nothing else.

"They used a nautilus from old Earth as the model," Matindi said.

"It's beautiful!" Tembi spun around in a slow circle, trying to take in the details. Around the shell were smaller auxiliary buildings with different designs. None of those smaller buildings were shells, but all of them had the same rounded symmetry. The whole place felt as though it had been grown instead of constructed.

A man was waiting for them in the crystal archway. He wore a suit instead of robes, and had the same timeless look about him as Matindi, but his skin was a normal healthy brown instead of green. And (Tembi had to check to make sure, but yes, there they were!) the left side of his face was painted in branches bending beneath the weight of new spring leaves.

He waited until Matindi had drawn close, and then asked, "What do you have to say for yourself?"

Matindi took her time. Her eyes moved from his dark hair to the painted branches, and then down to a pair of black leather shoes gleaming from an absurd amount of polish.

"I always wanted to be a teacher," she said.

"You could have come home to do that," the man said.

"Yes, well," Matindi said with a sniff. "I meant, I always wanted to be a *good* teacher."

They stared at each other. Tembi felt her fists knot tight as the man in a suit moved towards Matindi—

Matindi and the man fell into each other's arms, laughing.

"Oh, it's good to see you, Piki," he said, his arms moving easily into place around Matindi's wrong-jointed elbows. "Been far too long."

"Or not long enough," Matindi said, resting her head on his shoulder. She was smiling. "It's Matindi now, by the way."

"Noted. Oh my." The man's eyes had turned towards Tembi. She realized she was still ready to start punching, and stood as tall as she could, her ears flattened back against the sides of her head. "You're a fierce one, aren't you, Tembi Moon?"

"You have no idea," muttered the boxy-faced Witch.

"Dismissed," the man in the suit said to him.

The other man nodded, and there was a brief rush of air as he vanished into the Deep.

"Sir?" asked the bald woman.

"Not you, Leps," he told her. "You're Tembi's guide for the rest of the afternoon."

Tembi glared at the spotted Witch (*Did he say her name was Leps?*), who waited until the man had turned away before she stuck her tongue out at Tembi.

Well. *That* was unexpected. But now she had to deal with the man in the suit: he had crouched down in front of her so they were of the same height. This close, she could see that he had kind, dark eyes that looked much older than the rest of him.

"Hello, Tembi," he said. "My name is Matthew. I'm sorry we had to meet this way."

"Why is your painting like Matindi's?" she asked.

He smiled. "Why do you have birds?"

Tembi's hand moved to the side of her face. She had all but

forgotten her own new paint. "I don't know."

"Neither do I." Matthew stood, smoothing his suit coat over his hips. "You'll find many answers here, Tembi, but in some ways, we're at the whim of a vast alien intelligence. Sometimes it doesn't explain itself.

"But with the paint," he added, still smiling, "I like to think it's trying to show its love."

Tembi glanced over at Matindi in time to catch her rolling her eyes. "You never change, Matt," Matindi said.

"You know me and tradition," he said quietly. "Sometimes, it's the only thing that's stable around here."

"Yes," Matindi said. "On that note, I was wondering if my old quarters are available. I was thinking of staying on for a few years."

"Of course they are." Matthew nodded towards one of the smaller buildings around the Tower. "I make sure they're cleaned once a week, in case you decide to grace us with your presence."

"And do you still have a day school for the community's children? Or did you finally decide they should attend the schools in the city?"

"We still have our own school," he said. "It's turned into a very good one."

"Walk with me, Matthew," Matindi said, setting both of her long-fingered hands on his arm. "I want to see what you've done with the gardens."

"Yes, dear," he said, placing a kiss on Matindi's cheek.

Tembi watched Matindi leave—watched Matindi leave *her!*—and told herself it was okay, that she shouldn't panic, that she was just fine standing here in front of a giant sliced-open shell with a stranger who had tried to *kidnap her*—

"C'mon," Leps said. "I'll show you around. But let's start at the bathroom."

"I don't have—I don't need a bathroom," Tembi said quickly.

"You gotta wash those birds off before someone sees you," Leps said. "Otherwise you won't fit in with the other Witches' children. Hang on," she added, and laid a hand on Tembi's shoulder.

Leps jumped them both into the Deep before Tembi could prepare herself. It was a jump too fast to recognize; there was no rush of colors or song, only a brief pop of white light and then the smell of cleaning chemicals.

"Whoa," Tembi whispered.

Like the outside of the Tower, the bathroom was white and cream, but it was also trimmed in a deep sea-blue tile which moved into the white in patterns which resembled waves. The floor was another spiral, blues and whites and creams spinning off into smaller sunbursts. Anything made of metal shone like gold. (Tembi, semi-reformed pickpocket, thought it might actually have been gold, or at least close enough to gold to fool most buyers. She wondered if she could come back with a wrench.)

Leps pointed to the sink. "Water comes out of there," she said, and then she pointed at the toilet. "Everything else goes in there."

Tembi glared at her.

"Kidding," Leps said, with a little twist to her lips to show she wasn't quite kidding. "Serious kid, aren't you?"

Tembi didn't answer her. Instead, she got to work washing off the painted birds. The paint was like nothing she had ever seen; it stayed put until it finally seemed to recognize that she was serious about removing it, and then it came right off.

Once the birds were gone, she kept scrubbing. Her family's unit didn't have running water; they had a hydrosonic shower for cleaning and a packbin for waste, but this was like a trip to a bathhouse. Better than the bathhouse—the water was warm and wonderful, and it kept coming out of the tap.

There were towels when she was finished, plush squares of cotton with gold stitching which were softer than clouds. As Tembi patted herself dry, Leps killed the time by inspecting her own face in the mirror. Both of her eyes were slightly bruised, and there was a distinct pattern of widespread toes across her forehead.

"Be sure to thank your sponsor for me," Leps muttered, and then noticed Tembi staring at her. "I shave my head," she said. "I like the spots."

"I know," Tembi said.

"Then why are you staring?"

"I'm not." She began poking the walls to locate the hidden laundry service or garbage chute, or however the Witches concealed their used towels. It was probably rude to point out that she could see the blood moving beneath Leps' pale skin, and it was very disturbing. Leps didn't act sick, but nobody could have skin that thin and still be healthy, right? Was she contagious? Matindi wouldn't have abandoned her with someone who had a plague—

"Stay here," Leps said, and disappeared.

Don't panic, Tembi reminded herself. She found the laundry bin beneath the sink, and threw her towel inside; it vanished almost as soon as it crossed the threshold.

The Witches use the Deep for laundry duty, she realized, and was beginning to revisit the idea of panicking when Leps reappeared. The bald woman was carrying a set of linen robes in different shades of blue.

"I can get you a shirt and pants if you want those instead," Leps said, as she handed the robes to Tembi, "but you seem to be a robes kind of kid."

"Thank you," Tembi said. She stared at Leps until the woman sighed and turned to face the wall.

"You'll like it here," Leps said. "It's got everything you could need."

Tembi didn't reply.

"I grew up poor too, you know. The Deep almost always chooses rich kids. Nobody knows why. But you and me and a few others? We're different. They won't let you forget it, but that's fine—here, you always know where your next meal is coming from, and that's what matters."

"I always know where my food comes from." There was an enormous lump in Tembi's throat. The linen robes were thick and soft, and fit her better than any secondhand clothing from her sisters. But dressing in them felt…it felt wrong, somehow. "My mom…my sisters…"

"Oh. Hey, don't worry about them." For the first time that day, Leps sounded as if she wasn't ready to fight someone. "If Lancaster's Tower Council treats you like they did me, they'll give your family a huge chunk of credit. You'll have to work it off, but they'll be rich."

Tembi swallowed, hard. "You can turn around now."

Leps did, and smiled. It was a nice smile and did pleasant things to her face, even though it exposed a set of pointed canine teeth. Her people must have lived on a meat-rich planet. "Good color on you," she said. "Didn't think you'd like the green. Not after the grass."

That grass…Tembi kept her face still. "I'm used to cities," she said.

"Yeah, you'll definitely like it here." Leps put her hand on Tembi's shoulder again. This time, the jump took them to the top of the Nautilus.

Tembi didn't scream—she didn't even *gasp!* Not even with the sides of the shell sloping away in long tumbling lengths of white and cream, and nothing between her and thin air but—

Oh, never mind. There was a railing right in front of her.

"The Deep won't let Witches fall," Leps said. "But we like to bring visitors up here, and I hear our insurance premiums are already just ridiculous."

Tembi barely heard her. She was overwriting her hastily formed opinions of Lancaster and its grounds. She had assumed Lancaster was a small city itself, or at least a town straight from a program on the storybook channels, with great green pastures all around and a single road winding through to connect it to the outside world. Not so. The road was there, yes, and so were the great green fields. Beyond those were thick groves of trees, evergreens with huge woody trunks, each of them growing almost as tall as the Tower.

Beyond that…

A city. Yes, a massive city, all around Lancaster! She had thought the school was set in the woods, but it was merely a giant stretch of green within a city!

Tembi's heart leapt. Grass or not, forest or not, she was still inside a city.

"That's Hub," Leps said. "Biggest city on Found.

"That's where we are, by the way," she added. "The planet's name is Found. That word means the same thing in about eight languages beside Basic, so Lancaster's founders decided to use it."

"Can—" Tembi wasn't sure how to ask. "Are we allowed to go to the city?"

"Yup," Leps replied. "As long as you keep your grades up, there's no curfew. There's a hopper service that runs every twenty minutes. It's free for all untrained Witches.

"And Hub's very safe," she continued. "The Deep makes sure you're never in any danger, and the folks out there treat Witches like their lives depend on it." Leps must have seen the expression on Tembi's face, because she quickly added, "Wait, no—I should have said their livelihoods depend on it. Everything in Hub exists because of Lancaster, so we get the royal treatment when we're in the city."

Tembi found she was able to swallow again. Respecting someone because they controlled your credit? That was fine. That happened all of the time. And it was much better than learning the Deep would murder anyone who wasn't nice to her.

"Wanna go check it out?"

Yes, *of course* Tembi did! Her feet itched to be on solid ground again. Instead, she asked: "Why are you being so nice to me?"

Leps chuckled as she laid a hand on Tembi's shoulder, and she jumped them into the city.

talk
Lancaster
talk
talk talk talk
talk talk talk talk talk
talk talk talk talk talk talk talk talk talk talk
talk talk talk talk talk talk talk talk talk talk talk talk talk talk

Excerpt from "Notes from the Deep," 24 July 3490 CE

Chapter Seven

That was the end of Tembi Moon, but it took Tembi Stone-skin several years to realize she had left her old self behind in that classroom on Adhama.

Those years should have been an easy time for her. For Matindi, too—her old teacher had walked back into her old life at Lancaster as simply as singing. Tembi thought Matindi had moved from Lancaster to Adhama to become her teacher, but no, Matindi had left the Witches a long time before. A very long time before. Decades? Definitely. Centuries? Maybe. Some Witches did not age. To them, time had as little meaning as space. Matindi's return meant she took on the duties of the senior Witches, joining Matthew on the Tower Council as one of the oldest and most respected voices of the Deep. Tembi met these Council Witches with her chin and ears held high at a formal dinner with inedible food served on tiny golden plates. She was poked and prodded, and, once they had decided she was an entirely ordinary child, ignored. Lancaster was a busy place, and even the immortal Witches had no time to spare for her.

Tembi was introduced to everyone else at Lancaster as Matindi's ward, a stray she had taken in while touring the galaxy on sabbatical. She stayed in a spare room in Matindi's quarters (the room was larger than her family's entire unit, and had carpets!). Each morning, she wiped the golden birds from her face and went to school with the Witches' children.

She fooled no one: every single soul at Lancaster knew about the too-young Witch.

Matindi told her that some things had changed in the years she had been gone. Young Witches, for example, were now allowed to return home and see their families, even spend their breakdays with them! Not like before, when a new Witch was

swept away to Lancaster and locked away for her own good…
The green-skinned Witch shook her head as she told this to
Tembi, her eyes fixed on a long-gone past that Tembi couldn't
see.

But Tembi could go home! She could visit Adhama, and see
her mother and her sisters, and spend awkward meals pretending everything was normal until enough time had gone by that
life finally became normal again. It helped, a little.

When she was on Found, she learned the history of the
Witches.

It was odd and distorted, as all histories are, made more
complicated through the presence of the Deep. Lancaster was
not just a school and a business but also a home: Witches lived
there, behind its high walls. There were hundreds of them,
maybe thousands, Tembi couldn't keep track. Each Witch was
different, made from strange bodies and stranger words. Some
Witches married; some did not. Some raised a family within
the walls of the school; some did not. Some rode the Rails at
whim; others stayed, their roots running deep within the soil of
this, their adopted planet.

When Tembi asked questions about why Lancaster was the
way it was, Matthew took her to a little museum next to the
hopper platform, and took her on a guided tour of Lancaster's
history.

She learned that Found was a second choice, as the first
Witches had wanted to build their school on Earth.

No. Even after the Deep and its Witches had changed the
shape of the galaxy, the good people of Earth were having none
of their nonsense. Build your school somewhere else, they said.
We'll help you finance its construction. Just not *here.*

The Deep had shown the first Witches a rocky planet in the
base of the Cygnus arm which it thought might be suitable. It
was in a great location and the environment was very close to
Earth-normal, it told them, but there was one problem: the
planet had four moons in fixed orbit and a minor axial tilt so
there was almost no weather to speak of. It rained at nights but

the days were clear, and the average daily temperature was approximately 24 °C year-round, except near the shorelines where it was a degree or two cooler. But with minor investment in terraforming—

Thank you, the first Witches had told it. We will try and make do.

They named the planet Found, designated its moons as shipping docks, and began construction on the finest school in the galaxy. Lancaster, they called it, as the names some of the first Witches had suggested were too hard for others to pronounce.

They built Lancaster as a pastoral fortress. Large, beautiful, set within a city that would boast it was the home of the Deep. Ships came from across the galaxy to meet with the Witches; if you had Lancaster's blessing, the worlds would open to you.

Except…

…except that wasn't what Tembi *saw*.

Matthew and the rest of Lancaster told her one thing; her own eyes told her another. She knew what she saw as she stood at the hopper pad, waiting for a lift into Hub. Each hopper flight was full of off-worlders who had come to Lancaster to plead their case before the Witches. After a time, she could read their expressions and know which ones had to go home and explain why they wouldn't have a new shipping port in their community, or tell their employers that the Witches wouldn't move their cargo, or any one of a hundred reasons the Tower Council might reject a petition.

She supposed there was sense in it. In the museum, there were great, brilliant paintings which showcased the Witches as guardians of the Deep. The Witches served as its stewards, Matthew had explained, and Witches made sure the Deep was only used for peaceful purposes. Education. Trade. Tourism. Diplomacy.

Never for war.

At the time, it had sounded lovely—it had sounded *pure*. Like magic.

(And she had finally understood why they insisted on calling themselves Witches, even though the term still sounded ridiculous to her.)

But Tembi decided she wanted nothing to do with the Deep.

It wasn't a conscious decision. Not at first. At first, she watched daily life at Lancaster unfold around her, and saw how the Deep was involved in everything they did.

It was...

...it had begun that first day in the Tower bathroom, when she had learned the Deep was used to whisk the dirty linens away.

It wasn't just dirty laundry, oh no. When the Witches had a mess to be cleaned up, the Deep did it for them, vanishing the filth through its own sorcery. Witches never went shopping unless they wanted to, or waited in line to mail their post, or any of the hundreds of tasks that Tembi had heard her mother complain about on a daily basis.

There was nothing in that museum about how the Witches made the Deep do their chores for them.

The more Tembi saw, the less she liked Lancaster. During her first few weeks at the school, she didn't understand why she never saw Witches around campus. There were gardens, and a lake, and places to rest and play and eat, but she never saw Witches moving from one location to another. Then, she realized that most of the Witches didn't even walk! They used the Deep to move across Lancaster, across the whole campus, yes, but even for journeys as short as moving from room to room.

At eleven, Tembi lacked the words to describe the nature of Lancaster's relationship with the Deep. If the docks on Adhama had been overrich with its presence, Lancaster was a thousand times more so. The Deep was always *there,* nudging her at her mind, begging for her attention. It would gladly do anything for her, or for any of the other Witches. All they had to do was ask.

And they did. They asked for everything!

They asked over and over again, until the Deep was...

...was...

...Tembi couldn't describe it.

All she knew was that she couldn't bear it, and after several months of watching this…*thing*…she couldn't put into words, she turned away from the Deep.

For the first few years, Matindi kept the Deep away from her. Tembi needed to adjust to her new life, she told it, and pushing too hard right now might drive her away forever. The Deep seemed to accept that, and kept its distance.

But while Tembi no longer spoke to the Deep, or allowed it to enter her dreams, she couldn't help but notice how the Witches treated it.

Her skin began to harden.

While Tembi climbed trees and crashlanded on pavement like the other children, she didn't come home with skinned knees. The fighting? Well, Tembi was only caught once, and given enough chores to make sure that getting caught would never happen again, but the Deep told Matindi tales about sneaking into Hub and brawling with the locals. (Once, it had jumped Tembi back to her own bed when she went into Hub, needing the heat of a good fight to burn off some stress, but she had shouted at the air for *hours* and it never did that again.) And when she began taking martial arts, she was never bruised or broken.

Matindi tried to help. Long holidays with Tembi's family on Adhama, or shopping excursions across the galaxy. Even concerts, which caused the other Witches to wonder aloud at whether Matindi should be permitted to raise the Deep's favorite child.

Matindi pushed back; Tembi got to keep her music.

The music was important. If Tembi had music, she didn't have to feel the presence of the Deep, and, for reasons she still couldn't put into words, that was what Tembi wanted most of all. She hid from it during the day, and at nights she slept with her soundkit on, and woke with the song of another human being in her head so it could no longer come to her in dreams.

Two years.

Three.

Four.

Tembi at fifteen, her skin nearly as hard as the stones of Marumaru. Taller now, with gold rings in the holes her sister had pierced in her ears, and a scarf wrapped around her head to hold her curly hair out of her way.

Tembi at fifteen, and the Deep was tired of waiting.

It began to bring her gifts. Little tokens at first; exotic flowers, mostly. Especially pretty beetles. The odd brightly colored bird, or serpent. A piece of wood, cut and polished to show its gleaming heart.

Matindi had a rule—No using the Deep as a garbage disposal in her home!—but Tembi opened that sealed cupboard to return these items to its sender.

The Deep started to get pushy. It started leaving its gifts where she couldn't simply throw them away. At the table while she was eating breakfast with Matindi (and Matthew, if he had spent the night). In class, in front of the teacher and the other students. Tembi yelled at the air; this would buy her a few days of peace, but the gifts would soon start up again.

Sometimes, she would catch Matindi quarreling with the Deep. This was usually in Matindi's native language—Tembi would understand her own name and nothing more—but once, just once, Matindi had said: "Of course she's not talking to you! You took her away from her home before she was ready! How would you feel if she took you away from *me?!*"

That seemed to make an impression: the next morning, Tembi found a mother cat and a litter of newborn kittens sleeping beside her. The mother awoke and fled in terror; she never returned. Tembi bottle-fed the kittens until they could live on their own, then found them new homes in Hub. One of them, a white male with gray stripes running across him like a saddle, kept returning to Tembi's room. She thought the Deep was bringing the kitten back, until she saw the kitten walking by itself in the direction of Matindi's quarters, and realized it was too stubborn to accept it had a new home. After that, Tembi had a pet. She named it Taabu and drew little eyebrows on his face with a cosmetics pencil twice a week, and allowed it to prowl around Lancaster.

Emboldened with the success of the kitten, the Deep began to bring her other things. Artwork, gemstones, large quantities of credit chips from all over the galaxy, and so on. Items of value, at least to most people. Tembi began to schedule time into her day to track down their rightful owners so Matindi could return them.

The last straw was when Tembi and Matindi returned from their shift in the gardens to find an ancient Earth vehicle in their common room. The Deep had been courteous enough to move the furniture to make enough space for it, but it had stacked wooden shelves on top of old-fashioned glass ornaments, and the wreckage was profound.

Matindi shook her head, very slowly, and then started shouting. "We're not dealing with this!" She waved her fists in the air. "Do you hear me? This is officially a managerial issue! You now need to speak with our manager!"

Tembi went to put the vegetables away. When she returned to the common room, Matindi was gone and Matthew was sitting on the couch.

"Hello, Tembi," he said, and gestured to the chair across from him. "Please take a seat."

Oh. This Matthew. The version who brought papers over for Matindi to sign, not the one who made them excellent griddle cakes on breakday mornings. She didn't like this Matthew nearly as much.

Tembi sat. She was still wearing her gardening clothes: under normal circumstances, Matindi would throw a fit for tracking dirt around the common room, but as most of her house was groaning under the weight of the vehicle...

"Do you know what this is?" Matthew said. "It's a Frazer Nash-BMW 328. There were only six of these to have survived an old Earth war. We traced this one to a museum on Caulda. They're eager to get it back.

"This can't go on," he said quietly.

"I don't want it to," Tembi said. "I've been trying to get the Deep to stop."

"We all have," Matthew said. "But it's escalating, and sometimes we can't get the Deep to understand that what it does can hurt us.

"It doesn't understand larceny," he said, pointing at the car. "It doesn't understand that there's a director at a museum on Caulda who wants to press charges against you."

"Wait, what?"

"Why not?" Matthew shrugged. "Everyone knows the Deep does what it's told. So you obviously told it you wanted this car."

"I didn't!" Tembi was outraged. "I don't even know what a car is!"

"You know that and I know that," he said. "But the Deep is how the galaxy functions. It has to be dependable. Nobody wants to hear that it's breaking its patterns and stealing items to get a young woman to like it again. So—"

Tembi stood, furious. "I will *not* take the blame for this!"

"If you don't, then someone else will," Matthew said, deeply serious. "It's not fair to you—it is in no way fair to you!—but what happens if the galaxy loses faith in the Deep? Or in its Witches? This is a balance we've maintained for thousands of years, Tembi. Trust is built over time. Routines and tradition are built over time!

"But here you are," he said. "You shouldn't be. Not for another few years, at least. Matindi and I don't know why it chose you so young, nor do we know if you'll be unique. That's a big part of why we're worried."

The little lines around his eyes that appeared when he thought Matindi was mad at him were there; worry lines, standing out as if cut by razors from centuries of use. Matthew was worried—maybe even scared.

Tembi took a deep breath and sat back down. "What do you mean?" she asked.

"The Deep has picked others since you," Matthew said. "It's gone back to its old ways—all of the new Witches-in-training are young adults. But what happens if it chooses someone younger than you were? A toddler, perhaps, or a baby?"

Tembi slumped back into her seat. She had never considered the Deep in the hands of a baby. "Matthew—"

"It brings you cars when you don't ask for them," Matthew said. "What would it bring a baby?" He paused. "Matindi and I have tried to give you enough space so you could grow without the Deep. But, Tembi? It's time. We need to know why it came to you, if there's something it wants that we haven't been providing it. It's time you learn how to live with it, so you can find out what that might be."

"I don't want to." Tembi's voice was a whisper. Taabu strolled into the room, sniffed at the strange vehicle, and left to see about activating its food bowl.

"I know," Matthew said. "That's another difference between you and everyone else who's been chosen—we were all ready to join with the Deep."

"What do you mean?"

"All of us Witches? The only thing we've ever had in common was we had broken hearts. We had recently gone through the loss of first love. Myself? I've always thought the Deep felt the pain of our loss, and it chose us because of that. Filling a void, if you would.

"You'll be sixteen next week," he continued. "Still younger than any other Witch here, but I think you know that you need to take control of this situation. If you don't, someone else will have to. And if you're in control, you can at least make sure the situation is a little fairer for you, right?"

Tembi nodded.

"The Deep is going to be with you for the rest of your life," Matthew said. "It's time for you to learn how to make it live with you on your terms. Not its own."

painted woman
knows
mother father
painted woman knows

Excerpt from "Notes from the Deep," 7 August 4013 CE

Chapter Eight

On the day she turned sixteen, Tembi left the golden birds on her face and went to take her place with the Witches.

Lancaster Tower. Tall and white and gilded, and no Matthew at the door to greet her this time.

Chin up, she told herself, her head and ears held high. The doors in the spun crystal spirals parted for her, and she entered the Tower. *It's not like they can kill you.*

(Maybe they could? Matindi had been awfully keen on wishing her luck that morning, but—No. The Deep didn't let its Witches die in accidents. Or get murdered. Or—)

No. Hush.

Across the white marble floors. Down the third hall to her right. Why did the Witches need such huge overdone hallways? It's not like they ever bothered to walk anywhere. She was wearing black and gold. Maybe she shouldn't have gone with the gold scarf for her hair? It matched the birds but maybe that was bragging? Nobody else had gold paint. It wasn't too late to take it off, dump it in one of the potted plants, pick it up on her way home—

"Hey, Tembi!"

Leps!

Four years older than when Tembi had last seen her, still bald, still in her Spacers' uniform. The Deep hadn't yet frozen her in time; she looked more in control than before (And honestly? Slightly less like a carnivore from an ice planet, which was comforting.).

Tembi picked up her pace, her bare feet padding across the marble.

"Hey, kid, you look good." The bald woman fell into step with her. "Did you know I'm your teacher for the prep course?"

Tembi shook her head.

"Basic stuff," Leps said. "Introductory Deep work. But here's the thing—the other students in this class? Most of them completed their educations before the Deep tapped them. So I'm going to be referencing data you might not have covered yet. Let me know if you don't pipe in, 'kay?"

Pipe in...? Some kind of slang, probably. Moving to Lancaster had dumped Tembi into a cross-cultural nightmare of regional dialog. At least in this case she could understand Leps' intent from context.

"Okay," Tembi agreed.

"Good." Leps nodded. She stopped in front of a large door made from a deep brown wood. "Now, I'm gonna be hard on you in there. It's just how it goes. But you're tough so you'll be fine."

Leps touched the doorplate and the door pulled open on silent hinges. The low sounds of conversation flooded out, then stopped as Leps led the way inside.

"Attention," she said, using the two-toned voice of the Deep. "Newest student in; most experienced student out."

Leps' voice shifted to normal. "Putnam, you're gone. Move up to the next class. Try not to disappoint them like you've disappointed me.

"Everyone else, this is Tembi."

Muttering from the students: too much to have hoped that they wouldn't have heard of her. Tembi walked past them, head and ears high, and took the empty desk that had been vacated by a smallish man (whom she assumed was Putnam, but how could she say for sure?). She settled herself crosslegged on the chair, her robes concealing her bare feet.

Tembi had expected a classroom, but this was more like a small training facility for athletes. With desks. There were glyphs taped off across every available surface; the tops of the black desks had been taped in white, while patterns in colored tape chased each other across the floors, the walls, even the ceiling had been marked in targets.

There was no desk for a teacher. Instead, Leps paced the front of the room like a great white cat.

"None of you can hear the Deep," she said. "That's not a personal flaw, or a failure—it's physiology. In Earth-normal humans, the prefrontal cortex doesn't finish developing until your mid-twenties. The prefrontal cortex is responsible for both rational thinking and telepathy, so you're twice at a disadvantage.

"But while you can't hear the Deep, it can hear you. The purpose of Lancaster's beginner's program is to train you to talk to the Deep as if it were an extension of your will. You will master control now, so that when you can talk with the Deep, you have the confidence and skills needed to manage it.

"Who's my training dummy this week?" she asked, her hand on a rack of foam balls.

A hand went up. Its owner, a stunning young woman with long black hair and deep blue eyes who was a few years older than Tembi, stood. "I am," she said.

"Scheisse," Leps said. "May the gods save us all. Fine. Bayle, take us though the first mantra."

The young woman—*Is her name Scheisse or Bayle? Maybe it's both.*—moved to the front of the class. The paint on her face was a blue fern with long, broad leaves, and her eyes kept darting towards Leps, as if expecting the pale woman with the spots to strike out at her without warning.

"We are the Deep," she said, her voice decidedly Deep-free. "We are its Witches, we are its voice—"

Leps hurled one of the foam balls at the woman's head. The woman didn't cry out, but the ball vanished before it touched her.

"Fail. And you knew it was coming. Bayle, sit down," Leps snarled. "Tembi, get up here."

Tembi's stomach dropped through the floor. The feeling of going into a fight against a much larger opponent (one the size of a planet, maybe, with fists like stony moons) broke over her. She stood and moved to the front of the classroom, and turned to face the room full of young Witches.

They were all very pretty young people, in rich, colorful clothes. Forty of them, watching her with varying degrees of interest. Almost all of them were Earth-normal, but here and there—*Oh, that boy has scales!*—were some adaptations.

She looked past them to the far wall, focusing on the glyphs painted across the back. There were racks of foam balls all over the room, and between these were long wooden sticks in messy stacks.

"This is Tembi. The Deep came to Tembi when she was…how old were you, Tembi?"

"Eight."

"And yet nobody at Lancaster knew about you until you were…?"

"Eleven."

Yes, oh yes, this was definitely the worst-case scenario. First day at Witch school and the scary predator lady was making her tell her embarrassing personal history to a room full of pretty people.

"Tembi, tell the class why you got caught."

Oh, this kept getting better. The edges of her vision blurred; she felt as if she might black out. "I wasn't paying attention. Two ships looked like they were about to hit each other. They weren't, but I thought they were, so I…"

"Speak up!" Leps slapped the end of her stick on the floor. "Tell them why you got caught!"

"I thought two ships were about to crash. The Deep heard me, and it moved the ships." Her voice sounded pathetic in her own ears.

"You hear that?" Leps shouted. "She panicked and jumped some ships. That's the kind of mistake we can forgive in a little kid with no training. It's unforgivable in an adult. You will be responsible for moving food and medical supplies. Sick and injured people. Entire families looking to begin new lives on distant planets. Tell me who loses control."

The rest of the class stood. "Witches lose control," they said in a raggedy unison.

"Again."

"Witches lose control." Louder this time.

"Again!"

"Witches lose control." The class had locked together in their rally.

"Correct." Lep's stick whacked the side of the nearest desk. "The Deep does not lose control. We lose control. We are here to learn how to *maintain* control, no matter what."

Leps whipped the tip of her stick towards Tembi's face.

The end of the stick shattered against her rock-hard skin.

Tembi stared bloody murder at Leps. If this was a test to see if she could resist strangling her new teacher with her bare hands—

Leps froze, staring at the broken end of the bamboo staff. It took her a moment to recover. "Pass!" she said. "Tembi, do you require a trip to the physician?"

"No," Tembi growled through clenched teeth. She touched her cheek; her skin was unbroken. The muscles beneath it were sore, but that was nothing a medical nanopack wouldn't fix when she got home.

"Tembi, return to your seat. Andon! You're up."

The next four hours were spent doing drills where they moved objects across the room. The glyphs and taped areas were targets: Leps would bark orders, and then the young Witches would ask the Deep to move a foam ball from point to point.

Tembi turned out to be extremely good at this. The Deep rallied to her requests, bouncing the balls across the room with precision. She even managed to keep one of the balls floating in mid-air for thirty seconds before the Deep let it fall.

"Child's play," Leps would say as she walked around the room. She had obtained a new stick, and was whipping this behind her like a tail. "Wait until you have to juggle a dozen objects at once while also keeping the Deep in your head. You think it'll be easier when you can actually hear what it has to say to you? No. It doesn't speak in words. It has its own language, and that's hard enough to understand when you aren't trying to move a starship across the galaxy."

Colors and song and emotion, Tembi thought, and remembered meeting the Deep in her dreams. In spite of herself, she thrilled a little to the idea of seeing it again, as if a friend were about to return from a long journey.

Every foam ball in the room vanished, then reappeared in a large, precise pyramid floating a few centimeters above Tembi's desk. The last ball hovered in mid-air above the highest point on the pyramid, spinning slowly.

Leps sighed. "Fifteen-minute break," she said, and disappeared.

The class scrambled for the doors. Some of them grabbed bags from beneath their chairs; a few paused, eyes closed, before their own lunch bags dropped into their hands.

Tembi watched this, slightly horrified.

"Don't worry," came a voice from behind her. "You're doing great. A few weeks and you won't have to pack your lunch."

It was the young woman who Leps had ripped apart at the beginning of class. Scheisse? Or maybe Bayle? She was smiling. "C'mon," she said. "We usually don't get more than one bathroom break a day. If we miss this one, it'll be a bad afternoon."

"Your name is Scheisse?" Tembi asked.

The woman's eyes went wide and she pressed her hands to her mouth. Her fingernails were perfect works of digital art, with detailed moving scenery showing images of the sea. "Oh," she said. "Oh, no. No. It's Bayle—Bayle Oliver. And maybe don't say that word around anyone else?"

Tembi winced. "Sorry."

"It's fine, I do stuff like that all the time," Bayle said. "C'mon, we need to hurry."

Tembi followed her through the heavy door and down the marbled hall. Bayle was practically running, her skirts pulled up to her knees. Her feet were bare, too, but much wider than Tembi's at the heel. Her people weren't Earth-normal.

"I like your manicure?" Tembi offered.

"Thanks! It's the view of home from my window. I wanted

to bring it with me to remember it," Bayle said, and folded her fingers in so she could inspect the digital display. Like her feet, the balls of her hands were a little too wide to be Earth-normal. "It's overcast today. Usually it's much nicer."

A continuous streaming feed from another planet? Tembi couldn't imagine how much something like that would cost.

"I can't believe you passed the stick test," Bayle said. "I don't think anyone's ever done that before."

"How was *that* a test?" Tembi asked, her fingers poking the sore spot where the stick had shattered across her face.

"You had enough control over the Deep to let the stick hit you," Bayle replied.

Tembi rolled that idea over in her mind. "Well…I don't think you can call it control if you don't know what you're supposed to do. Besides," she added, "when I started martial arts, my guardian and I convinced the Deep to allow me get hit!"

"Hah! Never tell that to Leps!" Bayle laughed. "Let her think you're a prodigy."

The bathroom was similar to the one that Leps had jumped her to on her first day at Lancaster. In this one, there were multiple stalls and toilets, but the white and gold were still dominant. Bayle went straight to the sink and began to scoop water from the tap to her mouth.

She was still drinking when Tembi finished with the toilet. "One moment," Bayle said, her hands splayed out in front of her like a bowl. There was water where there shouldn't be; Bayle's fingers were webbed.

"Toes, too." Bayle lifted one foot and spread them so Tembi could see the translucent skin between them. "Can't stand wearing shoes."

"Me neither." Tembi grinned.

Bayle vanished into one of the stalls. "I get a lot of crap from the Earth-normals," she said.

"Yeah," Tembi agreed, and spoke louder so she couldn't hear the other girl while she was in the midst of peeing. "I've been here for a while. They don't like my ears, but I live with a bright green Witch and she manages, so I can't complain."

"Sure you can." Bayle opened the stall door and went back to the sink. She washed her hands, and then started drinking again. "Poor treatment is poor treatment," she said around huge mouthfuls of water. "It's not a competition. Ugh, this world is so *dry!*"

"Matindi says it's something to be fought by living your best life in spite of them. Oh, and," Tembi added, "that grace is where you find it."

Bayle laughed. "What does that even mean?"

"I don't know, but people usually leave her alone after she says it."

"Oh, I've got to try that!"

They two of them left the bathroom and retraced their steps to the classroom.

"Are you hungry?" the older girl asked.

"A little. Is Leps really going to keep us all day?"

"Not if you can do that pyramid trick again." Bayle did a little jump and a kick, her robes floating down around her as she landed. "That threw her. Usually she spends a full eight hours tearing us down. We get one short break—the Deep help you if you have to use the bathroom and you haven't learned gastric movement yet."

"What's gastric movement?"

"Really?" Bayle sniffed. "You've been living with the Witches and you haven't heard about that? It's asking the Deep to dump your…um…contents…into the toilet for you."

Tembi stopped dead. "That's awful. That's so *awful!* Why would anyone make the Deep do that?!"

"*I* don't do it!" Bayle sounded defensive and offended, all at once. "That Witch you live with never told you about that?"

"No…just…*No!*" Tembi felt nauseated. "That might be the worst thing I've ever heard!"

"Well," Bayle paused, her head tilted as if trying to hear something. "The Deep doesn't mind. From its point of view, if… if food is energy, then what's left over from food needs to be turned back into energy so it can be put to use again."

"Sorry, but I want to hear that from the Deep." Tembi suddenly didn't want to go back into that classroom. "Not from the Witches who use it."

"That's smart." Bayle got an odd little smile on her face. "That pyramid trick was incredible, by the way. It usually takes years before we get that level of coordination with the Deep."

"That wasn't me." Tembi shook her head. "I'm not exactly on speaking terms with the Deep these days."

"But…" Bayle glanced at Tembi, her eyebrows knitting together and her head tilted to the side again. "Maybe you should be, if it's willing to listen to you."

Tembi opened the door to their classroom, but didn't reply.

---

fireboy
alone
with painted woman

Excerpt from "Notes from the Deep," 9 April 3410 CE

Chapter Nine

The months blurred.

Classes were hard—almost impossible. Leps drove them to exhaustion every day. Morning lessons were tedious: move one foam ball to a target; move two foam balls to two targets; move three foam balls and one stick to the ceiling and make them rotate clockwise. And so on.

Tembi did learn where the term "clockwise" came from, but that was about the only thing she learned during those morning lessons. The rest was training and endless, *endless* repetition.

"The Deep understands specifics," Leps said, swinging another long stick. "You will learn to be specific in your requests. Short, tight sentences. Zero ambiguity. The Deep is a partner, not a friend!"

That stick was an effective distraction; each student had gotten whacked at least once, and they instinctively kept an eye on it. It had taken Tembi several weeks to recognize that the goal was to be aware of the stick while not thinking about the damage it could do. This was (just the slightest bit) easier for her than the other students, but she still found her mind returning to that damned stick if she didn't keep herself focused on the task.

"Do you want to risk jumping yourself?" Leps would ask, as she cracked the stick against the metal legs of the black-topped tables. "Do you know what happens when a jump goes wrong? No, you don't! Nobody does! The Witch never comes out of the jump—she's gone forever! Do you want that to happen to you?! No? Then don't try to jump your fool selves until you can talk with the Deep!"

It was a lecture that came at least once a week, and never failed to send chills up Tembi's spine. She could move foam balls across a classroom room with unerring precision, but the idea that she would one day send herself through the Deep? Or... or...*other people?* Matindi and the other Witches could jump across the galaxy without a second thought; Tembi couldn't stop thinking about what might happen if the Deep lost track of what it was doing, or decided to listen to another Witch instead of her. She might end up stranded on an alien planet. Or worse.

Those were the mornings. In the afternoons, it was star charts and practical telemetry.

"You need to know where your cargo is coming from, and how it needs to land," Leps would say, as she swung her stick around the room. "We take all of this for granted," she would say, banging the stick on the desks. "What happens if the Deep decides it doesn't want to land a ship? Or takes the afternoon off? That's on you, to get those people somewhere safe until you can get the Deep to behave again. You are their lifeline to a planet, and you will *not* scrape this up!"

Some of the students would roll their eyes. The Deep, stop working? Please.

Tembi, who would never forget the half-mad look on Leps' face when the Deep had temporarily stranded her on Adhama, memorized star charts and trade routes until they were burned into her mind.

When class finally ended for the day, Tembi was usually too tired to do more than shuffle back to Matindi's quarters and collapse on her bed. But today, at the end of a five-day work session, she and Bayle didn't make it more than a hundred steps from the Tower before they flopped face-down on the lawn.

"Breakday tomorrow," Tembi said. She couldn't feel the grass against her face, but the ground was soft and forgiving. Like a mattress. Oh, to sleep...

"We need more than a breakday or two," Bayle groaned into the grass. "We need a breakmonth. Breakyear. Breakdecade."

"Breakcentury," Tembi giggled.

"Five on, two off," Bayle said, mimicking Leps. "You work for five, you rest for two. That's how it's always been. That's how it'll always be. Tradition!"

The ground trembled ever-so-slightly as another body crashed to the ground between them. "Tradition can bite me."

"Steven, we're starving," Bayle muttered. "Don't tempt us."

Tembi turned her head. The young man who had collapsed between them had deep brown eyes, and light brown skin covered with a fine dusting of scales. His skin wasn't any harder than her own, but it was certainly more noticeable: Steven's people had chosen a different bioforming option to help them survive on a world nearly as unforgiving as Adhama.

"Food run?" Steven asked. His paint took the shape of bronze leaves floating on the breeze. The leaves looped up into his dark brown hair and down again, ending just above the opposite ear. "Go into Hub for some tumbarranchos?"

"I don't have the energy," Bayle sighed.

"Sure you do," Steven said, poking her in her ribs. "Food first, then maybe we'll go swimming."

"In a nanocleaned *pool*." Bayle snapped out that last word as if it was a curse. "It's an insult to water."

"Or the lake," Tembi said quickly. It was always best to head off Bayle's complaints about treated water as fast as possible. The girl could rant for hours. "Or...or we could catch a hopper to the beach for the weekend?"

Bayle and Steven exchanged one of *those* glances. One of those glances which suggested she was being silly. One of those glances which couldn't help but remind Tembi that however nice Bayle and Steven were, they were still three years older than her, and three years mattered a lot right now.

"But tumbarranchos sound good," she added.

"Yeah," Bayle said, standing. She was in robes of storm gray, and stray pieces of dried grass stuck to the fabric. "Let me run home and get some shoes."

Tembi did the same. She would have preferred to stay barefoot, but Hub had citywide ordinances about food and shoes. Besides, people were not nearly as sanitary in Hub as they were in Marumaru. Tembi knew she had grown up in a poor neighborhood, but she had never once stepped in fresh human waste until she had started exploring the back streets of Hub. Shoes had more than one purpose.

They met back at the Tower, in the line for the hopper shuttle. Some of the older Witches shook their heads as they passed, bemused by the idea of Witches who weren't yet skilled enough in talking to the Deep to risk jumping themselves to the nearby city.

"Scrape 'em." Steven said, as they joined the queue of travelers moving from Lancaster to Hub. "They were us, once. If they can't remember what it's like to worry about accidentally stranding yourself a million light-years from nowhere, that's their problem."

"The Deep wouldn't do that," Bayle said, as she examined her manicure. Her fingernails flashed a deep blue-black with streaks of moonlight through them: night had settled on her homeworld.

"You want to risk jumping yourself to Hub?" Steven asked her. "Not me. I'll meet you there."

Tembi stared out the window of the hopper at the setting sun. She was pretty sure the Deep would take her anywhere she asked, but she still couldn't hear it. There was the physical risk, yes, but... How was it fair to ask it to jump her all over the galaxy without knowing what it wanted from her in exchange?

The feeling of wings brushed the sides of her mind.

All right, she thought to herself, as loudly as she could. *If you want to talk, I'm listening.*

"Tembi?" Bayle was watching her, blue eyes wide. The girl reached out and touched Tembi's hand; Tembi unclenched her fists.

"I'm okay," she said. "Just thinking."

"Careful, kid, your brain might get stuck like that," Steven said. Bayle swatted him across the back of his skull.

The hopper's warning bells chimed. The doors slid shut, and the machine lifted into the air like a bird taking flight. Below, Lancaster's rolling lawns swept towards its woods and the city behind them, with little flecks of light and shadow the only signs of human habitation.

This hopper was a different creature than the one on Adhama, made of unblemished plass and gold-colored metal, and so much faster! The trip took all of three minutes, a short hop that took them the twenty kilometers from Lancaster to the station nearest their favorite restaurant. The doors opened, and the three young Witches joined the other passengers as they moved into the city.

Tembi felt better the moment she stepped onto the pavement. Hub welcomed her like Lancaster never would—cities had their own heartbeat, and she never felt truly alive when she was at the school. She wanted to scrub the birds from her face, throw off her shoes and run barefoot through the streets, tear the gold trim from her robes and the scarf from her hair and sell them for enough money to—

"Good," Bayle said, as the restaurant came into view. "There's no wait tonight."

They ordered: Steven was a vegetarian; Tembi and Bayle got their meals with meat. Their food was up, almost as fast as if had been made by the Deep, and they went outside to sit on the steps of a nearby office building to eat.

Tembi had never had tumbarranchos before moving to Hub, but now she couldn't imagine her life without them. A thick slab of fried corn arepa, cut in half and loaded with cheese and vegetables and all kinds of other flavors, then pressed between an iron and a hot griddle until the edges were seared. Sandwiches were a tumbarrancho's poor cousin.

Bellies full, the three of them went to wander the streets until they felt they could face Lancaster again. Any one night was like all nights on Found, but if Tembi had been back home, she would have said it felt like late spring. Some of Lancaster's fireflies had found their way into Hub's windowbox gardens many generations ago, and had since thrived; the city was full of small floating lights. Steven caught one that was drifting by, snatching it from the breeze as easily as catching a ball, and then tossed it back into the air unharmed.

They stopped for drinks. Bayle finished hers, then Tembi's, and was eyeing Steven's with malicious intent when a tall man with red flames painted on the side of his face cut in front of them.

"Tembi," he said, grinning. "The Deep said you were nearby."

Her ears perked up. "Moto!"

"C'mere, little girl" he said, and she flung herself into his arms. "Where've you been?"

She tapped the golden birds on the side of her face. "I started class."

"Oh, congratulations," He looked up and noticed Bayle and Steven. "Who're your friends?"

Bayle was staring at Moto, open-mouthed. Which made perfect sense to Tembi: Moto was gorgeous, about five years older than Bayle, with the type of smooth features that would have earned him a steady paycheck on any of the romance channels. His worn black Spacers' uniform fit him like a second skin. His ears, like Tembi's, were longer and more tapered at the tip than Earth-normal.

(Tembi thought her own ears made her look like a moth, but on Moto, his long ears were *exotic!*)

Tembi made the introductions, showing off this Witch from her homeworld who put everyone and everything else in Hub to shame. Bayle and Steven did their best, but a little voice inside Tembi snickered at how her friends were as off-balance around Moto as she usually felt around them.

"I'm going to steal Tembi for a few minutes," Moto said, and the two of them moved aside to let the people using the sidewalk pass them by. He caught her hand in his own and inspected it, then pressed the palm of his own hand against her face. "Tembi—"

"Don't say it." She knew she sounded waspish, and pulled away from him. "I know, Moto, I know."

He said it anyhow. "Our people wear our lives on our skins." His hands were gentle on her shoulders as he drew her back, and she forced herself to look at him. "What can I do to help?"

"You went through training," she said, and tried not to resent how his skin was nearly Earth-normal. "You know what it's like."

"I know it wasn't this bad for me," he said softly. "And you know I'm here for you, right?"

Tembi nodded once, quickly.

"You *know* you have to keep yourself under control. When was the last time you went to the gym?"

"Who has time?" Her voice sounded bitter.

"You make time," he said. "In fact, we're going to make time right now."

She wanted to scream at him. Instead, she said, "I'm out with my friends."

"Bring them along," Moto said. "They probably need to burn off some stress, too."

"Moto—"

He grabbed her hand and pressed his fingernails into her skin. When he took his hand away, there were no indentations. He did the same to himself, and showed her the small half-moon marks as if they were trophies. "You need to be able to *feel*, Tembi," he said. "The worst it got for me was that I could walk on hot pavement. But this? This is bad."

"All right," Tembi sighed. She turned to Bayle and Steven, who were pretending not to eavesdrop. "I need to go somewhere," she said. "Moto can jump you back to Lancaster if you don't want to wait for the hopper."

"We're with you," Bayle said, as her eyes darted sideways to take in the curves of Moto's butt. Spacers' uniforms didn't leave much to the imagination.

Moto gathered them together in his arms, and jumped. It was a short trip, with none of the signs of the Deep within it. They passed through a space that existed nowhere in the physical realm, and emerged in a room which reeked of cedar shavings and sweat.

Steven clasped his hands over his nose. "Oh, *nooo*," he

groaned.

"Give it a minute," Tembi said, patting him on the back. "You'll adjust."

"Oh gods, no I won't!" His eyes were watering. "Some idiot decided my planet needed a whole population who could smell a dog fart from a kilometer away."

"Fine." Tembi grinned at him. "Get Moto to jump you home. You'll miss the fun."

She nodded towards the open floor in the center of the room. It was elevated, and two men were standing on it, trading blows. Their fists had been wrapped in thick mitts and they moved around each other, snaking punches when they could.

"Old-school boxing," Tembi said.

"That's barbaric!" Bayle shook her head. "They're *hitting* each other!"

Tembi laughed, and went to change into her sweats. When she returned from the locker room, Moto was waiting for her in the ring.

"Ready, little Marumaru girl?" he asked, pacing back and forth in his corner.

She jumped up on the platform and stuck out her tongue.

They bowed and closed.

Tembi had taken to martial arts like a fish to water. It was different from the street fighting of her childhood: that was sloppy, just punching and kicking and hoping you managed to break somebody's nose so you could steal their stuff and run. Martial arts had a rhythm to it; it was a music of the body, each fighter playing their own song.

She didn't fight to win; she fought to keep the music going as long as she could.

Moto knew this. He was twice her size and had the training to put her on the ground without trying. Instead, he let her set the music.

Kick, block, kick…

Tembi started low, her blows aimed at his shins. Moto caught them on his legs, twisting so her attack glanced off. She spun, her small fist whipping towards the soft spot on his ribcage; he slapped it away, and countered with a quick backhand. She caught this on her forearm and pushed it down, leaving Moto's left side exposed to an elbow jab—

"Good one!" Moto said, as her elbow landed. "C'mon, harder!"

Punch, punch, block...

Moto sussed out her rhythm and moved with her, turning as she did. He began to block and respond more quickly, turning each punch and kick into a rally of counterattacks. A fist flew at her face; she parried and turned it into a grab, then turned to smash her own fist into his sternum. He blocked with his free hand and spun her away, putting a roundhouse kick in her path. She saw it coming and dodged, but this put her off-balance, and Moto's roundhouse kick turned into a snap kick which clipped her chin hard enough to knock her down.

She tackled Moto around his knees and brought him to the mat. A dumb move on her part: he had longer limbs and the weight advantage, and he quickly pinned her. She tapped out, and they rose and moved to their corners before bowing and closing again.

So it went. Back and forth, across the mat and down, until Moto finally called it.

"Okay, Tembi," he said, breathing only slightly harder than normal. "Good match."

Tembi bowed to him, her eyes closed, smiling. She felt better than she had in months.

She jumped from the mat to the ground, landing heavily. The muscles of her legs were barely more than tenderized meat, and she wobbled over to the chairs where Bayle and Steven waited.

Neither of them were paying attention to her. Steven was rubbing Bayle's back, trying to get her to pick up her head.

As Tembi came closer, Bayle looked up.

She was crying.

stonegirl
stonegirl come
stonegirl fight
patience

Excerpt from "Notes from the Deep," 4 January 2994 CE

Chapter Ten

"Some people can't bear to be around violence." Matindi nudged the mug of chamomile tea towards Tembi with one long green finger. "Drink."

"Sparring isn't violence," Tembi insisted. "It's…it's like dancing. Or singing!"

"You don't have to convince me," Matindi said. "Well, you might have to convince me how it's like singing, but I understand the dancing part. How it registers in Bayle's head, though? That's her business, and it sounds as if she thinks that sparring is too violent."

Tembi made a rude noise and plopped her head on the table.

The kitchen smelled of cinnamon and sugar. Matindi didn't cook, but she loved to bake, and she had been putting the finishing touches on cinnamon buns when Tembi arrived home. These were cooling on the countertop, waiting for the icing. It had been a lovely scene to come home to, especially after the awkward moment between when Moto had jumped them to Lancaster and when Bayle had run off towards the dormitories, tears still streaming from her eyes.

"Drink," Matindi said again, as she bumped the mug against Tembi's arm. "*Driiiiink.*"

Tembi scooped one hand around the mug and pulled the tea towards her. "Bayle and Steven are my only real friends," she muttered from the crook of her arm.

"For now."

Tembi raised her head and glared. "You're supposed to say, 'Oh heavens no, Tembi, everyone at Lancaster loves you!'"

Matindi lifted one dark eyebrow, and Tembi collapsed into giggles.

"Personally? I think you should be glad that your friend has a gentle heart. There are too few people willing to put peace before war." Matindi got up to pour herself some more tea. She liked to make it the old-fashioned way, with a kettle and a mesh strainer, and she busied herself with these at the sink. Every night, for as long as Tembi had lived with her, they had finished their day sharing time over chamomile tea.

"It was sparring, 'tin! Against *Moto!* That's not exactly going to war."

"Right, right." Matindi returned to the table. "Sorry, I've got work on the brain."

Tembi's eyes shifted to the stacks of folios and holocubes scattered around the kitchen. Matindi tended to bake when she was stressing about work. When she had come home for the night, Matindi had been sliding the cinnamon buns onto a cooling tray with one hand, while scrolling through a holo with the other. Tembi hadn't done too much classwork using action reports, but it looked as though Matindi had been reading something about casualties resulting from an armed conflict. Matindi had snapped off the cube and refused to talk about it, but Tembi was willing to bet it was a report about the war in the Sagittarius systems. Again.

"Everything okay?" she asked.

Matindi nodded. "Nothing to worry about," she said. "I'm only involved because a pack of fools want to use the Deep to move military forces, and they're making some good arguments.

"But don't worry," she assured Tembi. "I won't let the Deep be used that way."

Tembi smiled at her teacher. They had resumed their dreamtime lessons once Tembi had started her training, and the Deep seemed...agitated. Happy, but agitated, as if it needed to talk to Tembi but couldn't figure out how to do that. Matindi said that the Deep had begun pestering her during Tower meetings, too, trying to call her attention to something important, but it wasn't able to communicate anything more than bursts of too-complex song. The Deep kept circling back to agitation whenever the Sagittarius conflict came up; they were sure it had something important to say, but it couldn't—or wouldn't—tell them what it was.

"How about that Steven boy? It's time you started dating."

Matindi was usually much more adept at changing the subject. Tembi sighed and let thoughts of a distant war slip away. "Got dumped right before the Deep picked him, and I don't want to be a rebound fling," she said. "And, like everyone else in my class, he's at least three years older than me!"

"Oh gods, yes, I keep forgetting." Matindi squeezed her eyes tight in embarrassment. "I'm sorry, Tembi. I'm twenty-six hundred years old—anyone under a hundred and fifty looks the same age to me!"

"It's okay," Tembi laughed. "No one's lining up to date a girl with skin like mine."

Matindi pointed at her own face.

"Yeah, I might look Earth-normal, but…" Tembi rubbed her fingertips together, and a sound like small rocks grinding underfoot filled the kitchen. "They say I don't give kisses, I give abrasions."

There was a mortified cough behind them. Matthew, clad in one of Matindi's bathrobes with his bare hairy legs sticking out beneath the hem, scurried out of Matindi's bedroom. He waved hello to Tembi and scurried down the hall to the bathroom. The sound of the shower kicking on was a loud burble before it dissipated into the white noise of daily life.

"Did I say I was twenty-six hundred?" Matindi said, sipping her tea with her pinkie finger extended daintily. "I should have said I'm twenty-six hundred and twenty-eight."

Tembi groaned and dropped her head to the table again.

That night, her dreams were full of colored wings.

She stood in the middle of a plane of white nothingness. Most nights, this was where she would meet Matindi, and the two of them would talk to the Deep.

Tonight, Matindi was occupied with her paperwork (or, possibly, Matthew), so Tembi walked into the void alone.

She thought about calling for the Deep, but that never worked. Not in the dream. Instead, she sang.

It was an aria stolen from a planet far across the galaxy, a melody full of high notes which carried across the plane. She didn't understand the words—the language was dead, or maybe dying, which turned the song into a lament of itself.

But it was beautiful.

L'amour est un oiseau rebelle, Que nul ne peut apprivoiser,
Et c'est bien en vain qu'on l'appelle, S'il lui convient de refuser.

Music, arcing and wild, full of brightly-colored notes and the smell of deepest night, echoed back to her from across the plane. She could not hear its voice, but she could hear its song; she kept singing and let the Deep fly alongside her, tumbling within its own music.

L'oiseau que tu croyais surprendre, Battit de l'aile et s'envola.
L'amour est loin, tu peux l'attendre; Tu ne l'attends plus, il est là.
Tout autour de toi, vite, vite, Il vient, s'en va, puis il revient.
Tu crois le tenir, il t'évite, Tu crois l'éviter, il te tient!

The Deep joined its song to hers, and colors rained from them upon the featureless plane. Their song went on, reaching a crescendo. By then, Tembi was flying too, riding on the soft and downy back of the Deep.

Si tu ne m'aimes pas, je t'aime; Si je t'aime, prends garde à toi!
Si tu ne m'aimes pas, Si tu ne m'aimes pas, je t'aime;
Mais si je t'aime, si je t'aime; Prends garde à toi!

And so the song ended.

Tembi pressed her face against the Deep and whispered, "I'm still mad at you. A little."

The Deep blew a cloud of bright pink smoke that sounded like a wet bowel movement.

"Stop it," she said. "You never even asked if I wanted to be your Witch! Everyone else gets a choice. You picked me and that was the end of it."

The pink smoke went gray, and spiraled up towards where the sky should have been.

"Is that an apology?"

There was a smell of fresh mango and vanilla, spun into sugar and frozen cream.

"Yeah, I love you too, you giant... What are you, anyhow?"

The Deep spun her around in the void in tight pirouettes until her sides hurt from laughing, and they flew on.

They sang together for a while; that was enough for Tembi, but the Deep began to slow down.

"What's happening?" she asked.

It answered by throwing a fountain of deep blue bubbles at her. The color seemed familiar, but she couldn't place its source. Before she could ask for clarification, there was a sense of falling; then, she was standing.

Bayle was in front of her, hunched over and crying as she had been in the dojo earlier that night.

"Is this a vision?" Tembi asked the Deep. "I didn't mean to hurt her."

Bayle's head snapped up. "Tembi!"

"Oh, you're really here." She held out her hand to help the older girl up.

"Where are we?" Bayle stood and wiped her face on the sleeve of her robes. "Where *is* this?"

"It's...I don't think it matters," Tembi said. "It's where Matindi and I go to train with the Deep at night."

"Is this a real place? It doesn't feel real!"

Tembi shrugged. "It's real enough, and private."

"There's no up, there's no down, there's—Wait, what do you mean, you come here to train? The Deep's not here! I can't hear it!"

Tembi felt as if Moto had landed a solid kick to her stomach. "You can hear the Deep?"

"I—well—" Bayle cocked her head to the side, as if listening, and then shook her head. "Yes. Not now, but yes."

"Why are you in the beginner's class?!"

"Can we talk about this later?" Fresh tears were starting to stream down Bayle's face. "This place scares me! I just want to get out of here!"

Tembi was about to argue when the Deep sent a gentle storm of green triangles to tumble like playful kittens around their feet.

"I don't know what that means," Tembi told it.

The triangles scrunched up their surfaces to glare at her in disgust, and then disappeared.

"It means I want to leave," Bayle said. "Please, Tembi."

"You didn't see the triangles?"

"All I see is you, and me, and nothing else." The other girl closed her eyes. "If you know how to get me out of here…this is a prison."

"It's not, but—" Tembi didn't know how to put Bayle at ease. She gave up. "Just wake yourself up."

"This is just a dream?" Bayle took a deep breath. "How do I do that?"

"You do it every night," Tembi said. "Your mind already knows the way out. Let yourself follow it."

Bayle stood quietly, eyes still closed and breathing deeply. After a few moments, she vanished.

"All right," Tembi said to the Deep. "What was that about?"

The sensation of being nuzzled by a gigantic friendly dog came and went in a cloud of warm woody brown. This was replaced by more of those deep blue bubbles—Tembi realized with a start that these were the same color as Bayle's eyes.

"Go to Bayle?" she asked.

The Deep pushed at her with that head-butting sensation again, very gently.

"This would be so much easier if I could hear you," Tembi muttered. "Maybe." She gave the Deep a hug, and woke herself up. It was night—so late at night that morning was an earnest threat—and Taabu was curled beside her in a nest made from her knees and the sheets. She petted the cat, dressed herself in yesterday's robes, and slipped out the window.

(Matindi didn't have a curfew. She said that putting rules about how and when Witches could come and go was busy-work for fools, and that Witches needed to know how to police themselves. On the other hand, Matthew would roll his eyes and sigh at Tembi when the quiet got to be too much and she left to go to Hub when he thought she should be sleeping. So, when he slept over, the window it was.)

She hit the ground outside the window with a hard *thud!* This was followed by a quiet *prap-prap* of paws as Taabu joined her.

"Coming?" she asked the cat.

Taabu glared at her before it stalked off in the direction of a nearby clump of bushes.

Tembi wasn't sure where to go next. There was the dormitory where most of the Witches-in-training stayed, but—

At the back of her mind came the smooth, soft press of water. *Oh. Right. The lake.*

The lake was a quiet walk towards the east. Sheltered within a grove of Earth-normal redwoods, it was the ideal spot for young Witches to rest and play after classes. Tembi had never visited the lake this late at night; it was empty except for a streak of white cutting through the water.

Bayle did a dozen quick laps in the time it would have taken Tembi to swim two, and then beached herself on a floating dock. She dressed, and then appeared beside Tembi on the shore in a quiet **whump** of displaced air.

"So you can jump, too," Tembi said. She wasn't jealous. Not really. "If you've got this much control, why haven't you told Leps and moved out of the beginners' class?"

"Because I want to go home." Bayle was holding herself as if she was made of ice. "I want to be a Witch, but I don't want to be posted anywhere except Atlantis."

Atlantis: Bayle's homeworld. All water except for great spikes of land, with cities built in spirals around them. Not to Tembi's liking, but Bayle could stare at her fingernails for hours, meditating on those tiny windows to her sea.

"And if Leps learns you can jump?"

"Then I'll be bumped up. Probably posted to an apprenticeship on a big station in a year or two. Atlantis is a nowhere planet. Nobody wants that duty. They'll assign a third-rate Witch there, especially if she asks for the post, but…"

"…but not a really good one." Tembi pulled her robes flat against her legs and sat. Light sparkled off of the lake and got tangled within the early morning fog gathering in the air, gleaming like one of the Deep's sensory thoughts. "How long are you going to keep faking?"

Bayle gathered her own robes around her legs and sat beside Tembi. "Figured I'd wait until you and Steven moved up to the next class, then join you."

A dark thought poked Tembi straight between her eyes. "Were you… Did the Deep tell you to be my friend?"

"It tried," Bayle said with a grim chuckle. "I told it I'd talk to you first, and then I'd decide what I wanted to do."

Tembi groused a little at that, but… Well. Given the options, it was the best outcome.

"I also told it that if I pretended to be your friend and you found out, you'd never forgive it. Or me," Bayle added. "I don't think it understands humans."

Tembi felt a prism of unreal feathers fluff at that statement. Bayle's gaze drifted away, and she said, "I'm allowed to have my opinions, and you *don't* understand us! Sorry."

"What?" Tembi asked.

"Oh, the Deep is complaining," Bayle said, waving one hand as if brushing the Deep aside. "It says we're too…simple to understand.

"At least, I think it means simple," she added. "Sometimes it mixes up its intentions."

Tembi picked up a pebble and tossed it into the lake. The water and the mist above it broke into shards of liquid light, and then fell back into their usual ripples. "But you can hear it," she said. "Can't you make it explain itself?

"Not really? It's not conversation," Bayle said. "When it speaks in words, it's… It's like the Deep doesn't really understand what it's saying. It gets most of the words right, but I don't think it fully recognizes what they mean."

"Matindi says it likes to talk about shipping and schedules, because those use straightforward terms. Anything more complex, and it starts to get confused. Especially if it needs to talk about concepts like friendship."

"Poor thing," Bayle sighed. "Imagine if you could only talk about work."

Tembi felt the Deep settle around them. She reached out with one hand and began to scratch an invisible…something. "And never took any time off," she said, wondering if she was actually feeling the Deep lean into her fingertips, or if she was imagining it. "And had to talk to twenty thousand Witches across the galaxy, all of them at once—"

"Poor thing," Bayle said again, then added, "What are you doing with your hand?"

"Oh, it likes to be scratched in the dream," Tembi said. "Maybe it enjoys it here, too."

Bayle stared at her as if she was mad, but then stretched out her own hand and began to scratch the air. "It does enjoy it," she said quietly. She sounded almost awestruck.

They stopped talking. Or, Tembi stopped talking: Bayle seemed to be having a conversation with the Deep. Tembi quit scratching the air, threw a few more smallish rocks into the lake, and then lay back to watch the edges of the trees appear as the sun began to rise.

"Hey, Tembi?" Bayle asked, almost shyly. "I think it wants you to teach me how to sing."

they come
mother father
far
far
they come

Excerpt from "Notes from the Deep," 16 December 3439 CE

Chapter Eleven

The next few weeks had nothing to do with music. Instead, it was classwork during the day, and at nights Moto would teach Bayle to spar.

"The Deep doesn't want you to sing," Tembi had told Bayle. "Not really. Singing is just one of the ways it talks. It wants you to learn how to move with it. Sparring helps me focus on moving with another person, so maybe it'll work for you."

Bayle listened to the Deep for a moment, and then said, "It says yes, but also no, and then I think it threw up in purple?"

"Yeah, that sounds about right."

"What does the purple vomit mean?"

Tembi shrugged. As far as she could tell, the colors didn't have meaning. Neither did the motions, or the textures, or the smells, or…or any of it, really. Those differed according to the Deep's mood: one day, it would use deep blue bubbles in place of Bayle's name; the next, the wild smell of the open sea.

Music could keep pace with the Deep, because music was always changing. To Tembi, it made perfect sense that music was part of the Deep's language. But she couldn't understand why nobody at Lancaster tried to sing along with it, or why music wasn't part of their training. In fact, she had been astonished (and bewildered, and more than a little dismayed) to learn that when the Deep was new, music had been forbidden to its Witches! Not just in their school, but in the entire city of Hub. It had been thought that a song in the mind could crowd out the Deep, so when the city around the school was built, the Witches demanded that music—all music—be excluded.

A mighty feat, that. Among all the peoples of all the worlds, music was their shared constant. The Deep bound those worlds together and allowed them to be as one, so they could cross the

Rails without ships or fuel or the other burdens of travel. And, as the Deep allowed them to bind their fortunes, so they had given the Deep this one vast city to seal music away from its Witches.

As for the Witches themselves, they had built their school behind walls and forests and gardens and great green lawns not for safety or beauty, but to dilute the sounds of the city, as cities make their own music.

In Matindi's time—in Matthew's time—no Witch was allowed to sing. Or watch the channels. Or go to parties, or ride a lift on a different world, or walk into an unfamiliar store, or—

Well. Prohibiting music? A stupid move, an idiot's token gesture, and it was only a matter of time before the Witches were forced to accept that.

Music had always been there.

Music would always be there.

After a few hundred years of such nonsense, the Witches finally admitted they might have been a bit on the hasty side when it came to music. There were some traditionalists who swore that music led to the corruption of their bond with the Deep, certainly, and others who weren't as strict but still avoided music when they could. But music could now be found in Hub, in Lancaster, in the homes of the less orthodox Witches.

(Tembi very much enjoyed walking past those traditionalist Witches with her soundkit on and singing as loudly as she could, but only when she was sure Matthew wouldn't catch her.)

So, music.

Song.

And singing.

Since Bayle loved music herself and could already sing a passable tune, Tembi had decided the Deep couldn't have meant *singing*. No, not actual singing. It must have meant…something else. Something like singing, but something Bayle couldn't yet do. They pressed the Deep; it had no answers, and bubbled at them like a fish beneath the surface of a pond.

So. They needed to find something like singing.

It would be trial-and-error to find out what that was, so Tembi had decided to begin with sparring.

Unfortunately, Bayle had taken to martial arts like a fish to a frying pan, and after a month of hard effort, they had decided to give up and try something else.

"Don't get me wrong, I love what it's doing for my thighs," Bayle said over a round of tumbarranchos. She pointed her toe and flexed the muscles now dotting her legs. "Better than swimming. But Tembi? I'm tired of getting hit, and I don't like hitting other people. This isn't for me."

Tembi nodded. "We'll try something else. Does Pepper have any suggestions?"

Bayle checked the databand on her wrist, as if reading a message from a friend. They were trying to use "Pepper" as code for the Deep when they spoke about it in public, but they both knew they were too self-conscious about such silliness to make it work.

"No," she said. "Pepper doesn't have anything new to add."

Tembi shook a fist at the imaginary Pepper; this was met with the smell of a rampaging pack of enormous, soaking wet dogs about to crash down upon her in greeting.

"You smell that?" she asked Bayle.

The other girl shook her head and held up her dinner. "Only this," she replied.

"All right," Tembi said. "I'll check with Pepper tonight."

"Hey! Hey, look! Witches!"

Tembi and Bayle exchanged a bemused glance. The Venezuelan restaurant was on the outskirts of the tourist district, and the paint on their faces tended to garner attention from visitors. The two young men who had spotted them were dressed in worn Spacers' uniforms of dark black and blue, with streaks of red across their chests to denote fleet insignias and rank.

The men dropped into the vacant chairs at their table; the older (and better-looking) of the two tipped his chair sideways to talk to Bayle.

"Love the makeup," he said, smiling. He reached out to touch a lock of Bayle's black hair which was resting against her paint. She blocked with her right hand, and spread her fingers apart so he couldn't help but notice the translucent webbing between them.

"Hi," she said, with the kind of toothy smile that reminded Tembi of a shark.

"Hi yourself," he said, and spread his own fingers. He had webbing too, darker and more textured than Bayle's; he pointed towards his neck, and a set of rudimentary gills on his neck flared and closed. "I was just gonna ask you if that was a picture of kelp, but I'm thinking I guessed right."

Bayle looked him up and down with an appraising eye. "Lemurian?"

"You know anybody else with gills?"

"My mother always warned me about Lemurians."

"Really?" he grinned at her, and went to touch the lock of hair brushing against her face. This time, she let him. "What did she say?"

"That they're cheap and have terrible taste in drinks."

"Well, then," he said, flagging over a waitress. "Why don't you help me pick, and we'll prove your mother wrong?"

Tembi sighed into her meal. This wasn't an uncommon event: Bayle was beautiful, and radiated an aura of being the type of woman best approached through dinner and dancing. Men gravitated towards her. At least this time they weren't embarrassingly old.

She turned to the younger Spacer beside her to pass the time. "Hey."

He was busy fiddling with the levels on a brand-new sound-kit. "Hey," he said, idly.

"Tembi."

"Kalais," he replied. "You know how to make this thing work?"

She did, actually: it was a few models newer than the sound-kit she had brought with her from Adhama, but it was in the same family.

"Thanks," he said, as music began to chirp through the earpieces. He added, almost shyly: "I've never met a Witch before."

"I'm not really a Witch," Tembi said. "I'm still in training."

"What's the difference?" He had light brown skin but his eyes were almost black, and deeply earnest. They reminded her of a puppy.

"I can't jump myself or talk to the Deep yet."

"Why not?"

She shrugged. "Brain development," she said. "It's a prefrontal cortex thing. It's already talking to me, but I won't be able to hear it clearly until I'm at least eighteen. Probably older."

"Wait, how old are you?" He peered at her with new interest, and Tembi realized that he was probably her own age.

"Sixteen," she said. "You?"

"Seventeen." He held out his hand. "Kalais."

"You said that," Tembi said. She paused, and then shook his hand. He grimaced as he touched her skin. "I'm not Earth-normal," she said, setting her ears flat against her head as an example.

"Well, yeah," he said. "But who is?"

She looked more closely at him. Kalais' puppy eyes were a little larger than most, but they weren't too unusual.

"My planet's pretty dim," he said. "They call it a perpetual twilight."

"Sure." She had heard of low-light planets. Most of the people living on it needed special lenses to travel to worlds with standard lighting. Maybe his eyes—

He blinked, hard, and his dark irises vanished. Beneath those near-black lenses, his real eye color was almost white. Tembi jerked back in surprise, and Kalais laughed. He blinked again, and those dark irises were back.

"Whoa!" Tembi said. "Can you see in the light?"

"With the lenses down, yes," he said. "If they're up, everything's just blurs of different colors.

"I like your ears," he added. "They make you look like an elf."

"What's an elf?"

"Kalais, don't bore the poor girl." The older Spacer pushed

two drinks in front of them. These frothed a thick pink foam all over the table. "Here you go, kids. Two virgin rose petals, for two virgin roses."

Tembi felt the need to blush and stammer, but Kalais was doing a better job of that than she ever could. Bayle winked at her, and sipped daintily from a long-necked bottle of something that smelled of berries and spice.

"The boys are military. They're here on reconnaissance," Bayle told Tembi, and then nodded towards the older Spacer. "Rabbit's job is to set up meetings for his boss."

"What's your job?" she asked Kalais. She tried the pink drink; sweet, but with a strangely sour aftertaste. The flavors went well together.

"To learn *his* job." He nodded at Rabbit. "General Eichin says you always need a backup in key positions. Just in case."

"War?" Tembi tried to ignore the feeling of furious wings beating against the back of her mind in bright sparks of rainbows.

"You heard of the conflict in Sagittarius?" Rabbit asked. When she nodded, he said, "It's getting bad. There's a real humanitarian crisis happening—it's getting real bad.

"You Witches," he said, as he pressed an index finger lightly against Bayle's nose, "don't let the Deep move anything involved in war. But we're the good guys. No doubt about that. We're going to war to end a genocide, not cause one. I'm here to lay the groundwork for Eichin to come and petition the Witches for use of the Deep."

"It's not going to happen. The Deep wants peace," Bayle said. "That's the only request it's made from Lancaster."

"But if it helped us now, it'd be promoting peace," Rabbit said.

"This is a managerial issue," Tembi heard herself say in age-less Matindi's no-nonsense voice. "Bayle and I can't help you."

"I know." Rabbit rolled his head to stare up at the ceiling. "I'm just… I'm just blowing air. Read up on what's happening in Sagittarius, if you want to understand why we're here."

The conversation went flat for a moment. Bayle rescued it,

steering it deftly towards what Hub offered in terms of night-life. The men said they would be stationed on Found for several months, both to set the groundwork for Eichin's arrival and to support the general once he had arrived. Tembi asked a bunch of questions about why Eichin couldn't do any of this himself, and was told that there were some things that high-ranking military personnel had time to do, but grunt jobs? No, those were not among them.

As it didn't take much time to set up meetings or find a decent hotel room, Rabbit and Kalais expected to have some time to kill.

"We're looking forward to it, to be honest," Rabbit said. "My little buddy here got hurt in a battle a few weeks ago, and I've earned some shore leave. We want to live in a place where we don't have to worry about whether the ship's gravity's going to cut out while we're using the bathroom."

Tembi wrinkled her nose at that, but had to agree that he had a point.

They agreed to meet up again on the next breakday. Rabbit asked if they could escort them to the hopper back to Lancaster. It was such an old-fashioned thing to do that Bayle agreed on the spot.

They fell into twos, Bayle and Rabbit leading the way, their arms entwined. Tembi and Kalais followed; they talked about music, mostly, and about how they missed their homeworlds and families. Tembi listened more than she talked; she tended to keep Marumaru close to her heart. Kalais told her how he had enlisted young; most of his family were military personnel themselves and they approved of his decision to serve.

"Rabbit said you were hurt in a battle?" she asked.

"Yeah," he said, an almost wondering expression on his face as he moved his left arm. "I mean, I wasn't fighting in it. I was in a section of the ship that got hit, and my arm got wrecked. I mean, just scraping *wrecked!* I'm lucky I wasn't killed. I don't even remember how it happened—it was that fast! One moment I'm running errands for Rabbit, and the next I'm trapped under a metal pylon. I was there for hours until the battle ended and they could spare the time to cut me out."

Tembi didn't know what to say so she offered a weak, "That's terrible."

"I don't remember most of it," he said. "They shoot you up with a short-term memory blocker if you've suffered battlefield trauma. They say it keeps you from suffering post-traumatic stress disorders, but I think they do it to keep soldiers from going AWOL during recovery."

"Does it still hurt?" she asked.

"Nope. I got the full rehabilitation treatment," he replied. "But they didn't fix the cosmetic damage. It's really ugly to look at. Definitely second-date territory."

"Oh, so this is a date?" she asked.

"Well," he said, slipping his hand into hers. "Now it is."

She laughed.

"Your skin is amazing," he said, turning her hand over in his own. "It looks Earth-normal, but I bet you could stop a knife!"

"Probably not," she admitted. "It gets tougher when I'm under stress. It's been a pretty quiet month, so it's not as hard as it usually is. Besides, getting stabbed would still hurt."

"What do you mean?"

"You know when you bang your leg on something with a sharp edge? My skin might not show the injury, but I still feel it in the nerves beneath it."

"Can you feel this?" he said, as he ran his thumb over her knuckles.

"Sort of." She nodded. "Not through my skin, but everything under my skin knows I'm being touched."

Kalais put more pressure on the back of her hand. "How about now?"

"Now I'm worried you'll break something."

He laughed, and brought her hand to his mouth. He kissed the back of it. "How about now?"

Tembi shook her head. She felt awfully lightheaded.

He nibbled, very gently, on a fingertip. "How about now?"

That, Tembi felt. Along her finger, along every single centimeter of her body—

"Yeah," she said, grinning the slightest little bit. "I felt that."

Later that night, after the hopper flight with Bayle and a mug of chamomile tea with Matindi, after she had showered and changed and taken a few minutes to redraw Taabu's fake eyebrows, after she was safe in her own bed and watching the fireflies creep along the plass, Tembi thought about that simple, stupid, unhygienic nibble.

And wondered if Kalais would do it again the next time she saw him.

---

greenlove
stonegirl to greenlove
love
home
family
strength
FIGHT

Excerpt from "Notes from the Deep," 18 May 4042 CE

Chapter Twelve

"Tembi!"

Tembi looked up from her holo just in time to grab the foam ball flying at her head. She tossed it back to Leps, but before the ball reached her teacher, it stopped and hung in the air.

"Hands," Leps commanded. "Hold them up. High as you can."

Oh. Great. This again. Tembi obeyed. Leps had been pushing the class harder than usual lately, but no one could figure out why. Mornings and afternoons were now a blend of textbook learning and object movement, with the occasional pop quiz.

In this particular case, it was a literal pop quiz—the foam ball smacked Tembi in the face. Tembi blinked to get the dust out of her eyes; the rest of the class snickered.

"Did you even try to catch it?" Leps snapped.

A trick question, and one without any good answer. Too late, Tembi realized her mistake: if she said she had tried to catch the ball using the Deep, then she had failed the test; if she said she had asked the Deep to stay passive, then she hadn't instinctively understood Leps' lesson; and, if she said she hadn't tried at all, then she was dumb as a pile of flat rocks.

Three foam balls vanished from a nearby rack, and reappeared to smack Leps across the back of her head, *one! two! three!*

Leps closed her eyes and took a deep breath.

"I didn't—" Tembi began.

Leps held up one finger, and then pointed to the door.

Tembi decided to double down. "I didn't ask the Deep to do that."

"Oh?" Leps said coldly. "Then I want a two-thousand-word essay on why that's a bigger problem than if you had asked the Deep to hit me."

"But—"

"Three thousand words," Leps said. "By the time class is out this evening. And cite your sources. You pull anything off of the channels without crediting it, and I'll make you run errands for me. Literally."

Tembi shoved her chair back, taking perverse satisfaction from how one of its loose feet shrieked as it skidded across the marble floor, and left the room.

She stomped around the halls of Lancaster Tower for a while, listening to the echoing *pad-pad-pad-pad* of her bare feet against the stone. The Tower never failed to irritate her: all of its hallways were beautiful works of art, gleaming from gold and polished stone, and nobody except visitors and novice Witches bothered to use them. Fully trained Witches jumped everywhere. And she had never seen a person doing maintenance, not even to monitor a swarm of janitor 'bots—

"You clean these, don't you?" she said aloud. "You just…you just move the dirt and footprints away, don't you?"

Nobody answered, but she suddenly felt guilty about her bare feet.

Her feet had to be cleaner than shoes, right? She washed them three times a day—how often did shoes get washed?

…still…

Tembi left the Tower and cut across the South meadow. Orange butterflies soared up around her in a cloud; she thought about yelling at them, just on general principle. But that wasn't productive. *Nothing* seemed productive, not with three thousand words hanging over her head—

She turned east on a whim.

She was off to visit the Martian.

Lancaster Library was a goodly distance from the Tower. It was a warm, welcoming place…if you could get to it. It wasn't just the hike through kilometers of grass and wildflowers, oh no. Set within a maze made from giant boulders and strategically placed shrubbery, the Library stayed where it was, while the maze changed at the whim of the Librarian and the Deep.

(The Librarian said that since fully trained Witches could always jump directly to the Library, this was done to teach the students humility in the face of higher knowledge. Normally, Tembi could complete the maze within a turn or two, but that's because she actually enjoyed visiting the Library. If she was with another student, the maze usually continued to dump them back into the lawn until they had completed sufficient penance to show respect. Or, failing that, serious annoyance and swearing.)

Today, the Library allowed itself to be found without any twists or turns in the maze at all. Tembi ran down the gravel path to the too-small cottage with the old wooden door. Three quick taps on the doorplate, and the Library's front door swung open.

The single room inside the Library was small and square, with one wooden door set in each of its four walls. It reminded her of her family's unit back home in Marumaru, but made from bare gray stone instead of painted metal. She dragged her fingertips across the rough-hewn surface of the stone, delighting in how she could feel its bumps and crannies. Her skin was thinning; she was slowly regaining her sense of touch.

"Kiddo, that sound is like fingernails on a chalkboard."

The circular desk in the middle of the room was the oldest human-made thing Tembi had ever seen with her own eyes. Its wood had turned a deep, rich brown from being carefully oiled and polished once a month by the man who sat in its center. Born in the Mars colonies before bioforming had become popular, Williamson was tall, with light skin, short-cropped dirty blond hair, and blue eyes. Like most of the older Witches, he seemed almost ageless, but he did have some prominent wrinkles cutting across his forehead from a lifetime of squinting at text. As far as Tembi could tell, he was only slightly younger than the desk.

(And only slightly older than Matindi and Matthew.)

And he wore glasses! Actual reading glasses with silver frames!

"Hey, Williamson," she said, folding her arms and plunking her upper body on the desk. "What's a chalkboard?"

"You know digital displays and holoscreens? Like those, only made from slate."

Slate. She had never heard the word except as the name of another neighborhood way, way down in the Stripes, so far down that her sisters had threatened to beat her up if she ever went to explore it. But if it was in the Stripes, that meant slate was either a color or…

"They make digital displays from rock?" she asked.

"Not really," he said, as he leaned over and made a note on the plass tablet beside him. "It was a treated flat surface for semi-permanent content, used to display lecture notes during class and erased once they were no longer needed.

"But," he said, turning the page and skimming the content with an index finger, "it is said that when Earth-normal fingernails were applied to that surface, a shrill noise was generated. Which, for the purpose of this discussion, is all that's relevant."

"Okay." She peered over the counter. "What are you reading?"

"*De Caelo et Mundo,* by Aristotle." He glanced up, saw the expression on her face, and smiled kindly. The laugh lines around his eyes deepened. "An ancient philosopher's thoughts on how Earth's solar system works. It was written several thousand years before humans invented flight."

"You're a Witch, Williamson! Why are you reading *that?*"

"I think it's hilarious. What brings you here today, young Stoneskin?"

Tembi tried the nickname on for size and decided she liked it. "The Deep threw some balls at Leps. She blamed it on me and assigned me three thousand words."

"Ah, ethics. My favorite." Williamson said. He pressed a panel on the desk, and the wooden door to the left of his desk slid open. "Do you know what you're looking for?"

"I think so." It wasn't the first time Tembi had to write a lengthy essay about how she needed to be in control of the Deep and not the other way around. "But…"

Williamson arched an eyebrow at her.

Leps..." Tembi wasn't quite sure what was bothering her. "She's always been tough, but she wasn't mean. Except now, she's mean."

"Her first annual performance review is next week," Williamson replied. "She's nervous that she'll be told she isn't a good teacher."

He leaned forward and peered over the edge of the book. "It's not always about you, kiddo," he said, and winked.

Tembi giggled.

"No food, no drink, no open flames," the librarian said, as if chanting a prayer older than time itself. "You tear the books—"

"—you tear my hide." Tembi finished, and stuck her tongue out at him.

"Well, not *your* hide, young Stoneskin," he said, and paused to make another note on his plass tablet. "I'd have to find another form of punishment for you. There's a bathroom around here that's been in dire need of cleaning for at least twenty years. The Deep has been begging me to do it, but I'm saving it for someone who doesn't treat books the way they deserve."

Tembi grimaced.

"Shout if you need me," he said.

"Okay," she said, and vanished into the room.

She had no idea where this room was: there was no space for it in the tiny cottage in the center of the maze. Williamson was still in view, still sitting right there at his desk in plain sight, still no more than three meters away. As far as she knew, he was also halfway across the galaxy.

Tembi turned away from the Librarian and began to walk around the room. She liked books. The covers had a crunchy, solid feel to them that wasn't found in using holos or with scrolling on a tablet, and their pages had a sweet, woody smell. And, while they were extremely inconvenient and next to impossible to search, Tembi always felt like she belonged in the library when she was surrounded by books.

She had figured out a way to beat the search problem, though.

Apparently, the Deep liked to read, and it forgot nothing.

"Deep?" she asked quietly. "Can you recommend a book to help with Leps' assignment?"

A book appeared on a nearby table. She picked it up and checked the spine: *Ethical Challenges in Movement along the Rails: A Primer.*

She winced. The Deep usually didn't give her the basics. "Um—"

The book vanished. Another one appeared, with a brightly colored cartoon Witch on the cover. *What is the Deep? An I'm Curious!™ Guide for Children.*

Well. She could take a hint.

"Deep?" she asked. "Is there a book you want me to read?"

Immediately—instantly!—stacks of books appeared around her. A cage of books. No, whole walls of books on every side, covering the table, the floor, stacked so tightly that if she moved a centimeter they would collapse and crush her—

"Tembi!"

"Sorry, Williamson!" she shouted. The books vanished.

"Let's try this again," she muttered to herself, very quietly. "Deep? I can only read one book at a time. Is there one book I should read before I read the others?"

A pause as the Deep stopped to consider what she was asking.

She repeated the question, this time using different words, just in case.

A book appeared on the table in front of her. It disappeared before she could touch it, and was replaced by a different book. The second book vanished, and was replaced by a third…

This went on for some time. Tembi took a seat on the table and waited for the Deep to make up its mind. After a while, two books began to exchange places—a book with a blue cover was replaced by a book with a brown cover, then it was replaced by the blue, and then the blue was replaced with the brown…

The book with the brown cover settled on the table. It was massive, with glittering gold edging its thin pages. She sighed: it was the kind of book that no one other than Williamson would ever read for pleasure.

"This one?" she asked, holding her hands above the cover in case the Deep jumped it away again. When it didn't move, she flipped open the cover. *"A Foundational Treatise on the Use of the Deep in Conflict Conditions,"* she read aloud, and flipped to the first page.

> *"As the Deep is the first, and thus far only, sapient being discovered apart from humanity itself, the ethical underpinnings governing the use of this being for our own purposes has been a hotly contested topic."*

Okay. None of that sounded too dense. She moved on to the second sentence.

> *"The majority of ethical arguments made are solipsistic and do not consider the elements of accountability and shared communal purpose we have taken upon ourselves as the fourth-dimensional stewards of this being."*

Tembi stood and picked up the book. She knocked on the door frame and entered the Librarian's central room. "Williamson?"

The librarian took off his reading glasses and spun in his chair to face her. "Yes, kiddo?"

"The Deep wants me to read this, but…"

"Is that one of Rowland's?" he asked, and took the book from her. "Ah, yes. The eighth volume of fifteen. Only a Witch could live long enough to regurgitate the same tiresome point in several thousand brand new ways."

"The author was a Witch?"

"Oh, yes. Still is, most likely. He dusts himself off and comes to Lancaster to give lectures every decade or so.

"By the way, Rowland is younger than Madam Matindi," the librarian whispered conspiratorially. "But both of them are spring chickens when compared to yours truly."

"What's a chicken?"

"Gods save us," Williamson sighed. "What do you want to know about Rowland?"

"I don't know," she admitted. "The Deep gave me this book. Is there an abridged version?"

"Of Rowland? No, nobody would take the time to make one. As I said, he writes mainly for the satisfaction of seeing himself in print, and not for the purpose of contributing anything new to the field.

"But," the librarian added, as he turned the book over in his hands, "I suppose he did have one good point, several hundred years ago…" He paused as he turned the pages with gentle fingers. "Yes. He mentioned that as the Deep learns more about humanity, it might change its opinion of us. So holding on to the customs we use to interact with the Deep is about our self-preservation as much as its own."

Tembi blinked at him.

"Young Stoneskin," Williamson said, very patiently, "under what conditions is it prohibited to use the Deep?"

"To harm someone, especially during war."

"Correct." The librarian closed the book and pointed to the word "Conflict" on its spine. "Now, we assume we follow these prohibitions as the Deep has asked this of us. But tell me, young Stoneskin, in all of its time associating with us, do you think the Deep has ever made such a clear, coherent request?"

Tembi shook her head, slowly. The idea of the Deep saying outright that it wouldn't participate in a war…Well. That wasn't how the Deep communicated. At best, it would throw the smell of blood into their minds until the Witches managed to guess what it wanted.

"The biggest lie that Lancaster has told the galaxy is that while the Deep may be sentient, it relies on its Witches to make its decisions," Williamson said. "Everyone here at Lancaster knows that the Deep does what it wants. It's fully capable of making our lives a living hell if it wanted to. But it doesn't. It's got a playful streak, but it also has improved our lives immeasurably because *that's* what it wants for us.

"Can you imagine if it decides it wants something else?" Williamson's eyes were intent on hers, as if he was trying to drill the single most important message of her life straight into her brain. "Commerce would slow to a crawl, or even stop on some remote planets. The galactic economy would have to be rewritten to compensate for the relatively slow speed of starships. And, to go back one more link in the chain, we would have to build those starships first, as almost all of current galactic trade uses ships designed to work with the Deep.

"So we follow traditions," he said. "Because none of our traditions have caused the Deep to abandon us, and those of us who love this galaxy-hopping lifestyle of ours are terrified to our bones of that coming to pass."

He handed Tembi the book. "Go," he said. "Read. And don't forget to ask yourself why the Deep's decision to violate tradition and choose an eight-year-old Witch has shaken all of Lancaster."

talk

Lancaster

talk

talk talk talk talk talk

talk talk talk talk talk talk talk talk talk talk

talk talk talk talk talk talk talk talk talk talk talk talk talk talk

STOP

Excerpt from "Notes from the Deep," 4 January 3270 CE

Chapter Thirteen

Bayle's family had money. Serious, planet-purchasing sums of money. Bayle had a line of credit in her name, and she enjoyed spending it: Tembi and Steven usually came along for the ride.

And now, so did Rabbit and Kalais.

Even if she was one of those Witches who lived until she was a thousand years old or more, Tembi was sure she'd never be comfortable with the idea that she now had money. And she did! She did have money…or at least quite a lot of credit, borrowing against her future wages when she went to work for Lancaster. (Bayle had assured her that this was the same thing.) Indeed, Tembi's new position as a Witch had turned into the best thing possible for her family. As Leps had predicted, Lancaster's accountants had garnished Tembi's future earnings and set up a weekly payment plan for her mother. Her family had moved from their too-small unit in Marumaru to an apartment—an actual apartment! With running water!—in a neighborhood in Red, and one of her sisters had managed to leverage her new address to get a job as a clerk in a boutique up in Gold.

Tembi was convinced that it all might disappear in a heartbeat. So she let Bayle pick up the sums, and Tembi told herself it was fair because…

…fine. It wasn't fair—it was in *no way* fair! So Tembi had offered to teach Bayle things that the older girl had never gotten a chance to learn.

Like pickpocketing.

And while Bayle might never be good at sparring, she had the makings of an exceptional petty thief.

"You're making the Deep to do the lift for you," Steven grumbled. "I just know it."

"Whatever you tell yourself to make you feel better," Bayle

said, stretching out her long fingers. The golden badge she had lifted from the law officer vanished as the Deep returned it to the officer's belt.

The five of them had been enjoying the night air outside a small café, sipping on iced drinks and sharing a whole cake between them, when Bayle had leapt up and rolled the passing law officer under the pretext of asking for directions. Rabbit and Kalais had barely even noticed that she had left to talk to the law until she showed them his badge as her prize.

Kalais was shaking his head. "You do this for fun," he said, utterly bemused. "You steal people blind, and then return it?"

"The game is to not get caught," Bayle said.

"Why do you lift from the law?"

"We have a points system," Steven said. "Lifting from the law and from thieves is worth the most."

"Thieves?" Kalais asked.

Tembi pointed around the street, picking out the two (other) professional pickpockets working the crowd, and explained how they were a team which cut and lifted handbags. One would distract, the other would grab, and then they'd both fade into the alleys to repeat the process on the next block.

"This is really stupid," Rabbit said. "Really, really stupid." He looked at Bayle and Steven. "You should know better." Then he looked at Tembi. "*You* know better, don't you?"

She replied by sucking the last remaining drops out of the bottom of her plass cup.

"Witches don't steal," Steven said. "Everyone knows that."

"If you get caught—"

Bayle held up Rabbit's wallet.

"Hey—" he started to say, but the wallet vanished from Bayle's hand. He tapped his pocket, pulled out the wallet, and checked to make sure everything was inside.

"We don't steal," Bayle said. "It's just a game."

"It's a game to you," Rabbit said. The gills on his neck flared as he took a deep breath. "Not to anybody else. Not to you, if you get caught."

"It's just," Bayle said, as she smeared frosting on Rabbit's nose, "a *game*."

He growled and yanked her onto his lap. Tembi, Steven, and Kalais were suddenly very interested in the scenery several meters in the opposite direction of the two of them.

"Could you teach me how to be a pickpocket?" Kalais asked her, as they dropped their plates and utensils into the cleaner bins.

Tembi opened her mouth to say yes, but the word got stuck on its way out. Teaching Bayle and Steven had been one thing—she was still not quite sure why she had done that in the first place—but teaching Kalais…

"No," she said. "Rabbit's right. We gotta stop."

"Victimless crime!" Steven said, throwing his hands up. "And it's only, like, two minutes of crime, at most!"

"Then you teach him."

Steven grumbled about clunky fingers and missing easy grabs, and Tembi knew the discussion was over.

Bayle and Rabbit rejoined them a few minutes later, and they set off into the city.

"So…" Rabbit said, reaching over to ruffle Tembi's hair. "Want to drop the kids off with the sitter and go catch that show?"

Tembi pretended to punch him in the ribs. Rabbit looped one arm around Bayle's waist, the other around Steven's, and started running.

Tembi and Kalais let the others disappear into the crowd. He took her by the hand, and they walked without speaking, watching the fireflies blip in and out of the air.

After a while, he asked, "Is it like this where you grew up?"

Marumaru. Hard, wind-scoured Marumaru… "No," she said. "You?"

"I've already told you about my planet. You never talk about yourself."

"Ask yourself how a little kid learned how to steal," she said, as she snuggled her arms around his waist, "and you've got me figured out."

"I doubt that," he chuckled, and pulled her off to the side of the street.

They kissed under a shop's floating sign, slow and sweet. They had learned that if they took their time, she would start to feel Kalais's lips against hers (and he could keep his skin intact). When they broke apart, he touched her lips.

"Too rough?" she asked.

"No," he replied, as he ran his fingers across the curve of her face. "Your skin's getting softer."

"Good." She pulled him towards her—

Behind them, Bayle coughed. Loudly.

Tembi turned, and Kalais buried his face in her hair, laughing. "May we help you?" she asked Bayle.

"I'm sorry, I thought you wanted to see this show." Bayle was examining her manicure. "Was I wrong? I was obviously wrong."

The three of them set out to catch up with the others. The club was halfway across Hub, in the part of town that Tembi visited when she was missing home and Matindi wasn't around for a quick jump to Adhama. Tembi took them through the streets until they bumped into some people with their faces painted up in wild patterns. They all formed a pack, moving ever-closer to the club.

Most of the clubs in Hub played up the city's connection to Lancaster. Face paint was a must; so were tricks using anti-grav units to make it seem like the Deep was present and willing to bend to the whims of the dancers. Off-worlders loved the idea that there might be Witches in the room; Tembi and her friends loved how no one would ever suspect there were.

Music met them on the street: strong, powerful music set to a rainbow of near-blinding lights. They started dancing even before they got through the doors, catching the heavy beat and pushing forward with the rest of the crowd. Rabbit managed to talk the bouncers into letting Tembi and Kalais in, and the five of them danced their way into a room made of sound and light and the heady scents of alcohol and movement.

This club was in an abandoned warehouse. The room was a cavern, the air filled with various 'bots and dancers. They had entered at the top of a tall metal staircase; below was a floor lit in glowing bronze, nearly lost beneath the dancers.

Steven stood, eyes closed and taking in the layout of the room through his ears and nose, before he jumped over a railing and used the Deep to float gently downward, stopping just above the dance floor.

"Watch this!" Tembi shouted to Kalais, and pointed at Steven.

Steven began to dance. The colored lights from the 'bots overhead bounced off of his scales, turning him into a prism of moving color. He was riding the Deep, dancing a full two meters above the floor, moving above the heads of the other dancers. Hands reached up to grab him; he let two girls and a *very* pretty boy catch hold of his robes and pull him down to join them.

"Do they know he's a real Witch?" Kalais shouted at Tembi.

"It doesn't matter here!" she shouted back.

The two of them found the stairs and pushed their way down to the dance floor. They found an anti-grav field and let it carry them up to a patch of empty air somewhere near the bar. For Tembi, dancing was a little like singing—not as close as sparring, but not too far apart, either—she gave herself over to it and let herself move.

Kalais was self-conscious, holding himself rigidly tight as he stared at the dancers.

Tembi found this adorable.

"No one cares!" she called to him, turning a somersault in midair. She flew around him, put her arms around his waist, and pulled him into the dance.

The Deep was happy; it held up Kalais as it did Tembi, and they soared higher than the anti-grav units allowed.

Kalais finally let himself go.

He was a good dancer, taking advantage of the Deep to soar through the air. She barely noticed when the show started: the music changed, a fast switch from channel to live, and the band started playing. There was more emotion in live music; she felt the Deep surge around her, dancing along with her and Kalais, moving and playing and (she was sure, although she couldn't hear, not outside of its dreams) singing.

"Should we be this high up?" Kalais asked, as he pushed himself away from the ceiling.

Tembi shrugged and had the Deep take them a little closer to the floor.

This turned out to be a good thing, as the law raided the club a minute later.

"Scheisse," Tembi muttered, as she and Kalais watched the law officers crash through the doors.

The overhead lights went on. The false enchantments of the club were instantly dispelled; the reality that they were flying around a seedy abandoned warehouse blunted their good mood. The music stopped, and the anti-gravs slowly spun down so as to not dump the dancers onto the ground. Tembi asked the Deep to let her and Kalais down, slowly, and their feet touched down at the same time as the others.

There were strict warnings, but mostly the law just wanted the club to be emptied and the dancers to go home. Tembi and Kalais almost managed to make it through the door, but just as they had reached the end of the traffic jam, a heavy hand dropped down upon her shoulder.

She turned. The law was there, an Earth-normal man with light skin and light brown eyes.

"You look a little young to be here, kid," the lawman said.

"I'm eighteen," she said automatically.

"Sure you are." The lawman spotted Kalais. "You, too, right? C'mon."

The lawman began to steer Tembi away, expecting Kalais to follow. Tembi motioned him to fall back—she had no problems slipping the law in a busy club—but there was a harsh, "Kal!" and Rabbit was there.

"Oh, Kal, what are you doing here?!" Rabbit said, sweeping between the lawman and Kalais. He turned to the lawman. "I'm so sorry, officer! What did he *do?!*"

The lawman had seen this before. "His big brother, no doubt? Here to yell at him for following you to the club?"

"No, I'm his boss," Rabbit said. "We're not related. See?"

Rabbit flared his gills. It was sudden; the lawman wasn't expecting a man who looked Earth-normal to have an exploding neck. He dropped his hold on Tembi's shoulder; she grabbed Kalais's hand and started running.

The lawman shouted and started after them, but Rabbit was there, saying he wanted to help, he could give the officer their names, why wouldn't the officer just allow him to help?

Tembi ducked another lawman and dropped into the crowd of dancers leaving through a side door, pulling Kalais behind her. They broke into the evening air; two more of the law were standing outside, checking each face with a screener 'bot as the people left the building. She didn't stop to learn if they were waiting for her and Kalais. Instead, she reached out to the Deep, and the two of them began gliding up the outside of the warehouse as if they could run up walls.

Because with the Deep around them, they could!

"Tembi—"

"Don't look down," she told him, and ignored how the people below were gasping and pointing at them.

They didn't stop running when they hit the roof. Tembi and the Deep took Kalais in long leaping strides across the streets and rooftops, putting distance between them and the warehouse. She was laughing; Kalais was on the verge of screaming, but from terror or delight? She couldn't tell.

(Probably terror, at first. Delight was slower and always took some time to catch up.)

She stopped when they reached a giant floating sign advertising a popular brand of self-cleaning diapers for infants. She dropped into a quiet niche and pulled Kalais down beside her, still laughing.

Kalais was laughing, too: the terror had burned off and he was riding the adrenaline rush of their escape across the city.

"We didn't have to run," he managed. "They didn't care about us! We'll never find the others—"

"Shut up," she said, and grabbed his shirt to pull him into a kiss. And then they were laughing and kissing at the same time, and he was making little "ow!" sounds until they slowed down enough to leave the skin on his lips.

"Oh, that was fun," she said.

"The kissing or the chase?"

"All of it!" she shouted, and fell across his legs to look up at the stars. It was late enough so Hub's lights had dimmed across the city; even the diaper sign had stopped glowing. The sky was alive and brilliant.

"How are nights like tonight going to help your stress?" he asked. "I mean, I'm okay with taking things slow, but I thought you wanted to get yourself back to Earth-normal?"

Tembi started laughing again. "Why *wouldn't* tonight help?" she asked, and showed him her prize: the lawman's badge glittered against her open palm.

His eyes went wide, the dark lenses flipping up beneath his eyelids so he could see in the low light. "Tembi," he said. "The lawman must have missed it by now! You've got to give that back!"

"Why?" she asked, half-serious. "If it's the last time I steal something—"

—a push of colors against the back of her mind, like a very stern nudge, followed by the *tap-tap-tapping* of a multicolored many-taloned foot—

"—oh, fine," she sighed.

You stole a car for me, she thought, as loudly as she could. *You don't get to be judgey about this!*

Still, when she asked the Deep to take the badge to its rightful owner, the badge vanished from her hand.

She snuggled against Kalais's shoulder, her hands wrapped around his, and waited for the Deep to tell Bayle where to find them.

LISTEN

Excerpt from "Notes from the Deep," 6 November 3400 CE

Chapter Fourteen

"They're fighting again."

Kalais replied by snoring.

They had been watching channels in Tembi's room, but Tembi was exhausted from this new experience of multitasking her classwork and a boyfriend, and she had fallen asleep on the floor. Kalais had curled up against her, big spoon to her little spoon, and had fallen asleep as well.

She had woken to the sound of voices. Matindi and Matthew had gotten home from work about an hour ago, and had launched straight into the cold point-counterpoint rhythm of their strongest disagreements. The walls blurred their words, but Tembi was able to move her ears without waking Kalais, and she had been able to follow most of the conversation through the airflow partitions.

They were angry. They had been angry a lot recently; Matthew was spending more time than ever at Matindi's house, but much of it was spent fighting with Matindi, or asking Tembi when she was going to stop her strange habit of talking out loud to the Deep.

(Tembi didn't like how Matthew kept asking her when she was going to *stop*. Stop talking to the Deep like it was a friend. Stop going out to Hub at night. Stop drawing eyebrows on the cat. Stop, *stop, **stop!***)

Tonight, they were angry about the Sabenta.

Rabbit and Kalais were always willing to talk about the Sabenta, but while those conversations began easily enough, they turned into difficult ones very quickly. Tembi had decided to sidestep those conversations altogether, and, late one night after Matindi had gone to bed, had stolen her holo from the kitchen counter to read what Lancaster's Tower Council thought.

Lancaster's reports were exhaustive. Tembi reaffirmed the basic details she already knew, such as how the Sabenta were a community of people in Sagittarius, and they had been targeted by the system's government for eradication. There was a civil war throughout their system between those who wanted the Sabenta dead and those who didn't. The Earth Assembly hadn't put a stop to it because religion was a factor: under the codes of conduct followed by all members in the Assembly, a religious cause of conflict meant that the participants had to fight it out amongst themselves.

She also learned new information—or at least she had learned information which was new to her—such as how the Sabenta were likely to be the first of many different peoples targeted by the Sagittarius Armed Forces. The SAF had been pushing a religious ideology that bioformed humans weren't true humans and shouldn't be allowed to interbreed with Earth-normal humans; this seemed to have been accepted by enough Earth-normals within the Sagittarius system to result in war. As the Sabenta had put up the most resistance to the SAF and its leaders, they had become the first to be targeted.

(There was also one troubling report that Tembi wanted to talk about but couldn't, as she had accessed it with Matindi's personal passcodes and she didn't want to admit she knew those. In this report, many members of the Earth Assembly appeared receptive to the SAF's efforts to…uh…*remove*…bioformed humans. None of the delegates to the Assembly would come out and say that they were in favor of *killing*, oh no, but whoever had written the report had taken the time to note that they were Earth-normal themselves, and that fact alone had made many members of the Assembly willing to talk about possible futures.)

These action reports had helped Tembi understand why Rabbit wanted Lancaster to get involved. It wasn't just about convenience: if the Sabenta had access to the Deep, they could move in and out of the battleground more quickly than Sagittarius' armed forces; they could evacuate planets, or move supplies behind trade blockades without anyone's knowledge; and, since Lancaster would be opening transportation routes instead of joining the fighting, they could make the case to the Assembly that they weren't directly involved in a religious conflict.

All of this hinged on whether or not Lancaster decided they should help the Sabenta. And right now, Lancaster was staying out of it.

Matindi and Matthew each had opinions about that: loud ones.

"This is about your war," Tembi whispered to Kalais. She was amazed he could sleep through the shouting.

No response. Not even a snore.

Tembi listened until Matindi and Matthew changed and left, off to yet another fancy dinner for Lancaster's Tower Council. Then, she let herself drift back to sleep.

When she awoke, Kalais was gone. She stood and stretched, and went to find him. He was in the kitchen, standing by the table. The house was dark, and he was illuminated by the glow from the single worklight over Matindi's cooking station. He was flipping through a holo projection, taking in each screen at a rapid pace before flipping to the next one.

She moved quietly, bare feet padding across the warm wooden floors. When he heard her coming, he jerked away from the holos with an embarrassed grin, and flipped the display off.

"Those are Matindi's?" she asked. She didn't really need an answer. She had read those reports herself; besides, he was squirming.

"I don't know," he sighed. "You were sleeping and I wanted a snack, and the holo was on…"

"Sure," she said, as she plopped into one of the kitchen chairs. "Because Matindi always leaves her holo on."

He squeezed his eyes shut. "Caught."

"Yup. Reading reports about your war?"

"Yeah." Kalais pulled out the chair nearest to her and sat, head in his hands. He shot her a timid grin. "Moment of weakness. I won't do that again."

"How's it going?" she asked. "The war, I mean."

"I don't want to talk about it," he muttered.

Tembi opened her mouth and closed it, once, twice… She was sure there was a way to address this…this *hypocrisy* of catching him snooping around in Matindi's personal notes about the war, and then refusing to talk about that very topic!

There was probably a way to do it without starting a fight.

Maybe.

He saw her gaping like an angry fish. "I'm sorry," he said. "Listen, do you want to go for a walk? Drop me off at the hopper pad on the way back? It's getting late."

The clock on the wall put the time at just after sundown, but she had been the one who had fallen asleep first. It wasn't the first time he had taken pity on her and let her get to bed at a reasonable hour. She agreed, and they set out across the grounds.

It was dark enough for him to flip his protective lenses up and gaze at Lancaster in the dim light. "This place is really beautiful," he said. "You're lucky you live here."

"Yeah," she said. "Some parts of Lancaster are nicer than the others, though. The gardens around the Tower and the Pavilion? Those are wonderful."

"Have you shown me the Pavilion yet?"

"No," she replied. "It's usually occupied. I think that's where the Council is having their dinner party tonight."

"Can we sneak in? You can show me around real quick—I'd love to see the building."

"What? Crash a fancy party?" She feigned shock, then said, "Yeah, sure. The students do it all the time for the leftovers."

"Free food?" Kalais's eyes went dark as his lenses dropped down, and he offered Tembi his arm. "Lead on, Miss Stoneskin."

She took him across the grounds, to where the lawns blurred into tall grass and wildflowers. There was a path behind a tall rock wall, and they followed this until the sounds of chamber music began to reach them on the breeze.

"I thought the old Witches hated music," Kalais said softly.

"They do, but everyone else expects it. Off-worlders especially," she said. "C'mon, no need to whisper. They won't notice us."

They turned the corner where the rock wall ended, and bumped into a wall of floating white cloth. Tembi lifted the edge to make a hole, and they entered the Pavilion.

Kalais froze in his tracks with a quiet, "Oh, gods!"

If the Tower was modeled after a shell, the Pavilion was modeled on a thicket of white roses. The dome of the Pavilion crested above them, made from strands of woven white and gold, and supported along the ground by crystal pedestals carved into the shape of leaves. Some of the branches were translucent, and light shone from within these as the Pavilion's light source. The floor was white marble, and great sheets of heavy white cloth billowed across the entrances.

Across the room were tables covered in more white cloth, set in crystal and gold. The only colors were the bright gemlike clothing of the Witches and their guests. Across the room, Matindi stood out: she was seated at the head table and wearing her silver dress robes, which made her green skin shine like an emerald in a ring. The woman she was sitting next to was equally as bright; she was tall, with dark skin and long curled hair dyed in all of the many prismatic colors of the Deep.

Hmm... Matindi and the tall woman seemed to be arguing about something. Matindi had that too-stubborn look she got when she was pushed too far, and the tall woman had a familiar tilt to her chin that reminded Tembi of—

"Oh, I do *not* belong here," Kalais said.

Tembi snapped her attention back to her boyfriend. "That's a shame," she said. "The food's pretty good."

She nodded to where a group of other underage Witches were sitting on the floor, hidden from the eyes of the party-goers behind a catering table. They were all laughing and scraping food out of nearly empty serving platters. Bayle and Steven weren't among them, but she recognized the others from class. She and Kalais grabbed two plates from the buffet, and plopped down among the young Witches.

"Hey, Stoneskin," said a man with twisted stripes of purple

across his face. He was wearing a beaten Spacers' uniform, and he nodded appreciatively at Kalais's own Spacer kit. "I'm Ghent," he said. "Nice outfit! Where'd you find it?"

"I got it when I enlisted," Kalais said.

Tembi hid a little grin as Ghent tried to recover. "Military man," he said, and elbowed Tembi. "Where'd you find *him?*"

"He found me," she said, passing Kalais a platter of mystery meat. "Are there any rolls left?"

The other Witches couldn't pass her the rolls fast enough. There was even some butter (there was never any butter!). They started throwing questions at Kalais: where did he serve, how old was he—You can enlist at seventeen in Sagittarius? Wait, you enlisted at *fifteen?!*—and what was it like?

You know, what was it like? On the battlefield? In space, with the ships firing on each other? Is it just like on the channels—

This was the exact kind of situation that Tembi had imagined. Not about the war. No, she had imagined this curious inter-rogation of her boyfriend. She had an answer prepared to get them to back off (and in her mind it sounded *amazing!*), but Kalais beat her to it. He pushed up the left sleeve of his uniform, revealing the burned, ruined skin of his arm.

"It's not great," he said.

The Witches recoiled. Most of them had never seen a serious injury before.

"I fight for the Sabenta," he said. "They don't have much money. When my arm got crushed under a pylon during a battle, they could only fund functionality repair. I'm responsible for repairing the cosmetic damage.

"If I make it through the war, I'll get my arm fixed up," he said, as he tugged his jacket back into place. "Until then, I'll wear long sleeves."

"Did it hurt?" asked Vix, a woman from the Kowal system with silver runes on her cheekbones. She slammed her eyes shut as soon as the words slipped out, as if realizing how stupid her question had been.

"It did," Kalais said, almost kindly. "It doesn't anymore. The medics shut down the existing nerves."

The other Witches started asking questions. Slowly, at first, and then, once they realized Kalais was going to answer them honestly, as fast as he could manage them. Tembi sat back and watched: it was only after he had turned the conversation away from what *he* had done in the war to what *they* could do to stop it that she realized Kalais was...working? Yes. He was working, doing publicity outreach for the Sabenta.

And the other Witches? They sat, plates of food forgotten, hanging on the words of a boy several years younger than themselves.

"I know it seems like the war is too far away to matter, but it does," he said to Ghent. "People are dying. My commanding officer, General Eichin, is here to persuade Lancaster that their involvement will help save lives.

"In fact," he said, pointing, "he's right over there."

Everyone turned and rose on their knees to peer over the top of the caterers' table. Kalais guided their eyes to a man in a crisp black Spacers' kit with a red stripe across his chest. He was standing off to one side of the dance floor, talking to the tall Witch with the rainbow hair and robes.

"I love a man in uniform," Vix whispered to Tembi, nodding towards the general.

"Tell me about it," Tembi replied, as she glanced over at Kalais.

"Sorry, but we can't get involved," Ghent was saying to him. "I mean, I can donate money to get your arm fixed up, but we can't use the Deep to help you."

"It's one of our laws," agreed Tayler. "'cause if we help in this war, we'll have to help in others."

Ghent nodded. "And there will always be wars."

"Hey, we should probably drop this," Kalais said. "I'm just here for the free food—I don't want to bring everybody down by getting political. Did someone say there was quesillo?"

There was, and also cake and pie, and a squishy dish that was like an egg custard, only a little too creamy for Tembi's taste.

They ate and chatted until the buffet was broken down and the catering crew kicked them out, and then Tembi and Kalais slipped away into the grounds.

"Sorry if I sucked up the conversation," Kalais said.

"No, it's fine," Tembi replied. "They wanted to hear what you had to say. And you were…kind to them."

"Because they haven't—" He stopped himself before the next words came out.

"They haven't seen anything," she said. "Yeah. I know."

"Someday," he said, slipping his hand into hers, "I'd like to hear how you got to be so different from them."

"Let's just say that my biggest fear? It's forgetting where I come from." She stopped walking and took in the grass stretching out beneath her bare feet. The grass felt cool and wonderful; she knelt to run her fingers through it, and realized her skin had softened to the point where she could feel each blade of grass. She wondered when she had gotten used to something as alien as grass. "I think I might have already started."

"I hear you," he said. "I'm worried that I might have changed too much to go back home."

She stared up at the sky. The lights from Hub were still too bright; the stars wouldn't be out until after the city went dim at midnight. But she knew where the constellations should be, and while she knew Adhama's entire solar system like the back of her hands, she couldn't quite remember the position of the stars that shone in Marumaru's night sky.

"I'm worried that this might be home now," she said quietly.

"It's not a bad place to live," Kalais said. "Quiet. Safe. Your family probably doesn't worry about you."

"They do, but I can jump home to see them. Your family probably worries much more than mine."

"I doubt it." He shrugged. "We're military. Always have been. I got started a little earlier than they thought I would, but they always knew I'd leave to serve."

"When do you go back to the Sagittarius system?"

"I don't know," he said. "It's not up to me."

She turned them down another path and into a secluded area of the garden. A fountain in the center of a close-mown patch of grass held a bronze statue of a girl playing a pipe. The night-blooms were especially sweet-smelling at this time of year, and their large bell-shaped heads reflected the path lights like tiny floating moons. Beneath these, the gardeners had planted breeze reeds, which sang a soft tune as the wind blew through the holes in their fronds.

"I can see why you like this spot," Kalais said, his eyes closed, listening.

"It's peaceful," she said, settling herself on the grass. "Nobody ever comes here."

He opened his eyes. "Really?"

"Not at night."

"Really?" he asked again as he knelt beside her.

"Yes," she said, as she pulled him into her arms. "Really."

Sometime later, he asked her another question.

She said yes.

stonegirl
sings
stonegirl
listens

Excerpt from "Notes from the Deep," 18 February 2997 CE

Chapter Fifteen

There was no winter on Found; the planet didn't have enough of an axial tilt for true seasons. That didn't stop its inhabitants from celebrating Earth's winter solstice with some truly remarkable parties.

Lancaster Tower was glowing. Thousands of tiny lights moved across its surface in preplanned patterns, mimicking the ebbs and flows of a snowstorm. Across the grounds, white dunes of nanotech snow blanketed the greenery, moving aside for pedestrians using the footpaths and sweeping over the hoppers' landing docks when they weren't in use.

Strange robotic animals with exotic names were set to roam the school's grounds. The Library's maze became the temporary home for enormous four-legged creatures with crowns of bone antlers, and small canids with red fur and little white tufts on their tails. Tembi and Bayle had an unexpected encounter with something called a bear, which wandered out of a bathroom and sniffed them before disappearing into the school's hallways.

Gifts were exchanged. Pastries were baked. Religious customs were celebrated. But mostly, it was an excuse to get dressed up and hold parties.

Matindi tended to go a little overboard.

"The problem with living for twenty-six hundred years," she said, as she added yet another plass storage box to the stack in the center of the common room, "is that you tend to accumulate the most baffling junk."

Tembi, who had just discovered what appeared to be a string of several freshly severed cat heads at the bottom of a box of ornaments, agreed.

Matindi glanced at the cat heads. "Plass and fiber replicas," she said. "There was a despicable tradition on…oh, some backwater throwaway planet I can't remember. It's been outlawed, but they still insist on displaying the replicas."

Taabu hopped off the sofa and stalked out of the room, tail twitching.

The false cat heads disappeared from Tembi's hands. Matindi sighed. "They were a gift," she said to the room at large, "from a dear friend who's long dead, and I think of him when I see them."

The cat heads reappeared, but began to tuck themselves under a pile of crinkled packing tissues.

"Criticism noted," Matindi said, holding up a stasis box of holiday lights. "Here. Decorate the roof. Be creative."

The box vanished.

"Would you mind?" Matindi whispered to Tembi. "It loves an audience."

Tembi grabbed a scarf from the rack by the door, and stepped outside. The Deep had been waiting for her. As she stepped into the (not all that cold) snowy night, the walls and the roof of their house lit up in golden constellations.

"Oh," she said, wonderingly, as she realized she could still recognize the night sky over Marumaru, "This is perfect. Thank you, Deep!"

"I thought Matindi didn't let you use the Deep for chores." Bayle was walking up the path, her bare feet padding on the pavement.

"We aren't doing chores," Matindi said from the doorway. "This is family time. Did you bring the cookies?"

"Oh," Bayle said. "I thought I'd just—"

"*That's* a chore," Matindi said, and went back inside.

Bayle and Tembi stared at each other for a moment. Tembi shrugged, and Bayle sighed and turned to retrace her steps down the front path. She passed Kalais and Rabbit, their arms full of packages, and grabbed Rabbit around his waist to drag him away with her.

"What was that about?" Kalais asked, leaning over the packages to give her a careful kiss.

Tembi held as still as she could, enjoying the feeling of his lips against hers. "Witch business," she said once they broke apart, as she gathered some of the packages into her own arms.

"Always with the Witch business," he said, as he pulled her against him in a one-armed hug.

The packages vanished, and they stumbled against each other.

"Matindi?" Tembi called.

"Not me!"

"Thanks, Deep," Tembi said.

Kalais shook himself. "You realize that's weird, right? An invisible…*thing* moving stuff around for you?"

"Says a man who puts himself in a spaceship and lets the Deep jump it across the galaxy."

"Okay," he said, hands held up in surrender. "Okay, don't make me think about that."

She laughed and led him inside.

They spent the next hour setting up. The Deep was in a playful mood, so there were several moments when they needed to stop and find missing items (such as the furniture), or shoo robotic animals out the door. But by the time the guests began to arrive, Matindi's quarters were sparkling clean and decorated like the houses on the Solstice channels.

This was Tembi's fifth Solstice party with Matindi, but her first as a Witch in her own right. She had pulled her hair back with a wide red velvet band to show off her golden birds. When they arrived, the Witches greeted her as an equal instead of Matindi's wayward charge.

The Deep was on crowd control. The same tricks it used to bend space at the Library were used to ensure that Matindi's quarters had enough room for all of Lancaster's Witches and their guests. Hundreds of people—thousands, maybe!—kept flooding in, and yet somehow there was always a picturesque, quiet place to stand and talk near the ice sculpture.

Bayle and Rabbit began to dance. Others joined them; the music wasn't live, but it was lively; even the oldest Witches who normally wouldn't tolerate music took a turn around the dance floor at the Deep's bidding.

Kalais bowed to Tembi and extended his hand; she took it, and they joined the dancers. It was a different kind of dancing than the wild-eyed excitement of the nightclub: not as much instinct, and with more of the mind invested in the purpose of dance.

Sway, swing, back and forth, back and forth, together.

Robes flared out and blended together as the dancers turned. Tembi's robe was a deep red velvet which matched her hair band, with gold birds stitched across the hem and sleeves. Kalais had abandoned his usual Spacers' kit for a dark blue suit with tails, and their colors twined together as they moved.

Kalais seemed to like her dress. He kept tracing the edges of her sleeves and telling her the color suited her; the two of them kept running their fingertips along the velvet to enjoy the feeling of its soft plush pile.

When the music broke, they went to help Matindi and the Deep restock the beverages. The supply had gotten a little low; Kalais commented on how quickly some of the Witches seemed to be emptying their wine glasses.

"Things are about to get exciting," Tembi said, and nodded to an almost dreamy-eyed Witch in formal robes who was standing across the room. "Watch."

The Witch took a long pull from a bottle. A few moments passed, and then a blissfully happy expression overtook his face. "I am attending a party!" he announced in the two-toned voice of the Deep. "This is a pleasurable experience!"

The Witch sobered up instantly, but the damage was done; everyone broke into laughter.

"Witches almost never drink," Tembi explained to Kalais. "Except when they're around other Witches. It's safe for the Deep to show itself here."

"I've heard the Deep talk through Witches before," Kalais said, as another Witch across the room loudly declared that everyone looked very nice tonight and that they should get dressed up more often!

"Yeah, but that's a mutual act—the Witch and the Deep have to be thinking about the same thing for it to work. This is the Deep taking over a Witch's body, if only for a moment," she said, and nodded towards the room. "It only does this at parties."

"Could the Deep take over a Witch for...I don't know... hours? Days? Permanently?"

"I don't think so," Tembi said, and shrugged. "I've never heard of that happening. Ask Matindi or Matthew. If it's happened, they'd know about it."

"That's kind of scary," he said. "Doesn't that bother you?"

She stood on her toes to kiss him, a quick bump of the lips, nothing scandalous enough to set the old Witches to gossiping "You're cute," she reminded him.

"Is that a yes?" he asked. "A no? I'm unclear on the whole issue of possession."

Bayle appeared out of nowhere; if Tembi didn't know better, she would have sworn the Deep had dropped her off. "You didn't tell me Moto would be here!"

"I didn't think I had to!" Tembi glanced over towards the front door. Moto was stomping the false snow from his Spacers' boots. She had assumed Bayle was over her crush on Moto. There was Rabbit, for one thing, and the fact that Moto had spent a month teaching Bayle how to spar by knocking her flat on her butt was another.

"Well, I would have at least made an effort to look nice," Bayle said.

Tembi stared at her friend. Bayle was always stunning, but tonight she looked like a vision from the sea. Blue, green, and silver robes fell nearly to her feet, belted with woven silver at her waist. Her hair was a single long braid, with silver and pale green shells moving through it like waves.

"And what would you have done differently?" Tembi asked her.

Bayle laughed and hugged her, and stepped away to greet Moto with a flying hug. He swept her off of her feet and swung her around in a circle before planting a chaste kiss on her head.

"'scuse me for just a second," Tembi said, setting down an empty bottle of wine. Kalais nodded and went back to refilling glasses.

She danced across the room, moving around the Witches and their guests, and stepped into Moto's arms as soon as Bayle had left them. But as soon as she touched him, she stopped, fear jolting through her. While her own skin was almost back to normal, Moto's skin was harder than hers had been when she began her formal training as a Witch.

"Moto!" she said softly, alarmed.

He hugged her; it was like being embraced by granite. "It's not something to talk about at a party," he said, resting his chin on the top of her head. "But now you know how I feel when your stress is showing."

"Are you okay?"

"It's work," he said. "It's just work."

She was about to tell him that there was nothing—nothing at all!—that could cause enough stress to petrify him, when he broke away. "Do you have a minute?" he asked. "There's someone I want you to meet."

He brought her across the room to a small group of ageless Witches. Matthew was there, along with Williamson and a few others on the Tower Council she had met over the years. Moto took one of them aside: a Witch with long white hair dyed in the colors of the Deep, with a prism of rainbows painted across the right side of her forehead.

She was the tall Witch who had been sitting next to Matindi at the Pavilion party a couple of months ago. The one who had been speaking to General Eichin on the dance floor. Tembi weighed the Witch's value in her mind: she had money, obviously; those robes were pure linen and silk. But there was more to that. This Witch projected a sense of being *there*—a central force within the room—that went far beyond her physical presence.

Moto returned, the tall Witch walking at his side. "Tembi,

this is Domino," he said.

The name was obviously supposed to mean something to Tembi. It didn't, but the way Moto had said it was touched with more than a little caution.

The older Witch smiled at Tembi, and brushed her multicolored hair away from an ear. It was tapered to a point, just like her own.

"You're from Adhama!" Tembi said, delighted.

Domino smiled. Her lips had been painted a pale blue, and against her dark skin and white teeth, this made her smile go on forever. "One of the first Witches chosen from our world," she said.

"Domino is my supervisor," Moto said. "She's Lancaster's delegate to the Earth Assembly."

Oh. Oh! Tembi realized her mouth had dropped open. The Earth Assembly. *The* Earth Assembly!

"It'sanhonortomeetyou!" she squeaked, and dropped into the low kneeling bow that Matindi had taught her, just in case, you'll probably never need to use it, but better to know it than not.

"None of that, sister of Adhama," Domino said, holding out a hand to help Tembi rise. Domino's skin was so hard it may as well have been stone made flesh. It was cool to the touch, and felt much thicker than her own. "The Deep chooses us, and we find our place within its order. At no point does it demand we must kneel."

Tembi knew she was nodding so hard her head might pop off and roll away, but she couldn't seem to stop.

"So, Miss Tembi…?"

"Stoneskin," she answered, before realizing that using that particular name in front of these two particular people was a very stupid decision. Moto put a hand on her shoulder and grinned at Domino; instead of embarrassed, Tembi was surprised to find she felt very much at home.

"Miss Tembi Stoneskin," Domino said, nodding, with only the slightest grin. "Have you given any thought to what you want to do when you pass your certification?"

No, she hadn't, not really—certification was years away! But she nodded and said, "I haven't decided yet. I know Lancaster doesn't think I should be a pilot."

(True. Every time the Deep did something without her direction, Leps unloaded with one of her speeches on Witches and responsibility and how Tembi was likely to get a starship full of people killed, or at the very least stranded on the galactic edge, and how she should only risk jumping a ship if every other Witch in the galaxy was dead or dying.)

"Well." Domino leaned down a little to bring herself closer to Tembi. "Did you know that Witches from Adhama often begin their careers as personal assistants for Witches on the Tower Council, or the Earth Assembly? Our skin makes us harder to injure, so we also serve as their bodyguards. I've been watching your progress in class, and Moto says you are quite skilled as a fighter. With more training and experience, you'll be an excellent assistant.

"It's how I started," she added, her grin growing wider. "And I think Moto might be considering a career in politics himself. I'll hate to lose him, and I'll need a replacement."

Moto pretended to cup a hand to his mouth. "She's offering you a *job*," he said in a terrible stage whisper.

"I *know!*" Tembi whispered back, and elbowed him in the ribs.

"Hey Tembi, want to introduce me?"

She turned. Rabbit was standing there, looking…different. He had a glass of wine in his hand, but he wasn't drunk. No, he was the opposite of drunk—he was focused like a laser, staring straight at Domino, looking…

…looking *violent!*

Moto put himself between Rabbit and Domino, pulling Tembi behind him as he moved.

"Easy, friend," Rabbit said to him. "We're all friends here, right? I'm just here to make some conversation with my friends."

"Where's your boss?" Moto asked.

"Who, General Eichin? He went home for the Solstice," Rabbit replied. "He's Sabenta, so it's probably the last one he'll have with his family, you know?" He turned to Tembi. "Did you know I've sat in on meetings with my good friends here? They've said there's nothing they can do to help the Sabenta. Witches are most powerful people in the galaxy. They can empty an entire planet with a *wish!* But they say there's nothing they can do."

"This isn't the time or the place," Moto told him.

Rabbit ignored him. "You could end this," he said to Domino. He was so angry that his words sounded clipped, like they were full of teeth. "You could end this right now. Choosing not to act doesn't make you moral—it makes you complicit."

Moto went to answer, but Domino held up one long, graceful hand to stop him. "There are always wars," she said to Rabbit. "There will always be wars. We cannot get involved."

"You mean you *will* not get involved. Have any of you gone to the front of *this* war?" Rabbit asked. "Have you seen how they treat the Sabenta? Have you seen the camps? The mass graves?"

"Yes," Domino said. She seemed frozen in place, her head and ears held high. An Adhamantian statue in rainbow paint. "I jump there at least once a day. We know what's happening— we make sure we understand the price that is paid through our inaction."

Her answer rattled Rabbit. He recovered by moving closer to Domino, his hands held tight at his sides. Moto stepped forward; Rabbit didn't back down. "Liar!" Rabbit hissed. "You can't see that and still say you're apart from it! Millions have died! *Millions!*"

"They're not lying. They've seen it." Tembi didn't realize she was speaking until she had stepped out from behind Moto. Rabbit blinked at her; he had forgotten she was there. She closed the short distance between them, and stared at him until Rabbit—funny, snarky Rabbit, who never failed to make Bayle smile, who was always there for Kalais, who had carried her on his back through Hub when her ankle had twisted while dancing—took a step away from her.

"They're like me, Rabbit," she continued. She moved closer; Rabbit's eyes had locked on hers. "They're from Adhama. They've got my skin. Just…just calm down, okay? Shake their hands, and you'll know what they've seen. Or…or if you have to? Throw that punch you're sitting on—you'll break your own hand."

She knew what she was saying was cold truth. It was the only reason Moto could feel like stone, Domino could be like granite. They were carrying death in their skin.

Rabbit knew it, too. He stared at her for another long moment, then shook himself, as if breaking from a spell. "Those deaths are on your conscience," he said to Domino. "May you carry them every day of your gods-damned life."

He turned and walked away, brushing past Bayle and Kalais.

Oh, gods, Kalais! He had been standing right there—he had seen the entire thing.

"Let him go," Moto said, not knowing she had already forgotten that Rabbit existed. "He needs an enemy right now, and the one he wants to fight isn't here."

She pulled away from him.

Kalais was waiting for her: she already knew what he was about to say.

"Don't," she said.

"I have to."

He moved as if he was ready to kiss her goodbye, but stopped himself. Instead, he pressed a small brightly wrapped box into her hands.

"You don't have to leave," Tembi said.

"I do." He touched her cheek, the one without the birds. "I wish… I wish things were different."

And then he was gone.

She opened the box, mostly to have something to do that wasn't thinking about what had just happened. There on the spun fibers was a new soundkit, its earpieces sized for her ears. She nearly hurled the box away to go running after Kalais, but—

The Witches were watching. All of them.

Instead, she held her head and her ears as high as she could, and went to start cleaning up the party mess in the kitchen.

---

stonegirl
fireboy
the painted woman
fear

Excerpt from "Notes from the Deep," 19 July 3881 CE

Chapter Sixteen

The party was over. Tembi had retreated to her room as soon as the last Witch had left, and had broken down in a torrent of tears. Bayle was more stoic, and had very unkind things to say about Rabbit. Even though she kept trailing off into silence, and twisting the ring he had given her for Solstice around and around her finger.

Matindi had *there-there*'d as best she could, but she'd admitted that being twenty-six hundred and twenty-eight years old tended to distort a person's perception of healthy relationships. Instead, she had jumped to Earth and returned with chocolate cake from her favorite café, and left this on the kitchen table under a stasis cage set to keep the cat away.

The next few days were breakdays, which was for the best as Tembi spent them all in a deep sulk. She was supposed to go to a beach on Adhama with her family for the Solstice, but—

(…there was no chance of accidentally bumping into Kalais on Adhama, or him knocking on the door of the beach house to apologize, or…)

—she didn't feel up to it.

Steven came over. They watched some of the romance channels, ate popcorn, and shouted at the characters when they made stupid decisions.

Eventually, the self-pity burned itself off. This was helped in large part by the Deep, who had decided that if Tembi was going to spend her time holed up inside and petting Taabu to make herself feel better, then it should fill the house with hundreds of cats to speed up the process. Tembi tried to herd them outside, but that didn't work. Oh no, that didn't work *at all!*

She called Bayle; her friend jumped over to help. Between the two of them, they managed to convince the Deep to take the cats back to their homes. And then they cleaned, as hundreds of panicky cats could do a great deal of damage within a short amount of time.

They cheated, a little. Not with the Deep, even though it had realized too late the cats were a mistake and had offered to put things right. No, Tembi rented a box of commercial clean/repair nanobots from a large grocery store in Hub, set the controls to "All," and then she and Bayle went to lunch. By the time they returned, the nanobots had fixed everything except the broken glass and the scratch marks in the wood trim. The girls swept up and dumped the glass, and puttied and painted the scratch marks.

"No more cats," Tembi said to the Deep, as she coaxed Taabu out from behind the stove with a piece of fish. "I like this one. He's enough for me."

There was a petulant *clink* from the garbage bin as the Deep whisked the broken glass away.

Tembi decided to bury herself in the book the Deep had chosen for her in the Library. With the help of a dictionary, she cut her way through about twenty pages a day. Twenty pages on conflict, suffering, and the ethical implications thereof. She wasn't sure what she was getting out of it apart from a larger vocabulary, but at least her essays for Leps were definitely not copied off of the channels.

At nights, in the dreamscape, the Deep sulked and pouted at her. Its fur and feathers were mourning black, and it left a trail of red where it passed.

"I'm *trying*," she told it. "Would it help if you could talk to Matindi? Or Bayle? Maybe they could translate—"

Sometimes, it would flop down on the featureless ground and sigh. Other times, it would shake itself into rainbows and dance through these, singing.

"This would be easier if you had a face," Tembi said one night, as she rested against its back. "You have a body, you have wings and feet—I mean, I don't see where they begin or end, but you still have them—but no face? How can you even sing without a face?"

The Deep huffed and nuzzled her until she fell over giggling.

"Fine," she said. "I imagine you as a canine, though. I hope you know that. A big friendly fluffy dog, with feathers. And bird feet. And wings. Okay, maybe not a dog. Doglike. Dog... adjacent."

The air was filled with bright yellow *meows!* and a shower of glasslike cats rained down from the sky and shattered across the ground.

"Oh, stop," she said. "Everybody wants to be a cat! They're the sweetest, prettiest murderers. But you're definitely a dog. You want humans to understand you so badly and we...can't. That's definitely a dog trait."

The Deep tried a bark: it came out as the scent of sulphur and fruit. Then it tried a howl, and this worked much better; Tembi started to howl along, most of her lost in the silly freedom of the act, with a small sliver of self-consciousness that was glad Matindi and Bayle weren't around to witness this.

Well, maybe they would have joined in.

Well, maybe Matindi would have.

It was hard to feel tired in the dream, but this was a good, long howl. At the end of it, Tembi felt as if she had run for kilometers in the rain. A good, clean exhaustion.

She wondered if the Deep felt the same way.

"I wish I could talk to you," she sighed.

The Deep sighed back at her, a puff of pink and purple wind that tasted of mangoes.

"I don't know what to do for you," she said, idly scratching the Deep on what seemed to be an especially itchy spot. "I'm happy to just be your friend, but I think you want me to...do something. That book you want me to read? It talks about Witches as your emissaries to the human race. Is that what I am? One of your emissaries?"

That was too much information for the Deep to process at once. It grumbled and stood, dumping Tembi into the air in a wave of indistinct sensations.

"This is what I mean," she said, as the Deep paced in circles around her. "This is a communication barrier—I don't understand you, and you don't understand me. If we could just talk—"

Little puffs of fire appeared around her.

"Fine," she sighed. She waited until the fires died down, and then tried again. "You've shown me wars before," she said. "You've shown me those ever since I was a little kid. Generals who fought, and…those who didn't fight. I guess I didn't realize what you were trying to say."

Agreement, but in harsh brassy notes.

"All right," she said. "Can you take me to Sagittarius? I want to understand. I don't need to go there physically. Can you…can you just show me what's happening to the Sabenta?"

The Deep exploded in a shower of flowers.

"Yes or no," Tembi said, hands pressed against her head as the blossoms faded away. "Not a difficult question. Just answer yes or no."

A long pause, as if the Deep was thinking. Tembi felt her body make a quick turn sideways, and she was standing in—

"Oh gods!" Tembi whispered.

She was standing in a pit—

—there were bodies all around her—

—hundreds of them, maybe *thousands*—

—they weren't stacked or piled—

—*they had been dropped on top of each other like sacks of clothes stuffed with*—

"This is a grave," she said quietly.

She would not throw up. Her own body wasn't here. She was all the way across the galaxy, safe in her own bed. This was a nightmare—a real nightmare—but she had asked to see it.

She would *not* throw up!

Tembi kicked off of the ground and floated upwards. The Deep's dream-visions still behaved somewhat like dreams—she couldn't fly, but she could jump and glide, and wake herself up if things got rough.

She landed on the edge of the mass grave. It was an open field that was probably very beautiful, once, as there were plants still struggling to survive in the rain and the mud. But these streaks of green were dotted with torn earth.

More graves. Each as large as the one she had just left. And they had been recovered with dirt.

"Please tell me those weren't full," she whispered to herself.

"Yessss…"

The word was full of consonants. Tembi closed her eyes, counted to ten, and turned to see the body of a little girl haul herself out of the open grave.

"Deep?" Tembi asked, with a silent prayer to ward off evil. "Are you doing this so you can talk to me?"

The dead girl nodded. Her lips were gone; talking would be an appalling problem.

"Deep?" Tembi paused and tried to decide on the right phrasing. "Do you remember what this person looked like when she was alive? Maybe it would be easier to talk through that version of her, instead of this one."

The zombie froze, as if she was a holo on pause. Then, she stepped forward, her body whole, her robes as fresh and crisp as if they had just come from a shop.

"Thank you, Deep," Tembi said. "It will be easier to talk to her like this."

"Yes," the little girl said, and looked somewhat pleased that she was able to form the word. "Yes," she said again. "Yes."

Tembi started walking towards the edge of the field, where a series of ugly brown-and-gray buildings stuck out against the bare earth. These were set behind a metal fence that towered above Tembi and the dead girl. "I want to help," she said, and tried to ignore the sounds of clumsy footsteps as they crunched across the ground behind her. "But I don't know what you want me to do. Do you understand?"

"No."

Shipping and schedules, Tembi reminded herself. *It understands transportation, because to the Deep, the details required to move a starship across a whole scraping galaxy are simple—*

"Is this the only—" What did you call a place like this? She didn't think there could be a name for something this evil, but Williamson had showed her a history book once, about another war, and the name was right there in her memory. "—concentration camp?"

"No."

She took a deep breath. "How many more?"

"Five hundred, sixty, and two. Across eight planets in this system."

"Oh, gods," Tembi whispered to herself.

"No," the Deep replied. "No gods here. Only humans."

She set the metaphysics of that statement aside: if she unpacked any part of it, she knew she'd start screaming. "Deep? Do you want this to stop?"

"Yes."

Good. She didn't know what she'd have done if the Deep had said no, or had been indifferent.

"Do you want me to stop it?"

No response. Tembi turned to look at the little girl. The girl was nodding her head, her arms outstretched and moving up and down at the shoulders. It looked like a shrug, if the person had only seen shrugs and was doing its best to imitate them, but had no body to understand how the pieces went together.

"You do want me to stop it, but you don't think I can?"

The vibrancy went out of the little girl again as the Deep put the clauses together. Finally, the girl smiled. "Yes!"

That made sense. She was a sixteen-year-old Witch. Not even a fully trained Witch, either. Stopping something like this... "Okay," she said, turning to look at the heavy metal fence with the gray houses encaged within it. "Take me home."

Tembi woke in her own bed. Taabu was stretched out across her feet, and the windows were starting to shift from opaque to transparent as morning dawned outside. Taabu woke almost as soon as she did: the cat stared at her, and then fell over itself to hide beneath the bed.

She tried several of Matindi's meditation techniques to calm herself down.

Nothing.

"Deep?" she asked.

The book by Rowland that she kept beside her bed floated into the air, and then resettled itself on her nightstand.

"Okay," she said. "I'm going to cry now. It's because I'm feeling sad about the war." She paused to make sure the Deep had time to understand her, and then added, "You did nothing wrong. If you feel sad too, you can stay with me while I cry."

Nothing for a few moments. Then, the bedsheets around her crumpled as if pressed beneath a heavy weight, and the two of them stayed like that until the sun came up.

they come
mother father
far
far
they come

Excerpt from "Notes from the Deep," 19 January 3997 CE

Chapter Seventeen

The next few months were...odd. Tembi managed to convince Bayle to come to Sagittarius in the Deep's dreamscape, and they both walked through the graves and the camps in shared horror.

"This can't be allowed to happen," Bayle said. It was the only thing that she had said since she let out one brief scream at the start of the dream. "This is evil. There's no other word for it."

"The Deep wants it to stop," Tembi said. "I'll talk to Matindi and Matthew. Again." Matindi was willing to talk about what was happening in Sagittarius; Matthew wasn't. But if she cornered him while he was making breakfast for them on a breakday morning, he was usually willing to listen.

"I'll talk to my family," Bayle said. "Maybe there's something they can do."

That was one of the odd things: Bayle's family had more money than most of the people on Hub put together, but the ability to stop a war? That, Tembi wasn't sure about, and Bayle refused to elaborate.

Another one of the odd things was how often Sagittarius and the Sabenta came up in the channels, or in conversation, or in throwaway comments between strangers. Now that Tembi was aware of the war, it was *everywhere!* It was as if a veil had been lifted, and she could see and hear clearly for the first time. Worse, she knew the topic had always been there, but it just hadn't registered to her as...

...as what?

As something that mattered, she supposed.

(The idea that the Sabenta could be dying by the millions but she had been so blissfully ignorant that those deaths didn't even blip on her mental radar? That hurt. And then, when she realized she was feeling pity for herself instead of for the Sabenta? That hurt! Tembi decided to stop beating herself up about the past and try to put things right in the present, because if she didn't she'd never feel good about anything ever again.)

She felt impossibly frustrated, and found herself picking fights with Matindi for no good reason. This didn't help: Matindi would usually ignore her and talk to the Deep.

"It's adolescence," Matindi would say. "Her body's chemistry is all over the place. I could reason with her until my face goes from green to bright red, and it wouldn't make a difference. Just let her get it out of her system."

This didn't help.

After a long day at class, followed by a fight with Matindi that was truly spectacular in terms of how loud she got and how thoroughly Matindi managed to ignore her, Tembi stormed out of the house and headed to Hub.

She might have been hoping to bump into Kalais again.

(Emphasis on the "might.")

He had called once, a few weeks ago. Just to talk.

(And then he had come over, and they hadn't "just talked," oh no, they had done very little talking and quite a lot of things that didn't require any talking at all, and now Tembi was extremely mad at him and wanted to see him, all at the same time. But he wasn't returning her calls.)

She stepped off of the Lancaster hopper and into a swirling mass of angry protesters.

This was yet another odd thing, and Tembi realized she probably should have listened to what the hopper driver had been trying to tell her on the trip into the city.

The protesters wanted to shout at her—she got the impression they wanted to shout at any Witch they came across—but she was also sixteen and they weren't quite sure how to shout at an underage Witch. She was able to run down a side street and use the Deep to scramble up the nearest wall, and then watch the protesters from the rooftop. There were only about a dozen of them, all dressed in mourning black and holding signs in different languages. More protesters seemed to be streaming out of the hopper station, clustered together in groups and headed for a different destination.

Tembi licked the sleeve of her robe and scrubbed the golden birds from her face, and then jumped across the rooftops until she found another cluster of protesters. She dropped to the ground and began to follow them.

The main square of Hub was several kilometers from Lancaster. It was a center of commerce, with convention halls and tasteful hotels and restaurants scattered all around. Tembi had trained her friends how to pick pockets there, as almost everyone they saw was a visitor to Hub and had neither time nor attention for three young Witches. Today, there were very few people in suits but there were thousands of people in dull mourning black, surrounded on all sides by the law.

She walked among the protesters, unnoticed despite her robes being dark gray instead of black. They were chanting; she didn't recognize the language. The lawmen and women watched it all with careful eyes.

The next chant was in Basic:

> *Stand up—fight back!*
> *Stand up—fight back!*
> *Stand up—fight back!*

There didn't seem to be more to the chant than those four words, but a lot could be done with them: a woman, Earth-normal except for deep blue patterns covering every centimeter of her bare arms, took over the chant by shouting: *Stand up!*

The others rallied: *Fight back!*

Call and response, call and response.

Flat and loud, rather like an extremely boring song.

Enough of this, Tembi thought, and tapped on the shoulder of one of the nearby protesters.

The woman turned and said, in Basic: "Can I help you?"

She was friendly and her eyes were kind, but Tembi had problems hearing her over the chanting. "Is this for the Sabenta?" Tembi asked.

"Sabenta? No," the woman shook her head. "This is for trade route policy. There's a Sabenta rally later tonight."

"Thank you," Tembi said to her, and kept walking.

Trade route policy. Well, then. She thought she had studied enough trade routes during Leps' classes to know something about policy, but apparently she hadn't learned enough to get this…passionate about it. She moved off to the side and ducked into a small alcove between two buildings that didn't smell too much of overripe garbage, and pretended to adjust her sound-kit as she watched the protesters.

A quick rush of air blew past her as another Witch jumped into the alcove.

Tembi turned, expecting Matindi or Bayle, or maybe even Steven if he had found someone to jump him. Instead, a tall Adhamantian woman stood there in robes of dull mourning black. The woman pressed a finger to her lips, and Tembi managed to recognize Domino—the other Witch had stripped the rainbow colors from her hair and face, and had pulled her wild waterfall of long hair into a tight coil at the base of her head.

"I was across the square," Domino said, her voice more melodic than it had been at the Solstice party, "and I asked the Deep if anyone else was nearby. Do you mind if I join you?"

Tembi shook her head—No, of course she didn't mind if Lancaster's representative to Earth joined her!—and the two of them left the relative calm of the alcove. They didn't talk. They walked, and watched. Domino's eyes darted across the crowd, missing nothing.

"Do you know why I'm here?" Domino asked, as they made their second circuit of the protest.

There didn't seem to be a clever answer to that question, so Tembi decided on honesty. "I don't even know why I'm here."

The older Witch smiled. "You grew up in Marumaru, yes? Shipping containers for homes? A hydrosonic shower to get clean, but no water for drinking or cooking unless you had a rain cache, or carried it from the community pumps?"

Tembi didn't reply.

"I've never been to Marumaru," Domino continued. "I was born on the other side of Adhama. But I know what your home was like; I imagine it was very much like mine.

"Every year, there's an economic conference," she said. "It's done to help galactic leaders establish trade relationships and plan policy. You'll visit this same conference in your third year of training, but the location rotates so it won't be held in Hub."

"Why are the protesters here?" Tembi wasn't sure that trade relationships and planning policy merited the presence of several thousand angry people wearing mourning black.

"Because you grew up in Marumaru," Domino replied. "Because there is a Marumaru, and places that are much worse than Marumaru. The protestors want all children to have access to water, food, education… They want life to be fair."

Tembi burst out laughing. "Life *isn't* fair!"

"But that doesn't mean we shouldn't try to make it so," Domino said. "Also, some of these protestors want Lancaster to leave their planet alone, so they're protesting Witches and the Deep. And others want Lancaster to change their policies and pay attention to causes that are dear to their hearts."

"That's why you're here," Tembi guessed. "You're trying to find out what all of these different groups want."

"Very good," Domino replied. "You can only learn so much in a conference room, or through briefings. You learn so much more talking to people." The Witch smiled down at Tembi. "I wasn't always on the Council. My old job was more…direct. I miss it, sometimes."

"What did you used to do?"

"This and that," she replied, waving a hand as if the past was of no real consequence.

Tembi might have believed her, if Domino's ears hadn't perked up at the memories.

"Much of it involved talking to people on Lancaster's behalf," Domino said. "I suppose my job hasn't changed too much, just the setting in which I've found myself."

"I must say," the older Witch added, "I was impressed at how you handled that young man at the Solstice party."

"He's—he was a friend," Tembi said. "I think he's gone back to Sagittarius. To fight in the war."

"Ah," Domino said.

Tembi couldn't read anything in that little word. The silence grew awkward; it was a relief when Domino asked her what she thought about the war.

"I don't understand why we aren't doing anything about the Sabenta," Tembi said. "There're five worlds involved, and millions of people being killed, and Lancaster's not…not doing anything."

"There have always been wars," Domino said. "It's easy to ignore one more war. It's easy to ignore images you can't see with your own eyes, or stories you don't trust to be true. By the time we learned this war was—Well, no war can be better or worse than another, and there is always some element of genocide in war. We didn't understand that this was a system-wide extermination of the Sabenta throughout Sagittarius until it was too late to intervene."

"You're lying." The words were out of her mouth before Tembi could slam her own face shut.

Domino stopped. "Oh?"

Nothing to do but own the damage of her stupid mouth. "I can read your ears," she said, meeting Domino's eyes as best she could. "They… When you said you learned after it was too late to do something about it? They drooped."

The Witch stared at her, unmoving, and for no reason she could put a finger on, Tembi was suddenly very, *very* certain that Domino had intended to let her ears—

Wind, soft and sudden, blew past Tembi. She spun and found Matindi, dressed in woody green robes from head to toe, different (and more much formal) than the t-shirt and sweatpants she had been wearing when Tembi had stormed out of their house several hours earlier.

Matindi was several hands shorter than Domino, but she carried herself like a queen as she greeted the other Witch. "It is good to see you, sister," she said, moving her head the slightest bit downward.

"As to you, sister," Domino replied. Her chin and ears stayed level. "I have been enjoying young Tembi Stoneskin's company this evening. She is quite observant."

"Yes." It was a flat word, its only feature bland agreement.

"I should be leaving. Thank you for sharing this time with me," Domino said to Tembi. "I hope we get to do it again, very soon."

A flash of dark robes, and Domino was gone.

"Stoneskin?" Matindi asked, as she started walking. "Not that I'm judging—most Witches change their names at least once—but I thought you wanted to manage your stress."

Tembi shrugged. Between her dreamtime trips to Sagittarius and her breakup with Kalais, her skin was as hard as it had ever been. Williamson's nickname fit her like a stone glove.

"Okay," Matindi said, stopping dead in the center of the street. She spun and looked at Tembi. Tembi was now of a height with the green Witch, but it was yet another odd thing to realize she would soon be taller than her own guardian. "I need you to focus, Tembi. Pick a restaurant. Any restaurant."

Fine. Tembi picked one she hadn't tried before, a little place in the suburbs of Hub that Steven had eaten at on a date and raved about to her and Bayle. Astronomically expensive pieces of raw fish served over clumpy rice? Well, Tembi wouldn't eat something like that on her own credit, but if Matindi wanted to talk so badly…

The meal was served at low tables without chairs. Matindi flipped her robes tight across her legs and sat in a tight kneel, then ordered in an unfamiliar language. Tembi pointed at pictures on the menu, and pretended she knew what they meant.

Tea came, served in delicate porcelain mugs. Matindi savored the smell, and took a careful sip. "Good choice," she said. "I haven't had sushi in decades. I hope it's becoming popular again."

A normal conversation, Tembi realized. A peace offering, of sorts.

"Thanks."

"Tembi, can we have an honest discussion? None of my wise old lady nonsense, none of your angsty teenage rage?"

Angsty teenage rage? The term alone made Tembi want to start shouting again, but—

She nodded.

"Thank you," Matindi said. "You know I've always tried to let you find your own path. Being called to service by the Deep? That comes with responsibilities, and those responsibilities have limited your options. You were a Witch from the moment the Deep chose you. Not a dentist. Not a farmer. Nothing but a Witch.

"That doesn't mean you're going to be a pilot, of course." Matindi set down the porcelain cup and tented her fingers. "By now, you've realized that Witches have jobs that go beyond moving items across the galaxy. We're responsible for an entire industry, which means we play critical roles in keeping civilization itself moving.

"Not all parts of civilization are good." Matindi was staring at her, green eyes boring straight into Tembi's own. "At best, we follow paths which minimize the damage we do to others. But at our worst?"

"I've been to Sagittarius," Tembi said, as she dropped her eyes to her cup.

"In a dream, I hope."

Tembi nodded. There were small, almost unnoticeable flecks of brown within the green tea, very much like the colors of Matindi's eyes.

"Good," Matindi said. "And I'm not saying that because you aren't strong enough to handle the reality of that situation—I'm saying that I don't want anybody I love to put themselves in that much physical danger."

Love.

Tembi looked up and smiled at Matindi for the first time in… oh.

Too long.

Matindi smiled back. "I love you," she said. "I want you to be happy. But I also want you to be safe. And Domino is—"

"—not safe." Tembi finished for her. "I think I knew that."

Matindi nodded. "I know she's from your homeworld, and that you share a kinship because of that. But the reason I left Lancaster? It was because of something she did, a long time ago."

"What happened?" Tembi felt her own ears perk up in interest.

"I'll never be drunk enough to tell you the details," Matindi said. "Let's just say that there was a choice that could minimize damage, and another choice that would meet certain goals, and Domino chose the path which met those goals.

"There were costs." Matindi continued. "Lives were ruined. She had her reasons, and if I'm being honest with myself? I'll admit they were very good reasons. Sometimes I think Lancaster has only survived as long as it has because of people like her. But survival has a steep price, and I…I wasn't willing to pay it. So I left."

"But you're back now," Tembi said. "And Domino told me that she wants things to be fair. So what does that mean? Lancaster has gotten better?"

"Tembi? Honey?" Matindi said gently. "Domino has always wanted things to be fair, but fair doesn't always mean ethical. The only thing that's changed about Lancaster is that you're a part of it.

Tembi's heart dropped. "I'm sorry," she said. "I know you're trapped here because of me, but—"

"No, that's what gives me hope!" Matindi reached over and clasped Tembi's hands. "The Deep chose you, and brought you to me instead of to Lancaster. It wants something different than what is at Lancaster now. It wants change."

The book in the library…

"The Deep brought me a book by a Witch named Rowland," Tembi said. "Williamson said it was about how the Deep might be changing its mind about how it sees humanity. And then the Deep told me it wants the war in Sagittarius to stop."

The older Witch nodded. "I know," she replied. "I've had the same conversations with it. So have Matthew and the others on the Tower Council."

"Really?" Tembi was astonished. Matthew never mentioned the war, and dropped the subject whenever she brought it up. She had never imagined that he had spoken to the Deep about it. "What do they think?"

For the first time, Matindi couldn't meet her eyes. She looked away, out the window to the view of a tiny pond with silver fish swimming just beneath the surface. "What's happening in Sagittarius? They say it's terrible, but that it's an extreme, and if we get involved in this one war, we will have established precedent for the Deep to become involved in them all."

"Gods! If one more person tells me there have always been wars," Tembi said, her fingers tight around the mug, "I'm going to have to start a new one."

"Excellent," Matindi turned back to Tembi, her green eyes fierce. "When the time is right, I hope you do."

---

translator
translator translator
translator translator translator
translator translator
warrior

Excerpt from "Notes from the Deep," 22 May 3734 CE

Chapter Eighteen

"I tried something last night," Tembi said, as she and the Deep spun a sphere made from fifteen foam balls around Bayle.

"Oh?" Bayle was watching the balls with a cautious eye. Tembi had excellent control, but Leps had decided to combine mobility practice with the previous day's astronomy lesson. When she shouted out the name of a solar system, the balls stopped moving in their predictable orbits and would shoot up to form planetary charts.

"The Deep can read, right? It knows every book in the Library. So it understands the written word, no problem."

"Right—*oh!*" Bayle caught on. "So instead of talking to it, we write to it?"

Leps was prowling the front of the classroom. She slammed her stick across a desk, and shouted: "Stross Cluster!"

Tembi sent eight of the fifteen foam balls up into the air. These hung over Bayle's head until Leps nodded her approval, and then dropped back into their steady orbit.

"Exactly. We write to it," Tembi continued. "I left it a note on my tablet."

"Did it write back?"

Tembi shook her head. "I asked it to leave a reply, but it didn't."

"That makes sense," Bayle said. "If the Deep could write, Witches would communicate with it that way."

"But it can read," Tembi said. "So, tell me—what's the difference between reading and writing?"

"Iolanthe System!" Leps shouted.

Tembi launched the balls again: there were six this time, and she pulled in a smaller foam ball from a nearby desktop to simulate the path of the erratic comet that would someday plow into a dense-mass planet and gradually send the rest of the system into chaos.

"Stoneskin! That comet better be in its proper location or I'm docking points for showing off!"

Tembi had the Deep freeze the mock solar system and consulted her tablet. The comet jumped eighteen degrees to her left.

"Excellent," Leps said. "Resume."

"All right, I'll bite," Bayle said, once Leps had passed to yell at another group of students. "What's the difference between reading and writing?"

"I don't know," Tembi said. "We have to go to the Library."

Bayle sighed. "I hate the Library," she said. Three foam balls broke their orbits and beaned her in the back of the head.

"Stoneskin!"

"That was me!" Tembi shouted to their teacher. "Not the Deep." To Bayle, she mouthed: "That wasn't me."

"I know," Bayle whispered back. "I still hate the Library. Don't—" she said, holding up a finger as another ball sped towards her, "—do that again."

The ball stopped, then sulked its way back into formation.

After classes, they walked across Lancaster to the stone maze. The Deep took a few minutes to play its usual round of tricks with the boulders, but Tembi had gotten good enough at levitating herself that she could simply leap over the top of these and not get bogged down in the ever-changing maze.

"Coming?" she shouted to Bayle.

"You go ahead!" her friend shouted back. "I'm—*ow!*—taking the long way."

Good enough. Tembi knocked on the Library's wooden door and barged inside.

"Hey, Williamson!" she said, flopping her arms and head down on the ancient desk.

"Ah." The Martian slipped a long red string into the pages of the book he was reading, closed the cover, and set it down beside him. "Good evening, young Stoneskin. What do you need today?"

"Answers."

"This is the place for it," Williamson said. He removed his glasses and set them atop the book. "How can I help?"

"Why can the Deep read but not write? That doesn't make sense."

He smiled as Tembi tried on his glasses. "You're assuming that reading and writing are the same. They're not. They're part of the whole of literacy, and share many of the same processes, yes, but reading is consuming information while writing is communicating it. And the Deep…?"

"…is scheisse at communicating," she finished for him as she glanced around the small room. The world was very slightly blurry; she removed the glasses and dropped them onto the book.

"Indeed." The Librarian reclaimed his glasses and made a show of cleaning them. "Now, I'll save you some additional effort—why can't I let the Deep talk through me, and have it answer your questions that way?"

"We studied this in class," Tembi said. "Leps says when the Deep speaks through a Witch, it's because the Deep and the Witch want to talk about the same topic. If they're thinking about different things, the Deep can't speak through the Witch."

"Exactly," Williamson said, nodding. "It is excellent at taking information in, but it is extremely limited in how it can get information out."

"I understand how that works with speaking through a Witch, but how does that work with books?" Bayle said from the doorway. "I'd think that if it can read, then it could write."

"Good evening, Princess," Williamson said. "And yes, most humans who have at least partial literacy are able to both read and write to some degree. But the Deep is an energy field, not a human being. What goes into an energy field doesn't always come out, and if it does come out, it can come out changed."

"Scheisse," Tembi muttered as she banged her forehead against the wooden desk.

"Had the brainstorm that you could talk to the Deep through

text?" Williamson said. He held up the plass tablet he always kept beside him. "Good luck—I've been trying for several millennia."

"Does it ever answer?" Bayle asked.

"Single words, sometimes, or small groups of them. Never coherent ones." Williamson looked thoughtful. "I believe it gets frustrated at not knowing how to write, so I don't push it.

"Also…" He paused, as if not entirely sure he should say what was on his mind.

"What?" Tembi asked.

Williamson's head rose, as if he had decided something. "It's not the best at understanding emotional intent," he said. "Especially if it's in writing."

"Sir?" Bayle turned away from the third doorway.

"Shipping," he said, pointing at the first door.

"Ethics and Law," he said, pointing at the second.

He pointed at the third—the door Bayle was now leaning against—and looked at Tembi.

"Miscellaneous?" she replied. She had been in that room twice before, and found it too disorganized to be of any real use. The Deep seemed to avoid most of the books in there.

"I recommend a certain volume of poetry," Williamson said, as he put on his glasses and returned to his reading. "The author's name is Daughter Pihikan."

"Okay," Tembi said, waiting for the Deep to pluck the volume out of the stacks and deliver it, as it usually did.

Nothing happened.

"Discovery is a critical part of the learning process," Williamson said.

Tembi and Bayle glanced at the third door, which opened with the ominous creak of rusty hinges.

"Ignore that," the Librarian said without looking up. "I keep meaning to fix it."

The girls moved into the third room. The Deep's usual tricks of playing with the limits of physical space were at work, with shelves stretching far beyond the natural confines of the Library.

"What is this place?" Bayle asked, as she moved her finger across a series of cookbooks. "*Culinary Practices for Witches… Chopping and Paring with the Deep…*" She pulled one out, and flipped to a page at random. "Simmer oil. Do not bring to a boil. Jump oil to fish when skin is beginning to crisp… Tembi? This is a guide to cooking by using the Deep."

"Williamson says this is the room where he keeps anything written by a Witch that isn't about shipping, ethics, or law." Tembi glanced at a shelf which seemed to be full of books on naturalism and animal husbandry. "He says some Witches have hobbies, and others don't take to life at Lancaster."

"Y'know, surgery got so much more effective when we invented anti-grav," Bayle said. "I bet a doctor could think of a million different ways to use the Deep in medicine."

Tembi nodded. "Like setting broken bones before the 'bots are used?"

"Or purging infection, or poison, or—" Bayle broke off. "*Advanced Ceramics with Deep-Controlled Glazing Techniques.* Good gods, people have too much free time."

"And this is just the text that's been bound into books," Tembi said, searching the spines to find the poetry section. "There's probably a thousand times this amount of content in the digital archives."

"Maybe," Bayle said. "Or maybe all of the Witches who write this scraping stuff want to see it turned into books."

They separated after that, checking different sections of shelves, calling out interesting titles to each other as they went.

"Bayle? Tembi?" Steven's voice, shouted but small, as if he were calling to them over a great distance.

Tembi turned to see his silhouette in the doorway. He was much further away than she knew she had walked. "Over here!" she shouted.

Footsteps. A little more light began to shine in the gloomy room as Steven came near. He was holding a glowing plass ball in one hand. The light from the small ball bounced off of his scales and made him glow in a deep golden bronze.

"Pretty!" Tembi said.

"My people look amazing in the dark," he said, grinning. He liked to wear shirts and trousers, and by the end of each day these were woefully stained and wrinkled. These looked out of place with the rest of him glowing as if he had been dipped in gold.

"What are you doing?"

"Searching for this." Bayle came around the corner of the stacks, a thin book with a light blue cover in one hand. "*Beast of Burden,* by Daughter Pihikan."

Tembi took the book from her, and she and Steven flipped through the pages. "They're just short poems," Steven said. "Why did you want this?"

"You know how we want a better way to communicate with the Deep?" Tembi said. "The Librarian said this book might help."

"Uh-huh." Steven didn't bother to hide his skepticism. "Poetry."

"Emotional poetry," Bayle clarified.

"Yes, well." Steven pushed a lock of hair behind an ear. "Can we at least eat dinner while we read emotional poetry? Keep our strength up, and all that."

Matindi was attending yet another fancy dinner with Matthew and the rest of Lancaster's Tower Council, so the three of them ordered takeout and went back to Tembi's place. They crashed in the common room, Tembi on the couch, her friends on the floor, with Taabu begging for scraps.

"Don't give him human food," Tembi pleaded. "He gets the worst gas!"

Steven was pure innocence as he tossed the cat a chunk of seasoned tofu.

"I don't get any of this," Bayle said, paging through the slim book of poetry. "These are just weird poems about the Deep."

"Is it in code?" Steven asked, rolling onto his back. "A secret Deep code?"

"I hope so," Bayle said. She tossed the book to him. "If it isn't, we've been tricked into reading tragically bad poetry."

"It can't be that bad," he said, skimming with a finger beneath the words. "*Beast of Burden...* Okay, this is the title poem."

"Read it aloud," Tembi said. She was full of delicious tofu, and so many things that normally seemed important, didn't.

"Oh, I'm wrong," he said. "So very wrong! This is that bad! Here we go..."

> *Speak, infinite colors.*
> *Say, rainbow which bridges space...*
> *...maybe time...*
> *What do you want from us?*
> *You, who give so much, yet ask for nothing.*

Steven stood, book in one hand, cat in the other. He paced, gesturing dramatically with the book.

> *Speak, sharp as knives!*
> *Say, brilliant one...*
> *What do you want from us?*
> *We, who take all from you, yet give you nothing.*

By this point, Tembi and Bayle were laughing. A blanket floated up from where it lay on the couch by Tembi's feet, and draped itself in the open air, like a person wearing a cape. The cape twisted towards Steven.

"Deep! Hey, Deep!" Tembi cheered, and Bayle began to clap.

Steven turned to face the cape. He bowed and began to circle it, as if it were his partner on the dance floor. The Deep didn't bow in turn, but it did join in the circle.

> *Listen, friend.*
> *Hear me, I beg of you...*
> *...you, who are our friend...*
> *We are not yours.*
> *True friends would never treat you so.*

Now Steven was shouting, and the girls were laughing so hard they couldn't breathe. Taabu leapt from the crook of Steven's arm and took shelter beneath the couch. The Deep's cape kept floating higher and higher, and Tembi felt the joy of soaring wings beating against her mind.

> *Speak, please!*
> *Say, now…*
> *…why you allow us…*
> *…why would you ever allow us…*
> *To treat you as our beast of burden.*

It was a short poem, and by the end of it, even Steven was rolling on the floor, laughing along with them. The Deep swirled its cape around and around—

Pops of air, one louder than the other. Two Witches, arms full of leftovers, appearing in the kitchen, full and sudden witnesses to the scene in the common room—

Matindi, laughing.

Matthew, horrified, shouting: *"What are you **doing?!**"*

> *Lancaster*
> *mother father*
> *come*
> *LISTEN LISTEN LISTEN LISTEN LISTEN*

Excerpt from "Notes from the Deep," 14 November 3511 CE

Chapter Nineteen

"The Deep is not a toy!"

"I know!" Tembi shouted back at Matthew.

The two of them had been roaring at each other for the better part of an hour; Bayle and Steven had fled long ago. Tembi had learned that she was impulsive, reckless, a leech on Matindi's good nature, and would *never* become a pilot, especially if he had anything to say about it, which he did.

Matthew, in turn, had learned that he was too strict, untrusting, undeserving of Matindi's love, and his griddle cakes were filth. Oh, and he treated the Deep like a slave. That's right, she said it! A slave!

And Tembi, apparently, treated the Deep like a toy.

"The Deep isn't a toy!" she shouted. "It's a friend!"

That comment, more than anything else she had hurled at him, seemed to strike home. The fierce rage drained out of Matthew, leaving him cold and shaking in quiet fury.

"No. It cannot be your friend," he said, so softly that she had to move her ears forward to hear him. "It's a tool. Nothing more, nothing less."

Tembi stuck her fists against her sides to keep from punching him. "It. Is. A. Person!" she said, not quite shouting but still a little louder than was strictly necessary to get her point across. "And if you don't realize that, then there is something *wrong* with you!"

He flinched. Just a little, just the slightest bit around his eyes, but Tembi spotted it and locked on to that.

"You *do* realize that!" Then, as the impact of what she had said hit her, she stumbled a few steps away from him. "You *know* it's a person, and you still treat it like…like a *tool!*"

"Tembi—"

"That's even worse!"

There was a brief moment when Tembi thought she might actually hit him. Apparently, Matindi thought so, too; she was up from the kitchen table and forcing herself between them, almost as fast as if she had used the Deep.

"That's enough," Matindi said, her long-fingered hands spread wide to keep them apart. "I won't let you two come to blows under my roof."

Matthew turned to her. "This is your fault," he said. "I should have never left her with you."

"Matthew?" Matindi said. "Get out. Come back when you can have a decent conversation about what it means to be a human being."

Matthew readied himself to say something, thought better of it, and then—

"Kindly use the door," Matindi told him, as he gasped at not being able to jump. "The Deep is part of my family, and I will not have it used or abused in this house."

He turned and walked to the front door. It opened before he could touch the access plate. Domino, dressed once more in full prismatic colors from her hair to her robes, entered.

She stared down at Matthew with stony eyes. "I know I'm interrupting," she said.

"No," Matthew said. "You're not."

He left, pulling the door shut behind him.

Domino turned to Matindi. "I'll keep this short," she said, holding out one elegant brown hand. "Are you hurt?"

Matindi took Domino's hand as if it were a dead rat. "I'm well," she said. "So is Tembi."

"Good." Domino held out her hand to Tembi. She took it and gave it a gentle squeeze, as Matindi had. As usual, Domino's skin was as hard as rock, but tonight it was also cold.

"I was at Lancaster for the Tower Council dinner," she explained to Tembi, and held out a small plugin for a soundkit. "Matindi had mentioned you enjoyed music, so I wanted to give you this. It's a catalog of songs from Earth. I didn't realize my timing would be so awkward until the Deep jumped me to the end of your sidewalk, and no further."

Tembi was watching Domino's ears. They stayed slightly askew, the sign of an Adhamantian suffering from secondhand embarrassment. "Thank you," she said.

"You're very welcome." Domino turned back to Matindi. "Let me know if you need anything. I've heard how difficult Matthew has become in Tower Council."

"He hasn't," Matindi said. "But rumors have legs."

"Yes, they do," Domino said. "Please, reach out if you need to."

Matindi didn't reply. After a moment, Domino nodded to her, then to Tembi, and left.

Matindi threw up her hands and retreated to the kitchen table, where she sat and stared at nothing. Tembi, unsure of what else to do, started to make chamomile tea.

"The problem with living such a scraping long time but never becoming old," Matindi said softly, "is that you won't get to the point where it's easier to forget than remember."

Tembi put a cup of tea in front of Matindi, and took her own to the other side of the table. Both of them avoided looking at the chair where Matthew usually sat.

"What started all of this?" Matindi asked.

Tembi retrieved the book of poetry from the common room, and slid it across the table.

Matindi glanced at the cover. "Of course," she muttered to herself. She flipped through a couple of the pages and cringed. "Oh. Well. I suppose sometimes you do forget.

"All right, Tembi," Matindi said, as she closed the book. "What do you want to do now?"

"Go to bed, I guess," she said. The tea seemed to be working faster than usual; she felt a little lightheaded. Must have been from all of the shouting.

Matindi shook her head. "No," she said. "I mean, moving forward. Matthew isn't happy with you.

"Or me," she added, a little sadly. "He'll be fighting us every chance he gets."

"Why?" Tembi asked.

"Because all of this?" Matindi waved a hand in aimless circles to take in Lancaster. "If Witches start to think of the Deep as a person instead of a…an energy field that we can get to play tricks? All of this gets infinitely more complicated. And now that Matthew knows that I've permanently corrupted you with my wicked, wicked ways?" She sighed and took another sip of tea. "I suppose he expected both you and the Deep to fall in line once you started classes. You'd learn how to talk to the Deep, and you'd get it to obey and stop taking actions on its own."

"But the Deep's always done its own thing!" Tembi insisted. "It plays jokes…it shows up at parties—"

"And Lancaster tolerates those small deviations. Keeps us humble, I suppose. But it claimed you, and it brought me back here, and now Matthew knows you've managed to pull Bayle and Steven into our small anarchy…" Matindi trailed off and laid her head down upon the table.

She was silent so long that Tembi thought she might have gone to sleep. Tembi was thinking about sneaking off to bed herself when Matindi sat back up.

"They—" Matindi paused and looked to the ceiling, as if praying for strength, "—and by 'they,' I mean the well-meaning Witches like Matthew and his scientists, think the Deep has always been here. Part of our galaxy, I mean. They think it didn't bother to show itself until we had developed space travel. As if we were inferior beings who needed to become worthy of its attention before it bestowed its gifts upon us.

"That's what *gods* do!" She laughed, all edges, harsh and without humor. "The Deep is in no way a god! Nor is it an energy field. C'mon, Tembi. Energy fields don't play practical jokes. But another kind of creature? A living being that has the physical traits of an energy field?

"Matthew. The Tower Council…those idiots." Her voice suddenly sounded weak. "The Deep's nothing more than a sweet naive alien. It might even be a *child!* I think it came here recently... Keep in mind that 'recently' is relative, honey. For the Deep, 'recently' is after we had started to explore Earth's solar system. For us, it's...you know...Thursday."

Matindi let her head drop back down the table. "I am twenty-six hundred and...and... I forget. Old. I'm old. I've talked to the Deep every day of my life since I was twenty-two. I was called upon to help the most powerful and most innocent thing in our galaxy. That is an honor."

She tried to lift her teacup and couldn't; the cup tipped over and the tea washed across her hands.

She tried to stand and couldn't.

She *fell!*

"Matindi!" Tembi was on her feet, her own cup of tea spilling everywhere. The room twisted around her, and she grabbed for the table's edge to steady herself. "Deep! Deep, get help!"

Her knees hit the floor and she found herself on all fours, but the room was still spinning. She crawled beneath the table to find—

Matindi.

Lying on the cold tile.

Lying so very still.

"Matindi!"

The familiar *whump!* of displaced air.

Footsteps behind her, the table lifted and hurled across the room.

Voices she didn't recognize.

Tembi tried to pull Matindi into her lap, but her body didn't want to obey—

...Matindi, still struggling to stay conscious. Her eyes were unable to focus, but she was still trying to form the right words...

"...you've been called..." she said, squeezing Tembi's hand. "...it's your honor, too..."

"I know," Tembi told her. "I know."

As Matindi's eyes closed, she whispered, "Be worthy of it."

hear
see
know
mother father
come

Excerpt from "Notes from the Deep," 26 May 3781 CE

Chapter Twenty

A hospital.

A white bed.

Whispering—quiet at first, and then picking up in excitement as they realized she was awake.

"Tembi? Tembi!"

"Steven?" Her mouth felt like she had left it lying open during a summer windstorm on Adhama.

"Hey! *Hey!* Get the Councilwoman! She's awake!"

Puffs of displaced air moving on both sides. Her eyes didn't want to focus, but there was a cascade of rainbows floating in front of her.

"Hey, Deep," she said, smiling.

"Tembi? It's me." A woman's voice—not a stranger's, but not quite familiar. Not yet. "We need you to tell us what happened after I left your house."

Domino.

"This is important, Tembi. We need information. It looks like you and Matindi had something to drink. What was it?"

To drink? Yes, a spilled cup of— "Chamomile," she said. "We had chamomile tea."

"Moto, go. Have them check the container, too, in case the contents were jumped out." Domino's voice. An order. Another puff of air as someone else left the room. "Tembi? Did anyone come to the house? Did Matthew come back after I had left?"

"This is too much for her." Bayle. Angry?

"Let her answer. Tembi, did Matthew come back to the house?"

"No. Let her rest." Bayle. *Very* angry. "She's got a million 'bots swimming inside her! Come back when they finish scrubbing her kidneys."

"Young lady—"

"Yes?"

Tembi tried to pick her head up, but it was too heavy and the lights burned too bright. Still. She knew Bayle would be standing there, hands on her hips, staring up at the older Witch with polite murder in her eyes.

Domino admitted defeat. "She's in good hands."

Tembi agreed, and allowed herself to drift back to sleep. At the edge of consciousness, she realized there was something she was forgetting…

…something important…

She woke some time later, shouting Matindi's name.

"She's alive!" Bayle was standing beside the bed, a little distance away from several people in short white robes who were gathered near a large silver box. "Matindi's in bad shape, but she's alive. The Deep got her to the hospital just in time."

Tembi went limp. "Thank the gods," she whispered. "What happened?"

"Five more minutes," one of the people in white said. He had dark purple eyes and a slim cybernetic attachment running across his collarbones, and other than that he was all but indistinguishable from the other medical technicians.

She lay back and let them work. The nanobots were too small for her body's senses to register—she *knew* this!—but there was still a strange tingle across her torso as the technicians recalled them into the processing unit.

"Adhamantian?" Not a technician this time. A doctor? Apparently so; he wore silver diagnostic cuffs on each wrist, and was using one of these to review a holo of her chart.

"Adhamantian?" he asked again, moving his eyes to look at Tembi.

She nodded as she pulled the privacy sheet up over her body.

"Could you check your skin and let me know if it differs from your personal normal?"

Tembi pinched herself; the sensation barely registered. Then, she ran her fingertips across the sheet; she couldn't feel the cloth at all, and the sound it made was harsh and grating.

"Harder than normal," she replied.

"That's understandable. Your body has been in defense mode." He glanced at the technicians, and they packed up the 'bots and left the room. He glanced at Bayle. "Are you comfortable with your friend hearing this?"

Tembi nodded.

"All right," he pulled over the only chair in the room, and sat beside the bed. "You've been exposed to an organic toxin. We haven't been able to diagnose the source, but we were able to remove it from your body. The toxin was concentrated on your hands and around your mouth."

The tea. She hadn't drunk too much of it, but she had spilled it…

"If you weren't Adhamantian, more of it would have been absorbed by your system," he said. "I'm sorry to inform you that your guardian wasn't as lucky. She's alive, but in critical condition."

"I want to see her." Tembi stood and gathered the privacy sheet around her.

The doctor was having none of that. "Rest," he said. "We're doing the best we can, and it's already too crowded in her room."

The way he said that last part…

Tembi glanced over at Bayle.

Bayle grimaced. "The Deep is, um, helping."

Tembi pushed herself off of the bed. A pile of white hospital robes lay folded on a nearby cabinet, and she put these on as quickly as her aching body would allow. "Which way?"

"You'll know," Bayle said.

Tembi left the room, the doctor one step behind her and objecting the entire time. The moment she entered the hallway, she knew what Bayle had meant: to the right, the hallway was perfectly empty.

To the left, the air was thick with floating objects. Anything that wasn't bolted to a surface (and some that had been bolted down, oh dear, those appeared to be pieces of tile and wood flooring) was hanging in midair, ready and waiting if the doctors found themselves in immediate need. The cluster of objects didn't appear to be organized; medical supplies, of course, but also food and toys and—

"Is that *Taabu?!*"

"No, it's a different cat. Taabu was here for a while, but the Deep swaps them out when they get too cranky.

"Careful where you're walking," Bayle added, as they started down the hall to Matindi's room. "Some of these things have sharp edges."

From the other end of the hallway, Tembi could see technicians moving slowly, trying to reach Matindi's room but unable to get there because of the cluster of items blocking their way.

Tembi sighed. It hurt; her lungs felt stiff. "Deep?" she called. "Could you clear a path? We need to be able to reach Matindi."

The objects began to bob, very slowly, to either side of the hallway.

"Thank you, Deep."

Tembi and Bayle began to creep along the thin pathway, pushing past the overlarge pieces of medical equipment that didn't quite fit against the walls. The cat stared at them with bored unblinking eyes.

"Have you tried reasoning with it?" Tembi asked.

"Of course we have!" Bayle replied. "And Matthew can overrule it, but he must've fallen asleep. He's spending all of his time here."

Matthew!

The germ of an idea she didn't want to deal with grabbed onto the surface of her mind.

If there was a toxin…

If there was a toxin in a tea that Matindi drank every single night…

If there was a toxin in a tea that *Matthew knew* Matindi drank every single night…

Tembi was working her way towards fury before she knew it. She pushed through the microbe cage blocking the entrance to

Matindi's room and—

Matindi, on the bed. Looking small and fragile and a husk of her usual self, lost beneath the machinery keeping her alive.

Matthew, asleep in the chair beside her, holding her hand, wearing the same clothes that Tembi had last seen him in.

He looked up as she stormed inside, and said, "Tembi…"

His voice broke apart the suspicion in her heart, and then there was nothing else other than she was crying, and Matthew was crying, and both of them held each other by Matindi's bed as they wept.

Some time later, Tembi found herself sitting on the floor of Matindi's hospital room, Matthew sitting beside her. They hadn't spoken; she was unsure of what to say, and too emotionally drained to try and figure it out.

Matthew, twenty-six hundred years her senior, did know. "I'm not going to lie to you," he said. "The toxin bonded to the neurons in her cerebral cortex. They say they can remove it quickly using 'bots and screeners, but there's a small chance that doing so might damage her brain. The safest way to proceed is to do what they did with you, which is to help your own body process the toxins and allow you to recover naturally."

"Sounds good." It was a ghost's voice. Not her own.

"But she's much—" Matthew had to pause. "She's much older than you, and the doctors don't understand how the Deep prolongs our lifespans, so… So the risk of her not waking up at all is real, and…"

He couldn't finish.

"The Deep won't let that happen," Tembi said.

"Tembi—"

She looked up at him. "The Deep," she said, "won't let that happen."

"Okay." Matthew closed his eyes, unwilling to shatter her faith. "But you and I are listed as her next-of-kin. We need to talk about how we want to proceed."

Then it was meetings with doctors, and meetings with other doctors, and meetings with senior Witches on the Tower Council to see if the Deep could be used to separate Matindi's brain matter from the toxin. (Answer: Yes, probably, but when Tembi heard what "probably" meant, she decided the answer was no.)

After this, she and Matthew went down to the cafeteria, ate food without tasting it, and didn't talk.

That was where the law found him.

Four men in Hub's black uniforms were jumped in to appear beside their table. They were accompanied by another senior Witch, a woman who called herself Dale and who always wore a suitcoat over a long skirt. She couldn't meet Matthew's eyes as the lawmen arrested him for attempted murder.

Tembi shouted. She protested. She told them that Matthew *wouldn't* have done this to Matindi, *never!* And when it was clear they were going to take him away—that Dale was there to ensure the Deep wouldn't let him jump away!—she wrapped her arms around him and tried to jump them both home.

Home.

Matindi's house.

Her house.

Their *home.*

It didn't work, of course, but Matthew thought she was trying to hug him so he put his arms around her and held her. "It'll be okay," he said. "Stay with Matindi. I want her healthy so we can all go home together."

Tembi nodded, and let him go.

"Miss?" One of the lawmen had stayed behind, and was trying to get her attention. "Miss? How old are you?"

She didn't bother to look at him, her attention fixed on Matthew as he was escorted from the hospital. Everyone in the cafeteria was staring. Gods, Dale wouldn't even do him the courtesy of a jump, they were just walking him out into the street in front of everybody—

"Miss?" The lawman put a hand on her shoulder. "How old are you?"

Now she looked up at him; he dropped his hand and stepped away, quickly. "How old do I have to be to get you to leave me alone?"

"Eighteen, but—"

"Then I'm eighteen."

"Miss, you're not—"

She sent a mental request to the Deep, and two of the metal cafeteria tables rose in the air on either side of the lawman, then tilted so their flat tops were positioned on either side of him, like heavy hands ready to clap.

The lawman froze. Around them, the other people in the cafeteria gasped; some gathered their children and fled.

"I'm eighteen," she said.

He nodded.

Tembi asked the Deep to set the tables down, and walked back to Matindi's room.

---

bookman
bookman talk
stonegirl
stonegirl listen

Excerpt from "Notes from the Deep," 08 August 3116 CE

Chapter Twenty-One

Time passed; Tembi barely noticed.

Matindi was still in the hospital, still unconscious, still healing. Tembi had learned she could be reached in the Deep's dreams: even though she was mostly rambling and unintelligible due to the sedatives, Matindi had consented to the wait-and-see approach to her own medical care. She had also had the presence of mind to shout at Tembi for pulling the stunt with the tables in the hospital cafeteria, yelling about how the Deep was *not* a weapon, young lady, and *how **dare** you ask it to behave in such a way?!*

This, more than anything else, had assured Tembi that Matindi was on the road to recovery.

Knowing that Matindi was still here, still alive and present and able to connect with the Deep, made things easier. Not better, but easier. Classes didn't stop because Tembi spent her nights in a too-quiet house. Life didn't stop because the senior Witches kept dropping by with casseroles and pestering her to leave and move into the dormitories with the other students.

Life didn't stop because the law was keeping Matthew in a cell.

"He didn't do it," Tembi said to Bayle and Steven for what might have been the hundredth time that day. They were in class, and the usual tasks of moving foam balls around the room held no appeal for her.

"We know," they replied in unison.

"This isn't right!" she shouted at them. "I need *help!*"

They didn't—couldn't—give her a good answer.

She walked out of class, ignoring Leps' protests. When the Deep floated her back to the classroom, she sat at her desk, unmoving, staring at the far wall.

Leps let her go early. Tembi had expected another essay in punishment; instead, Leps had put one hand on her shoulder and told her to take a few breakdays to get her head together.

Tembi walked to the hopper station and flew into Hub. She wasn't sure where she was going, or why, but her feet knew: once they hit the pavement, they took her straight to Matthew's holding cell. The law was keeping him in a small apartment located in the center of their offices in Hub. It was run down and smelled slightly of bodily fluids, but visitors were free to come and go.

Not just visitors, it seemed. When Tembi arrived, Matthew was walking back to his apartment in the presence of a law officer and another Witch, a small bag of leftovers from lunch in his hands.

"Um…" Tembi pointed to the bag after they had exchanged a quick hug.

"Oh," he said, and handed it to her. "I'm sorry, Tembi. If I had known you were coming, I'd have picked up extra."

"No," Tembi said, shaking her head. "Why are they letting you walk around?"

The law officer nodded at Tembi, unlocked the door to the apartment, and left.

"C'mon in," Matthew said, as he opened the door for her. "Do you know Maxwell?"

"No. Hello," she said to the other Witch. He gave her a little wave but didn't bother to speak. He was a few years older than Moto, probably somewhere near Leps' age, and was typing away on a holo-projection generated by a databand on his wrist, all but ignoring her and Matthew. "Why are you—"

"Basically a free man?" Matthew said, as he motioned for her to sit at the seedy kitchen table. Tembi sat, and he went to scavenge utensils from the drawers. "Matindi wasn't the only Witch on the Tower Council who's been poisoned."

Tembi, who had been unwrapping the bag to see what was inside, snapped upright. "What?!"

"We're keeping it quiet," he said, as he slid a plate and a mismatched knife and fork over to her. "The law has decided I'm most likely not responsible, but until a better suspect comes along, I'm under their supervision.

"And Maxwell's," he added, nodding towards the other Witch. "He's here to make sure I'm not using the Deep to jump poison into anyone's meals while I'm locked up."

Maxwell waved, but didn't bother to look away from his holo.

"Okay..." Tembi said, a little hesitantly. She would never understand Hub's legal system. If they had been on Adhama, Matthew would be in a small room with bars instead of walls and a hole in the floor for his bodily fluids.

"Have you gone to see Matindi yet?" Matthew asked her.

"I came to see you first," she said. "I'll go by the hospital on the way home."

Matthew sighed. "I wish you could jump," he said. "All of this running around, that's got to be taking a toll on you."

"Not really," Tembi said. "I like to walk. And the Deep doesn't—"

She realized what she was about to say, and snapped her mouth shut and busied herself scooping the leftovers out onto the plate. They hadn't mentioned their fight, and she wasn't ready to return to the topic of the Deep. She knew she was wound too tightly as it was, and she didn't want to lash out.

Well. Not at Matthew, at any rate.

Matthew, apparently, was ready to talk. "It's fine, honey," he said. Tembi looked up and smiled at the archaic nickname Matindi used for her. "I was angry, and you were angry, and we took it out on each other. It happens—we're only human. The trick is to make sure it doesn't weigh us down from here on out."

Tembi nodded, slowly, and said, "I'm still angry, but..."

"...but other things got in the way," he said. "I understand. I've had a lot of time to think about why we were fighting over the past few days. Maybe we should realize that means we're not mad at each other, but at the situation."

"Yeah." She began to poke at the food. Some kind of fried rice dish with a lab-grown meat she didn't recognize. It tasted almost like dry seafood. "I don't know why you think it's okay to treat the Deep like your slave."

Across the room, Maxwell's head popped up, then dropped down towards his holos again.

"I don't," Matthew said.

"You might not think it's okay, but you still do it," Tembi said. "If it isn't right, then why do you let it happen?"

He spent a few moments examining the tabletop, then said, "Do you know the story of the first Witches?"

She nodded. "You took me to the Lancaster Museum when I was a little kid, remember?"

"All right," he said. "Tell me the story."

It came easily; she had told this same story to Kalais a few months before as she had dragged him around the orientation building next to the hopper platform. How, nearly three thousand years before, eight people working on the supply line between Earth and the Mars colonies found their shipments appearing on the other end of the line without any apparent human intervention.

They began to tell each other about strange sensations that appeared and disappeared without an obvious source.

The words which sidestepped their ears and appeared in their minds.

And the...well...the...the floating objects. Everywhere.

Had they gone mad? No, they decided. Not if these things were happening to all of them. For a time, they thought the shipping docks were haunted by the ghost of a friend who had died in a loader accident.

Then, the news of similar events began to reach them. All across planet Earth, shipping companies began to report that items were appearing at their destinations as soon as the paperwork had been filed. Scientists were looking into the phenomena, and wanted to collect data from anyone with similar experiences.

The dock workers went to the scientists and told them about the ghost.

The scientists laughed, and thanked them for their time.

The dock workers looked at each other, and then asked their dead friend to lift the scientists up to the ceiling.

After that, they were taken seriously.

It took nearly a century to work out that the ghost was not a ghost at all, but an (here, Tembi scrunched up her nose and went with the accepted version of the Deep, for simplicity's sake) *energy field*. One that was sapient and wanted to help humans explore the galaxy and expand across the planets.

And so? They did.

"That hits the high points," Matthew said as she finished. "Now, think of that from the perspective of the owners of the shipping companies. The ones who employed those dock workers."

Tembi stopped with her fork halfway to her mouth. "Why?"

"Humor me."

"They must have been happy," Tembi said, thinking back on her classes. "Faster-than-light travel is slow. It can take weeks to reach a planet that the Deep can reach in seconds."

"True, but don't bring FTL into the discussion," he said. "We invented FTL after we began using the Deep—soldiers needed a quick way to get across the galaxy, and the Deep wouldn't touch them—so that's not a factor."

"Sure…" Tembi said, shoveling rice into her mouth. Whatever the meat was? Very pleasant. Natural seafood was always too soggy for her tastes. "Then they'd be even happier."

"No," he said. "The management at the shipping companies? Furious. Simply furious. They had lost control over their supply chains, and as the fundamental rule of supply chains is control, they had a planet-sized problem on their hands.

"Nobody out there," he said, jabbing a thumb at the city, "thinks about supply chains. They aren't exciting. They don't care how they get food, only that they *do* get it. Reliably. Consistently."

Matthew poked the edge of her plate. "Most people don't have enough food in their own homes to last them a week, Tembi," he said. "They take for granted that they can go shopping, or stop at a restaurant on their way home. Even very poor people who live off of scraps? They're at the mercy of rich people who have access to food.

"Supply chains aren't exciting," he repeated. "But they are necessary. Lancaster is a glorified shipping company—that's all we are. It's our responsibility to help the galaxy survive."

Tembi glanced over at Maxwell. The Witch had been nodding along as Matthew spoke, and towards the end, he had put down his holo to follow the conversation. He noticed Tembi watching him, shrugged, and went back to his reading.

"Can't we do this and not treat the Deep like a—" she stopped talking, not yet ready to throw loaded words around him. "Can't we treat it like a friend?"

"Tembi?" Matthew's face dropped, and he looked extremely tired. "I'm dealing with twenty thousand Witches. Many of them are old and stubborn and, to be honest? They can be pretty nasty people. I'm still forced to explain why we allowed music into Lancaster, and that's been a settled matter for over two millennia.

"There are so many moving pieces that would need to be changed," he said. "And the Deep tells me it's satisfied with how things are, except—"

He paused to let her finish his thought for him.

"—except for the Sabenta," she said.

Matthew nodded. "I've been trying, honey, I really have. But the Tower Council? They're older than I am, and many of them have forgotten that the Deep isn't just a convenient garbage disposal. They don't bother to listen to it anymore. And they won't tolerate any discussion that *they* might be the problem, not the Deep. And they most certainly won't listen to the younger Witches who came to Lancaster after them, and who might be more flexible to change."

"If I were the Deep, I'd throw them out," Tembi muttered.

"But you're not," Matthew said. "That's the Deep's decision to make. Not ours."

She didn't have a good answer to that. Instead, she got up and moved her dishes to the cleaner.

"I've been working on getting the Council to help the Sabenta," he said, as Tembi returned to her chair. "It's not easy, but I was making progress." His eyes moved towards the databand on his wrist. "In fact, I was supposed to be at a general hearing in an hour to plead the Sabenta's case," he said. "That hearing has been delayed until my release."

"Why didn't you tell me any of this?" she asked.

"Because I can manage Lancaster when we use the Deep as a tool," he said. "I can't manage Lancaster if the Deep is a co-worker, or a friend, or a family member. I can't reconcile the business of keeping the entire galaxy going with how you and Matindi want all Witches to treat the Deep. There are too many moving pieces for me to deal with."

"This is why you two have been fighting," she said quietly.

"Yes."

"But…this isn't *right.*"

Matthew nodded. "I know," he said. "But neither is letting fifty billion people starve while Lancaster fights amongst ourselves.

"Why don't you go and see Matindi," he said gently. "I'd like to talk about this some more once we've had a little time to process, if that's okay with you. I'm still trying to figure out whether I can consider the Deep a friend. I don't know if I can."

Tembi's ears went back; Matthew spotted this, and gave her a very sad smile.

"I'm old, honey," he said. "Please remember that it's hard for me to change, too."

friends
all
forever

Excerpt from "Notes from the Deep," 01 December 2714 CE

Chapter Twenty-Two

Her feet took her to the hospital, through its halls, and to Matindi's room.

Her brain wasn't in any way involved with the journey. No, her brain was busy trying to process the last few months, the anger and frustration that had gone along with almost every stray thought she had towards Matthew—

—the terrible things she had said to him—

—but all the while he was trying to change, or at least thinking about whether he *could* change, and…

…and…

…she found herself by Matindi's bedside. The green Witch was still buried beneath medical equipment, with monitors and dripping liquids and nanobot chambers humming all around her. Tembi stared down at the too-still face of her guardian and knew—well and truly *knew!*—that someone had tried to kill Matindi…and maybe her, too.

"No," she whispered to herself. "No."

Her entire world slipped behind a bloody red haze.

Tembi didn't remember how she reached the darker neighborhoods of Hub, with the golden birds washed from her face and her robes run through the dirt until they looked rougher than they were. She walked until the sun went down and two men a few years older than she was tried to roll her—for credit or her body, she wasn't sure. She laughed as she threw the first man against a building, and laughing turned to dark words and crying as she bashed the second man against a trash bin. She grabbed him by the hair and cracked his head against the thick plass, again and again, until the Deep seized her and hauled her from his unconscious, bleeding body.

She looked at what she had done…

…and fled.

A rooftop beneath her feet. Hub, long and low, its edges broken by buildings and light, below.

"You haven't done that in a long time."

Moto.

"How long have you been there?" she asked, using the filthy sleeve of her robe to wipe away the blood and tears.

"Not too long," he said. "I had to make sure the paramedics knew where to find him."

"Oh, gods." Tembi buried her face in her hands.

"He's fine," Moto said, as he came to sit beside her. "They popped a Medkit and he was as good as new in fifteen minutes. But—"

"—I can't go around hurting people," she finished for him without bothering to look up. "I know."

"You don't," he said. "If you did, you wouldn't be doing this."

She broke into tears again.

It was almost a replay of how they had first met. Tembi, rolling other kids in the alleys; Moto, called in by the Deep to clean up after her when a fight had turned too serious.

She was never sure why the Deep had chosen Moto—she assumed it was because they were relatively close in age and from the same planet—but he had been kind when she needed it, and put her on the sparring mat to channel her aggression when she needed that. He had always made the time to help.

And here he was today.

Moto took one of her hands away from her face to inspect her skin. "Oh, Tembi," he sighed.

She collapsed against him and wept.

He let her cry herself out, but he wasn't willing to be gentle. "You have to manage your stress," he said, as he rubbed her back. "It's not an option for you, or me, or anyone from Adhama. Our tempers run too hot—we're the best in the galaxy in a crisis, but long-term stress? That's our weakness. We might be made of stone, but stone can crack."

Tembi sat up and opened her mouth, but he slammed his

hand down on the rooftop between them. "Listen to me!" he shouted. "I know what I'm talking about! Before I learned to keep from breaking, I nearly killed someone."

She squirmed away from him. "What? *You?!*"

Moto nodded. "That's how Domino found me," he said. "I was eighteen, and had just come to Lancaster. Classes were too hard. I lost control. I was fighting, and I…" He shook his head. "The Deep had to intervene, and it grabbed a trained Witch to move the other kid to the hospital.

"They had to keep it quiet," he said. "Lancaster's sterling reputation, you know. But Domino heard, and she decided she wanted to meet the boy from Adhama who…"

His voice trailed off.

Tembi nearly asked what he had done during that fight to catch Domino's interest, and then just as quickly decided she could live a long and happy life without knowing the details.

"So, from now on, we're sparring," he said. "You and me, four times a week, until Matindi is out of the hospital and Matthew is out of his cell. We're going to beat ourselves bloody, so you don't find yourself doing that to anybody else." Moto took her hand in his; she noticed his skin was softer than it had been at the Solstice party. "Deal?"

He wasn't giving her a choice, but…

Tembi nodded.

"Good," he said, her hand still resting in his. "Let me jump you to Lancaster."

The Deep wrapped around them. Tembi felt the Deep's sadness, mostly directed at her, a little towards a general world-weariness that she had never sensed in it before tonight, and then they were standing on one of the garden paths which led to the Pavilion.

"I'm supposed to be with Domino at a party," he said. "I said I wanted to take a walk, so…" He nodded towards the white arcs of the building.

"Moto—" she began, but stopped, unsure of what to say.

He smiled at her before he headed down the path.

Tembi went home and showered, and felt a little better.

(And then she caught sight of herself in the mirror and remembered that s*he had beaten a man's head against a dumpster!* and then had *run away* and *left him there!* and didn't.)

She fed the cat.

She cleaned the kitchen and the bathroom.

(…*blood flying, the sound of screaming…*)

She tried to read, but more tears started to fall and the pages of Rowland's book began to turn into a blurry mess.

A soft **whump** of displaced air, and Bayle was standing beside her.

"Tembi, what—"

"I'm a terrible person!" she cried, and fell against Bayle.

Her friend heard her out, and still managed to say the right things. No, she wasn't a terrible person. No, she probably shouldn't have beaten up—Wait, hold on, you beat somebody up? How big was he? Whoa!—that man, but he shouldn't have tried to do whatever it was that he wanted to do to her anyhow, so he wasn't worth her tears. And wasn't everything okay now, with no real harm done?

"Consider it a learning experience," Bayle said, as she pushed a handkerchief towards Tembi.

"…maybe…" Tembi sniffed.

"Come on," Bayle said. She moved into the kitchen and began to go through the cupboards. "You know I'm right. When was the last time you had something to eat?"

"I had some leftovers at Matthew's—"

"Not good enough." Bayle slammed the cupboard doors. "Want to go into Hub for tumbarranchos?"

"No," Tembi said, squeezing her eyes against the image of the man and the dumpster.

"Okay. Pavilion leftovers it is," Bayle said.

"But—"

"I don't want to eat cafeteria chow, and the coffee shop is closed. If we go to the Pavilion, nobody except the caterers and the other scrub Witches'll see us," Bayle assured her. "Moto won't even notice you're there."

Tembi went to clean up (again), and made sure she avoided looking at her own reflection this time. When she entered the common room, Bayle was wearing a different change of clothes.

"Um…"

"Well, Moto might notice *I'm* there," Bayle said.

Tembi laughed, and felt slightly better about everything.

The Pavilion turned out to be a good choice. A large number of the untrained Witches had come to scavenge, and while that meant the food was scarce, they had also begun dancing behind the building. Tembi lost herself in the music, and the Deep, and for a while her life was nothing but Witches twisting in the night sky.

Around midnight, a loud cheer came from within the building. Tembi peeked inside to check out the cause, and nearly bumped straight into Moto.

"I'm not here!" she said quickly.

He didn't notice. Instead, he picked her up and swung her around and around, laughing.

"They've agreed to help!" he said, lifting her high into the air. "Lancaster's agreed to a treaty to move Sabenta refugees out of the war zone!"

"What?" Tembi could barely hear him over the noise. The Witches appeared to be evenly divided between celebration and disgust, and both sides were making their opinions known.

"It'll get better from here," he said, as he hugged her. "I mean, we're still looking at months of negotiations, but this was the biggest hurdle, and we're—"

"Moto." Domino, barely a meter away, spoke softly but that single word cut through the ruckus in the room like a knife.

"Right. Yes, Ma'am." He set Tembi down, but couldn't resist giving her a quick hug on the way. "It'll get better from here," he whispered. "We'll make it work. I promise."

After that, it became a celebration. The older Witches who objected to a treaty left, noses in the air and all but chanting prophecies of doom; their numbers were replaced by the young

Witches who snuck into the Pavilion to join in the festivities. Long after midnight, the music finally stopped. The older Witches jumped away; the young Witches began walking, or pushed off the ground in long leaping bounds towards the dormitories. Tembi and Bayle decided to take the slow way home, and meandered through the gardens towards Matindi's house, singing.

"I still don't know why the Deep said you need to learn how to sing," Tembi said. "You've got an amazing voice!"

Bayle did something that was close to a bow, but involved pulling her robes to the sides and a good deal of exposed ankle. "Thank you!"

"We've got to figure out what the Deep meant," Tembi said. "If it's not singing, then what?"

"Can we just pretend it actually just meant singing, and I've already mastered it?" Bayle asked with a sigh.

Tembi was about to reply when a loud noise somewhere between a snap and a *bang!* tore through the gardens.

"Wha—" Bayle began, but Tembi had grabbed her and yanked her behind the nearest rock wall, one hand over her friend's mouth.

"Popstick," Tembi whispered.

Bayle stared at her, confused, then nodded slowly. Tembi pulled her hand away from her mouth, and the two of them sat, as silent as shipmice.

"The Deep says there are two people in the clearing ahead," Bayle whispered. "One of them is on the ground."

"Scheisse," Tembi muttered. Popsticks were designed to be nonlethal, but if they had a full charge and if the person using it went for the back of the neck… "We have to go see if they're okay."

"But Tembi—"

"I already left one person on the ground today," she replied. "I'm not leaving another."

"Good for you," Bayle said, and gripped the back of Tembi's robes to keep her from jumping up and running towards the clearing. "But we're staying here until that other person leaves, okay?"

"Okay," Tembi agreed. "Can you ask the Deep to get help? There's got to be someone from the Council nearby."

"Yeah…" Bayle's head tilted to the side, and then she gasped. "The Deep says it can't. It's promised to keep this a secret."

Tembi swore again. "That means the other person is a Witch!"

"A powerful Witch," Bayle said, nodding. "But they just left."

"Jumped or walked?"

"Jumped." Bayle paused. "The Deep is really anxious about this. It's howling, and there's a terrible smell."

"That's not good," Tembi muttered. She could smell it her-self—sewage and rotting fish—and her body felt as if the Deep was trying to hold her in place. She began creeping towards the turn in the path. "Deep, ease off so I can move. We go this way?"

Her friend nodded.

The two of them kept low and moved as quietly as possible. They rounded the bend in the path and—

Nothing.

No body.

No popstick.

No villain.

"Um…" Bayle began, standing.

"Yeah." Tembi rose to her feet beside her. "Something isn't right. This feels like a—"

Something hit her.

She felt herself fall.

The nothing swallowed her whole.

---

look past
the stars
look past

Excerpt from "Notes from the Deep," 01 December 2714 CE

Chapter Twenty-Three

"Tembi!"

Her head was in open rebellion. She wondered what would happen if she opened her eyes—

—*blinding pain*—

—she closed her eyes again.

"Tembi!"

Bayle's voice. Whispering. Insistent.

"Tembi! Wake up!"

"No." Oh gods, just saying that word set the pounding in her head to a new level of pain.

"C'mon, Tembi, if you've got a concussion, you can't let yourself go to sleep." Bayle was shaking her now, very gently, but Tembi was sure her brain was leaking out her ears.

"I hate you," she said.

"Keep talking," Bayle answered. Tembi heard the rattle of metal doors opening and closing. "Where do you think we are?"

"Ask the Deep."

"I did. It's panicking. It wants to bring us both back to Lancaster but I don't want to move you yet." Another door slammed shut. "Where are the Medkits?!" A pop, followed by a small rush of displaced air. "Thank you, Deep."

Tembi heard the hiss of a nanopack as it was activated, and then a blessed burst of cold against her temples.

"Oh gods, yeah, that's a bad concussion," Bayle said as she read the nanopack's diagnostic display. "Lie still and let the 'bots work. And keep talking."

"That feels amazing," Tembi said.

"Good. I've got it cranked up as cold as it can go," Bayle said. "Will the cold hurt you?"

"No," Tembi said. She could practically feel the millions of submicroscopic 'bots knit the broken pieces of her head back together. "Where are we?"

"Give me a second," Bayle said, and fell silent as she spoke with the Deep. Then, quietly: "Oh."

"A ship bound for Sagittarius," Tembi guessed. "Using faster-than-light travel."

"How'd you know?"

"Seemed like the worst-case scenario." She opened her eyes. The pain wasn't as bad this time, but now Bayle was looming over her, her dark hair clumped with blood. "Oh, Bayle!"

"It's not mine," she said, and pointed to Tembi's head.

Tembi told her fingers to move. They responded, with complaints; she touched her head under the nanopack and found it sticky with blood. "How long have I been out?"

"I don't know. I just woke up." Bayle cocked her head, listening. "Stasis? We were in stasis?!"

Stasis with an open wound...

"Do you feel cold?" she asked Bayle. "Not counting the nanopack, does anything in the room feel cold to you?"

Bayle instantly understood what she meant. "No!"

Tembi tried to puzzle this through. If Bayle didn't feel cold, that meant the stasis field hadn't been antiseptic. Normal stasis fields weren't recommended for humans, and it definitely wasn't recommended for humans with serious injuries. It didn't suspend the body's condition; it merely slowed it down. The injuries would persist for as long as the person remained in stasis, and an open wound would be exposed to microbes, bacteria, viruses... These had a much faster lifespan than humans, and would replicate in spite of the stasis field. With the body's immune system slowed to a crawl...

She realized she had been lucky to wake up at all.

But she had, and she was here, and it was getting easier to think as the 'bots put her back together.

"Does the diagnostic say anything about infection or disease?" she asked Bayle.

The older girl had already been scrolling through the diagnostic. "Nothing serious," Bayle said. "Just the usual stuff. You're clear."

"Check yourself," Tembi said.

Bayle grabbed a second nanopack, and scooted across the room so the 'bots in her pack wouldn't conflict with the ones in Tembi's. She twisted the pack and it activated with another loud *hiss!* and set it against her lower arm so she could read its diagnostic. "I'm clear, too," she said.

Tembi stared at the ceiling. That made no sense. Not unless someone had gone to a lot of extra effort to...

...to what? She wasn't a doctor. All she knew was the channels said to never go into normal stasis if you could avoid it, because if you did, you'd turn into a giant raging plague monster. Maybe she shouldn't watch so much science fiction.

"The Deep wants to know if it can take us home," Bayle said. "It's frantic."

"I'm fine, Deep," Tembi assured it. "But we need to learn what's happening before you jump us. If we don't learn, this might happen again. Understand?"

A long pause, and then Bayle nodded. "It understands. It's not happy, but it understands."

Tembi was sure the Deep was curled up around her, singing its multidimensional heart out to try and make her feel better. She started humming, an old lullaby from Adhama. It had twelve verses about pear trees and golden rings, and by the time she was finished, the anxiety in the room had dropped away.

"Thank you," Bayle said. "It's quiet again."

Tembi's nanopack beeped. She sat up, very cautiously: her skull felt fine. Her fingers explored the area where her head wound had been, and found tender too-new skin that threatened to split open again.

She looked around the room. Painted metal, with stripes of plass to denote different spaces. Two bunks, placed near the ceiling; below these, desks and chairs, both fastened to the floor. The walls seemed to be made entirely of cabinets, and there were no loose objects. None at all. Even the mattresses on the bunks were strapped into place.

Oddly, several heavy plass coffee mugs had been strung together with twine and hung from a hook in the ceiling. They looked unused. Tembi reached out to poke them. The mugs dangled and clinked, like ordinary plass coffee mugs strung together with twine.

She had never been on a spaceship before. Was this normal?

Was *any* of this normal?

"What did you find in the cabinets?" she asked Bayle, as she (carefully) lowered herself to the metal floor.

"Not much," Bayle said. "Extra storage, mostly. Looks like this room isn't used."

"Okay." Walking didn't hurt. Turning her head didn't hurt. The 'bots had either fixed her or loaded her up with painkillers. She was hoping it was a full repair: she'd start hurting again if the painkillers wore off. "We've got to figure out what's going on."

"The Deep says it was told to put us aboard the ship."

Oh. *Oh.* That was information Tembi couldn't take standing up. She swung one of the chairs out on its rotator bar and sat down. "Can it say who gave it those instructions?"

"It doesn't want to," Bayle said. "No. Wait. It says it can't. It promised it would keep it a secret.

"It's starting to panic again," she added.

"Deep?" Tembi said. "Please let us talk. If we're in danger, I promise Bayle will ask you to jump us."

Bayle's eyes went wide.

"What?" Tembi asked.

"I've never jumped anyone besides myself," Bayle said quietly. "And we're on an FTL ship, so we're not in normal spacetime. I don't know if I can get us out of here."

Tembi closed her eyes. *Trapped,* she thought. *At least until the ship drops into normal space, but then we'll be in Sagittarius—*

"Have you told anyone else you can talk to the Deep, or can jump?" she asked Bayle.

The other girl shook her head. "You're still the only one who knows."

"All right. We're going to pretend to be trapped on this ship. Learn everything we can about who took us, and why. Then, once we've docked, we'll jump back to Lancaster."

Bayle started nodding. "We'll need some kind of evidence," she said. "Especially—"

"—especially if there's another Witch involved," Tembi finished for her. "One who's high enough at Lancaster to force the Deep to listen to them."

Bayle stared at the ceiling. "The Deep says it'll jump us if we ask," she said. "So whoever made it promise to ignore us didn't think we'd wake up before we dropped out of FTL."

"Or doesn't know you can talk to...Pepper."

"Pepper. Yes." Bayle walked over to the door and tried the latch. It was manual, not digital, and it turned easily in her hand. "Our good friend Pepper."

"Pepper?" Tembi asked aloud. "Can you please take the nano-packs back? We need to hide the fact we're Witches."

Bayle chuckled darkly as the nanopacks vanished. "None of this matters if this room is monitored."

"Whoever took us would have checked on us when we woke up," Tembi replied.

"I hope so. Let's get out of here," Bayle said. She opened one of the cabinets and took out a stack of folded Spacers' uniforms. They sifted through the gear until they found items in their size, and put the rest back in the storage cabinets.

"Pants," Bayle grumbled as she shifted the strange clothing around her legs until the seams were in their proper places. "Shoes are bad enough, but *pants!*"

They braided their hair into tight knots, and used spit and their robes to scrub the paint from their faces. Then, they stuffed their robes into an empty cabinet, and stared at each other.

"We look like little kids playing Spacer dress-up," Bayle said.

Tembi shrugged. "Same tricks as when we're thieving," she said. "No eye contact, no whispering or soft talk, no quick movements, and always be looking at something in your hands."

"Right." Bayle returned to one of the cabinets and took out two plass tablets. "Don't power them on," she warned. "They're probably networked."

They counted to ten, opened the door, and stepped into the corridor.

And realized they had no idea where to start.

"If we go somewhere public, like a mess hall, somebody might recognize us," Tembi said.

"I don't want to try doors at random," Bayle replied. "Especially if this is a small ship. There could be... Wait, let me ask Pepper..."

She paused, and then said, "Pepper says it can tell me if a room is occupied, and warn me if someone is coming towards us."

Tembi didn't much like the sound of that—the Deep was terrible at following instructions more complicated than *move this over there,* let alone focusing on a single task for more than sixty seconds—but they weren't in a position to be picky about their invisible friends. She nodded, and they moved down the corridor.

Like the cabin, the hallway was metal and plass, with no loose objects except for three silver balls on strings hanging from the ceiling at every junction. They reminded Tembi of the dangling coffee mugs, but she still had no idea what purpose they served. The halls themselves had exposed metal beams lining the walls, and these had been carefully rounded on the protruding edge, with small cutouts every dozen centimeters that reminded her of the handles on coffee mugs.

There was no one around them. Tembi had no reason to imagine the ship as small, but that was the impression she got from the size of the corridors and the lack of other people.

"Here," Bayle said, and moved to a door on their right. The latch was locked, but the Deep popped it open for them, and they ducked inside. It was another set of sleeping quarters, with the same layout as the first cabin, except this one had all the signs of residents. They searched the room, looking for anything of use, but quickly gave up and moved on.

They repeated this process a dozen times. All they found were personal cabins.

"We're getting nowhere," Bayle muttered as they searched the thirteenth cabin.

Tembi agreed. "We've got to find an office or something. Maybe if we leave the crew section?"

"There'll be more people around," Bayle said. "Or we can try to find a place to hide until the work shift ends."

Since they didn't know if the crew followed a day-night schedule or kept the same number of personnel on during all shifts, they decided against hiding. Instead, they found a lift and moved up a level.

They saw their first crewmember as they exited the lift, a broad-shouldered woman with tightly braided hair. She nodded to them and stepped on the lift without a word.

"Well, that's a good sign," Bayle said.

The ship gave a shuddering lurch, and a siren began screaming across the ship's sound system.

"Oh gods, please let that not be for us," Tembi breathed.

"The—*Pepper* says the first room is unlocked and unoccupied," Bayle said, and turned towards the door.

More people in Spacers' uniforms were starting to appear, most of them running. By the time Tembi and Bayle had reached the door, a dozen people had passed them.

And ignored them.

"This isn't good," Tembi said, as Bayle opened the door.

"Whatever's happening, they're not looking for two women," Bayle said, as they raced into the room and shut the door behind them. It was quieter in here; the alarms were in the hall outside.

"That's what I meant," Tembi said, as she waved her arms and tried to get the room lights to activate. The room was completely dark except for the red emergency light flashing overhead. "If they're not searching for us, something else is happening."

Bayle swore.

"Lights!" Tembi said. "Activate? Illumination?"

There was a sliding noise as Bayle groped around on the wall by the door. A click, and the lights turned on.

"That's quaint," Bayle muttered.

"Nothing is automated," Tembi said, as she turned to take in the room. It was messier than the crew quarters, with paper taped to the walls, and objects such as writing tools scattered across the tables and chairs. "Have you noticed?"

"Base model," Bayle said. "Whoever owns this ship didn't want to spend money on upgrades."

Tembi tried to open one of the cabinets. These, at least, were controlled by digital access; the door was locked. "Hey, Pepper?" she asked. "Would you mind?"

The cabinet slid open. There were paper files inside, dozens of them.

"Here we go," Tembi said.

Bayle joined her in sifting through the documents. Their training at Lancaster had made them experts in skimming the contents of shipping documents and bills of lading, and they raced through the files. A picture of the ship was coming together, and it wasn't pretty.

"This is a Sabenta ship," Bayle whispered. "That's why it's using an FTL drive. The Deep won't touch it."

They looked up at the emergency lights as the ship shuddered again.

"Are you sure you don't want to risk jumping out of here?" Tembi asked her friend.

Bayle's eyes were redder than normal, but she took a deep breath. "Not unless we have no choice."

Tembi nodded, and moved to another cabinet. This one contained personnel files: the crew of the Sabenta ship was small but diverse, numbering in the low hundreds. They weren't soldiers. Their files said they were diplomats, but…

She kept turning pages, searching for more information. There seemed to be a lot of blank spaces in these records.

"Something doesn't add up," she said to Bayle. "It says this is a diplomatic ship."

"Nope," Bayle said, without bothering to look up. "I'm from a family of diplomats. They always splurge on the upgrades, even if they have no resources for anything else. Showing off your credit convinces other people to give you more credit."

"But if it's not military, and it's not diplomatic…"

"Espionage," said a familiar voice behind them, as the sounds of the alarms grew louder.

Tembi and Bayle turned.

There, in the open doorway, stood Rabbit. He cocked his head, and asked, "Now, why are you aboard my ship?"

---

help me
help you
LISTEN
stonegirl
LISTEN

Excerpt from "Notes from the Deep," 16 July 3616 CE

Chapter Twenty-Four

Bayle stood and crossed the distance to him in three steps. They stared at each other for the space of a dozen heartbeats.

Then she punched him straight in the mouth.

"Oh!" Tembi gasped.

"Bayle!" Rabbit pressed his hand against his mouth and checked it for blood. His hand was wet and red. Bayle—the same gentle Bayle who couldn't last through a month of martial arts—had nearly knocked out one of his teeth.

"Why are *we* aboard *your* ship?" Bayle asked, and punched him again, this time in the stomach. "Maybe *you* should tell *us* why we're aboard your ship!"

"Crazy Witch!" Rabbit caught Bayle's next punch and sent her rolling across the room. "Don't make me stuff you in lockup!"

Bayle was up again; this time, she grabbed Rabbit by the throat. The plass-hard digital displays of her manicure dug into the delicate tissues of his gills.

He froze. "Bayle," he said, as calm as still water. "I know you're not an assassin. Why are you here?"

"We're *here*," she hissed, "because we woke up here! We were in stasis—Tembi was in normal stasis with an open head wound! So start talking, or I start squeezing."

The barrel of a popstick appeared over Rabbit's shoulder, pointed straight at Bayle's head.

Tembi had had enough. "Deep!" she shouted.

An unseen force grabbed Rabbit and Kalais—because *of course* the person holding the popstick *had* to be Kalais—and slammed them both into the ceiling at near-bonebreaking speeds. The Deep held the men against the ceiling, freezing them in place.

Tembi slammed the door shut and snatched the popstick off

the floor. It was so tempting to slam its round end against Kalais and unload the full charge into his—

"Talk," she said, as Bayle came over to stand next to her, arms crossed and furious.

"Can we do this later?" Rabbit asked. "We're about to be—"

The emergency light stopped flashing. In the hallway, the alarms stopped.

"—never mind," he said. "Can you let us down?"

"Deep? Put a little more pressure on, please." Bayle said.

The men grunted in discomfort.

"Why did you kidnap us?" Tembi asked, turning the popstick over in her hand. She had never held one before. The spiraling curves cut into its metal shaft made it feel almost alive, as if it was begging to be used.

"Tembi?" Kalais's voice was soft and measured. "We didn't know you were here. We didn't kidnap you."

"Like we should trust anything that comes out of your mouths," Bayle said. "You two *just happened* to bump into us, and you *just happened* to be...be...*compatible!* And you *just happened to also be a pair of spies!*"

Tembi closed her eyes against the reality that the chain of co-incidences over the past few months hadn't been coincidences at all.

"If it helps, Kal's a spy in training," Rabbit said, using his old grin.

"Give me the popstick," Bayle ordered, holding out her hand.

Tembi ignored her. "If we do believe you," she said to the men, "then why are we here? Somebody had to put us on your ship."

"Seems to me we're in a stalemate," Rabbit said. "You claim we kidnapped you, which I know isn't true, and you say you didn't jump aboard my ship, which I don't believe is true."

"You know neither of us can jump yet!" Tembi tried.

Rabbit shifted his attention to her. "Kid? I'm a spy, remember? Bayle's been jumping for the better part of a year."

A year... They've been watching us for a year! She wanted to cry.

"Then you know I've never jumped with another person," Bayle said, her voice like sharpened steel. "And if you know me at all, you'd know I'd never risk trying that for the first time aboard a ship traveling at FTL."

Rabbit and Kalais glanced at each other, then back to Bayle.

Rabbit nodded, very slowly. "Good point," he said. "But that doesn't mean you didn't get help from a more experienced Witch."

"Scheisse," Bayle muttered under her breath, and Tembi lowered the popstick.

Rabbit noticed. "Well, well, well," he said. "The Deep says there's another Witch involved, doesn't it?"

"Deep?" Tembi said aloud. "If they make any move to harm us, can you please slam them into the ceiling again?"

Bayle tilted her head as if listening, and then nodded.

"Thank you, Deep," Tembi said. "You can let them down now."

The Deep did, and it wasn't subtle about the process. The men came crashing to the floor. They picked themselves up, keeping a wary eye on Tembi and her popstick.

Tembi and Bayle put some distance between themselves and their exes, and watched as Rabbit settled himself on top of one of the metal tables. Kalais stood behind him, his body tensed like a coiled spring.

"Talk," Tembi said.

"It's an easy enough story," Rabbit said. "You already know it. We're working on behalf of the Sabenta, trying to enlist Lancaster's help in ending the war."

"Why us?" Bayle said.

"You're nobility, and Tembi's the Deep's favorite." Kalais was staring at Tembi, his dark eyes fixed on her face.

"You're nobility?" Tembi asked Bayle.

"Later," Bayle said quietly. Then, to Rabbit: "You gave up on us pretty easily."

He shrugged. "You weren't our principal objective," he replied. "You were a cover story and a secondary target. The first rule of espionage is never run a single job when you can run two."

"What was your principle objective?" Tembi asked.

Rabbit grinned at her but didn't answer.

"Fine," she said. "But you better start thinking about whether any senior Witches at Lancaster knew about your stupid secondary project, because if they do, it'll be easy for them to claim you planned to abduct us all along."

The speed at which the grin vanished from Rabbit's face was what finally convinced Tembi that he was telling the truth. "Oh gods," he said quietly. "It's a set-up."

"Why was the alarm going off?" Bayle asked.

"C'mon," Rabbit said. "We've got to get to the Deck." He hauled the heavy door to the records room open and began running.

"Why was the alarm going off?" Bayle shouted after him.

"We were under attack," Kalais replied. "We either escaped or they retreated."

"Who was attacking you?"

Neither of the men answered Bayle.

Without a better option, Tembi and Bayle followed them deeper into the ship. They were running, but everyone they passed seemed to be running too, or was busy in a task and didn't have the mental energy required to notice the four of them as they sprinted past.

The deeper they went, the more the ship felt…finished. This part of the ship fit into Tembi's expectations about star cruisers. There were 'bots, automation, all aspects brushed and polished to a gleaming shine. Several sections of the walls were also painted in peaceful patterns that Tembi recognized as typical of the Sabenta.

"*This* is what a diplomat's ship should look like," Bayle said, casting a practiced eye across the corridor as they ran. "I suppose this is the section they show off when they're trying to impress donors."

Oh, right. That. Tembi leaned over and asked, as quietly as she could without breaking stride: "You're a princess?"

"What? No, of course not!" Bayle said, the traces of a blush starting across her cheeks. "I'm just a lady."

"What does that mean?"

She gave a very unladylike snort. "It means my ancestors designed a game for the video channels about merpeople, got mind-bogglingly rich, and went off to live out their fantasies on their own planet."

"Um…" Tembi gave her friend a spectacular side-eyed glare. "That's not royalty."

Bayle shrugged as they took a sharp left turn down another corridor. "When you buy your own planet, you become your own royalty." She glanced over at Tembi and added, "It could be worse. Steven's ancestors were survivalists obsessed with dinosaurs."

Tembi shuddered, and touched the tip of an ear.

Three more turns, and they had caught up with Rabbit and Kalais. The men were standing with their heads together outside of a large plass door painted in more of those peaceful Sabenta designs, talking in quiet voices.

Rabbit glared at the two Witches as they pulled up to a stop. "His name is General Eichin, he doesn't have the time to deal with you, and if the alarms start again, you'll come with us, no argument. Got it?"

Tembi opened her mouth with a viper's swiftness, but Bayle placed a hand on her shoulder. "Got it."

Calm, Tembi reminded herself. *Stay calm.* Maybe letting the almost-princess talk to the general was the smart course of action.

Rabbit watched them both to see if Tembi was going to push back, and then opened the door to the Flight Deck.

Bayle nodded appreciatively; Tembi thought she might throw up.

At first glance, Tembi thought she was falling; then she couldn't understand why she wasn't. Every surface of the Deck was made of streaks of light, the floors, the walls, the ceiling, all of it cutting across her vision in stark bright lines. Here and there were people, apparently floating in space, waving their hands through holo-projections which (she assumed) controlled the ship. Others were standing in mid-air, talking.

She closed her eyes and entered the room. Anti-grav devices kicked on and stabilized around her, and she opened her eyes again.

The Deck was less of a headache once she was looking at it from the inside. There was more of an order to the streaks of light zooming around them, and it felt like…

Oh, she realized. *It's almost like the Deep.*

Good. That made it somewhat familiar. Not enough colors and not nearly enough music, but faster-than-light travel was definitely in the same family as the Deep.

One of the people examining a holoscreen stood and crooked a finger at Rabbit. Rabbit nodded, and then motioned Tembi and Bayle to lead the way.

The man was familiar. Tembi realized she had seen him talking with Domino at the party in the Pavilion. He was wearing a wrinkled, less-formal version of his dress uniform, and his face was sweaty. Not exactly what she had expected in her first close encounter with a general, but—

"I sent you to see what was breaking into the lockboxes in the Records room, and you return with two stowaways in stolen uniforms," he said. "And one of them has your weapon? Explain."

Rabbit gave the quick version of events, beginning with finding the Witches and ending with the likelihood that someone at Lancaster had moved Tembi and Bayle to the ship.

General Eichin had begun shaking his head about halfway through the explanation. "All right," he said to the Witches. "You've had your fun. They've managed to track you to my ship, so unless you want the deaths of every single Sabenta on your souls, get out of here."

"Sir, we cannot." Bayle was standing at her full height, fingers knotted together. She would have been a prim-and-proper princess from the storybook channels except for the Spacers' uniform. "Someone jumped us here, and we are not able to jump out on our own. We are too inexperienced, especially with your ship traveling at FTL. Please understand, it was not our intention to cause you such problems."

The general stared at Bayle. "Rabbit, what's this one's backstory?"

"Bayle Oliver, daughter of Lord Oliver, an Atlantean noble."

"The girl you were surveilling on Found," the general said. He turned aside. "Rabbit, come."

Rabbit and the general moved to the center of the bridge and began talking. Or, the general began talking, while Rabbit listened with the attention of someone who knows they have been caught doing serious wrong and are waiting to learn the conditions of their punishment.

"What do we do now?" Tembi whispered to Bayle.

"We wait," her friend replied, a small and peaceful smile fixed to her face.

They waited. Tembi watched. The dizzying views from the Deck were actually quite beautiful once you got used to them, almost like staring into an aquarium—

"Tembi?" Kalais said quietly.

"I don't want to hear anything out of you," she said.

"I want you to know, I really do care—"

"Are you really from a military family?" She pointed her stolen popstick at him so he was forced to move away from her. "How about the small town you grew up in? Was any of it true?"

"No, but—"

"Don't talk to me," Tembi snapped, and turned her back on him so she could keep watching the stars.

The general and Rabbit returned, with Rabbit looking slightly beaten.

"Witches," General Eichin said. The word had the sound of both a title and a curse. "Understand that my best-case scenario is that I throw you out an airlock and never get caught. That's where I am right now." He held up a hand before they could protest and plead for their lives. "As that's not something

I would do, I hope that tells you how excited I am about our options.

"Walk with me," he said, and left the Deck.

Tembi and Bayle followed, carefully: Kalais and Rabbit were just behind them, and after that comment about the airlock…

Tembi gripped her popstick and kept careful watch over her shoulder. If the general thought he was going to throw her and Bayle into space, she'd make sure their ex-boyfriends came with them.

The general began talking. "We were making progress," he said. "We were finally making progress! The *Moonstone* is carrying terms of use of the Deep from Lancaster. If the Sabenta and their allies agree to these terms, we'll be able to use the Deep on a conditional basis to move refugees to safe quarters.

"This is incredibly important to the Sabenta. We can move our families out of Sagittarius until the war is over. We can move thousands of people in an hour, instead of hundreds in a week."

Eichin stopped and turned to look at them. He seemed taller than physically possible, not with the hull of the ship curving over their heads. "With you aboard our ship, we stand to lose everything," he said. "When the Tower Council hears you're aboard, do you think they'll realize the error of their ways and start to help the Sabenta? At best, they'll think you're two willful, stupid girls who tried to chase their lovers across the galaxy.

"But I doubt it," he said, shaking his head. "Or even if they don't think we've abducted you, those sloths on the Tower Council who don't want to lift a finger will use this as a reason to stay out of the fighting. If they discover you on board, that's the excuse that'll be needed for the hard-liners in Lancaster to refuse any kind of assistance, even transporting refugees."

The alarms began to sound again. Overhead, the red lights burst into life.

"Gods take it all." The general shook his head. "Rabbit, with me. Kalais, put them somewhere out of the way. Make sure they get through this without so much as messing up their hair."

"Get through what?" Tembi asked.

General Eichin didn't reply as he turned and walked back in the direction of the Deck.

"Get through *what?!*" she shouted after the general. She would have started running after him, but the ship shuddered again, and she and Bayle were thrown to the floor.

Tembi lost her hold of the popstick. The weapon spun off down the hallway and lodged in a niche between the wall and a plass display of a map. She tried to scramble after it, but the ship lurched again and she felt herself slam against the wall.

A hand reached down. She grabbed it before she recognized that it belonged to Kalais; she pushed him away and went to help Bayle.

"Not now, okay?" he said to her, as he moved them both towards a smaller hallway running towards the ship's interior. "You can take it out on me later—I deserve it—but I've got to make sure you survive first."

"What's happening?" she snapped. The ship rocked from another impact, and she and Bayle staggered against the wall for support.

"I don't know," Kalais said, and paused. "But if I had to guess, the Saggs have found us again. We're under attack."

---

stonegirl
help
the painted woman
help
the painted woman
help

Excerpt from "Notes from the Deep," 18 July 4196 CE

Chapter Twenty-Five

"What are Saggs—*wait!*" Bayle said, trying to follow Kalais. It was close to impossible: he had his space legs and could walk in spite of the jolting of the ship around them, albeit unsteadily. Tembi and Bayle, however, kept careening off of the walls. "Wait! Do you mean the Sagittarius Armed Forces?"

"Yes!"

Tembi cracked her cheek against an exposed support beam. She gasped, and her head began throbbing again. The Deep grabbed her around the waist, and she and Bayle floated slowly towards the wall, where they slipped their hands into the openings in the support beams.

"Thank you," she whispered. The smell of a type of fresh fruit she couldn't recognize came and went in response.

"Over here." Kalais had reached a door. He tapped in a code on the panel, and it slid open. "C'mon," he said. "C'mon, hurry! There's anti-grav in here."

They pulled themselves along the exposed beams lining the hallway. Tembi was beginning to see how the ship was designed for this kind of abuse; the curved edge of the metal beams was easy to grip, and the smaller holes cut in the beams were placed regularly enough to be used as reliable handholds.

She looked up. The three silver balls on strings that hung over each intersection were dangling towards the right; she realized these were visual cues of the ship's orientation in emergencies.

The overhead lights began to flicker. Tembi and Bayle moved hand over hand along the beams, until Kalais grabbed them by their arms and hauled them into the room. There was a strange tugging sensation on Tembi's kneecaps as the Deep fought with the anti-grav stabilizers over her legs, but she shooed the Deep away so the anti-grav could lift her into the center of the room.

There were more silver balls on strings in here, and these were outside of the anti-grav field; as she watched, they whipped around in response to impacts she couldn't feel.

"This is why the Deck has anti-grav," she whispered to herself. "To hold the crew stable."

"What?" Kalais asked, glancing up from checking a report on a data device set into his uniform's sleeve.

Tembi pushed away from him and glided towards Bayle. There were other people around them. Not hiding, no, but they stared each other and flinched with each new noise, or withdrew into themselves when the ship twisted.

Bayle was speaking softly to a woman and her three children. "Hey, Tembi," she said. "This is the Lelain family. They're catching a ride back to Sagittarius on the…what ship is this again?"

"This's the *Moonstone*," said one of the children. She wasn't Earth-normal; her hair and eyebrows were feathery, and they trembled as she clung to her mother's arm. Her two siblings looked nothing like her; they both had heavily textured skin and lips, almost like the bark of an old tree.

An impact rocked the ship; everyone in the room made the kind of small worried noises that only come out when you aren't sure you'll ever get to make another one. The treelike siblings began to cry, and the mother pulled her children away to a quiet corner of the room.

"What do you want to bet that the ship is under attack because we're on it?" Bayle whispered to Tembi.

"I'm not taking that bet." Tembi looked around for a window or a viewscreen or…or *something!* Some connection to the outside world to let her see what was happening.

"Do you think they want to kill us?" There was almost no color in Bayle's face. As Tembi watched, the Deep began to repaint her cheek with the familiar long swirls of blue fronds.

"I think they want to capture the ship," Tembi said. "If whoever abducted us wanted us dead, they could have murdered us instead of jumping us here. If they catch us? Well, you heard the general. That ruins the possibility of a treaty between Lancaster and the Sabenta."

"But...." Bayle fidgeted, her hands turning over and over themselves. "But they can't catch us! Not if we're on a ship traveling at FTL speeds."

"Who told you that?" Kalais had overheard them. He drifted over gracefully, at home in the anti-grav. Tembi felt a flash of anger as she realized he had been feigning awkwardness when they used to go dancing. "Speed doesn't matter if you're using a lockship."

Tembi had to know. "What's a lockship?"

Kalais held up one hand in a fist. "This is the *Moonstone*," he said. He stretched out the fingers on his other hand. "And this is a lockship." His open hand wrapped around his fist, and clenched down so his two hands were locked together.

"Is that what's out there?" Bayle asked.

"Yeah," he said. "Those impacts you feel? That's not from any weapon. That's the lockship trying to drop down on top of us."

"When do you use a lockship?" Tembi asked. She was afraid she might already know the answer.

"When you want to take over another ship," he replied. "As soon as they lock on, they'll seal their hull to ours, cut through it, and enter."

"What happens then?" Bayle asked, her eyes moving towards the mother and her children.

"We'll try and hold them off," he said. "But we're not equipped for a siege. We don't have enough weapons. If they lock on, we'll be taken prisoner, or worse."

Another impact knocked the three silver balls into uneven orbits.

"Don't worry," he said, and almost sounded as if he meant it. "The Sabenta are the galaxy's best pilots. We'll be okay. Once we shake them again, they won't be able to find us again in FTL."

"Wait, what do you mean, shake them *again*?" Tembi asked.

He paused to make sure the mother and her children weren't close enough to overhear. "Well, that's the buggy thing," he said quietly. "Finding another ship while traveling at FTL is next to impossible. If that's really the lockship banging on us, they've done it twice."

"How?" Bayle asked.

He shook his head. "I don't know. New tech, maybe. A tracking system that moves in the FTL spectrum? We've been trying to develop that for our own lockships."

"A datasig?" Bayle said. "They could lock on to anything transmitting or receiving data on this ship."

"Bayle, come on. We're an espionage ship," he said. "Every datasig we need in order to operate is shielded, and we screen the *Moonstone* from fore to aft twice each twelve-hour cycle for unfamiliar datasigs that might be chatting with a third party."

Creeping dread was starting to curl up and make itself at home in Tembi's stomach. "When did the lockship show up?"

"Not too long before we found you."

The creeping dread tucked itself in for the rest of the night. "Oh no," she whispered. "Did we bring a datasig with us?"

Kalais recoiled as if she had unloaded a fully charged popstick into him. "Do either of you have an Identchip?"

"No!" Bayle said. "My people use databands, and mine's missing!"

"I don't, either. How do you screen a body for a datasig?" Tembi said, patting herself down. Bayle did the same, but they weren't in their own clothes, and unless the tracking device was hidden in their underwear, then— "What if they made us swallow it while we were asleep? Or injected it into us?"

"We have to get to a fully shielded room," Kalais said, as he darted through the air towards the door. "One that blocks all transmissions."

Tembi pushed forward until the anti-grav unit caught her movement and carried her towards the door. "Where?"

"There's a conference room one floor up from the Deck! General Eichin uses it for secure meetings."

Kalais hit the doorway and floated through the shield. The ship's gravity field caught him and he crashed against the floor, then was tossed into the air again as the full force of the lockship's attacks rocked the *Moonstone*.

"Deep!" Tembi shouted, as the ship's gravity field seized her and sent her careening towards a metal wall—

The Deep flowed around her, then swept back to catch Bayle and Kalais. The three (*Four? Yes, four.*) of them flew down the hallway, the humans grabbing hold of the exposed beams and using these to throw themselves forward.

It wasn't easy. Even wrapped in the Deep, the ship rocked around them. Easy grabs suddenly weren't; a handhold in close reach could twist away, faster than anything. Turn a corner, and a hallway that appeared to be empty could turn into a cyclone full of objects. Tembi and Bayle followed Kalais as closely as they could—

—*oh gods* her stupid manipulative joke of an ex-boyfriend had a *phenomenal* butt, shut up *shut up **shut up!*** This isn't the time for—

—and the Deep kept most of those objects from rocketing into them, but those objects still slowed them down, and—

"Oh!" Bayle cried out as she spotted a body tumbling across the hall. Tembi felt Bayle reach out through the Deep with the same kind of control that allowed them to yank a foam ball from midair and pull it to safety, and then her friend was cradling a strange man in one arm.

"Leave him!" Kalais shouted. "We don't have time for him!"

"Yes, we do!" Bayle yelled back, dragging the unconscious man along with her.

Tembi stopped, and saw her friend struggling with a man twice her size. "Deep!" she shouted, and pointed towards the nearest door. It flew open, revealing three worried faces. She didn't have time to process any more details than wide eyes and pink skin before the Deep tossed the body at them and slammed the door shut after it. "Thank you!"

"I've *got* to learn how to jump in FTL!" Bayle said, as she caught hold of a support beam and steadied herself through a powerful tremor.

Tembi didn't reply. That feeling of creeping dread hadn't left;

she was beginning to think there was only one way off of this ship in time—

Another impact shook the *Moonstone*. It was severe enough for metal to shriek in pain around them.

"Did they lock on?" Bayle shouted at Kalais, hands pressed against her ears.

Tembi stared at her. Something about her hands—

"Bayle!" Tembi gasped, as the answer finally hit her. "Your manicure!"

Her friend looked down at the tiny views of her homeworld. "Oh gods, Tembi!"

"Oh, come on—" Kalais began.

Tembi shut him down before he could say something about trivial concerns. "Bayle's manicure has its own datasig," she said.

Bayle's eyes moved between the two of them. "It doesn't come off," she said, her voice breaking. "And I can't shut it down."

Another impact; more metal screamed.

"I think they're about to lock on," Kalais said, staring towards the ceiling.

"We need to get off this ship," Tembi said to Bayle. "And we need to do it before the lockship latches on. If we don't, the Sabenta lose their treaty."

"Tembi—"

"You can do it," Tembi said. "You and the Deep. You can take us home."

Bayle stared at her, panicked tears falling. "Tembi, I can't jump us to Lancaster! It's too far, and I can't—"

"No." Tembi grabbed her friend's hands and held them so Bayle could see her manicure. "Not Lancaster. Take me to Atlantis. I want to see this view, from this window. And I want to see it *now*."

"Home," Bayle whispered. She closed her eyes. When she opened them again, the panic was gone. "Let's do this," she said, and wrapped her arms around Tembi.

They fell.

─────────────────────────

lost

Excerpt from "Notes from the Deep," 18 July 4196 CE

─────────────────────────

Chapter Twenty-Six

It was chaos. Bright, screaming chaos.

They tumbled across the Rails, moving in and out of space. Tembi and Bayle held each other as if their sanity depended on it. As the moments stretched out, longer and longer, Tembi realized that they were no closer to Atlantis, or Lancaster, or any escape from this nightmare—

"Deep!" Tembi shouted. *"Deep!"*

The Deep appeared. Scared. Wild. Twisting and tearing at them with its talons to slow their fall. Tembi felt the Deep grab her robes, cut into the meat of her legs, digging for some leverage that might—might—pull them out of this madness.

She didn't scream. If she screamed, she would lose control—

—and Bayle would lose control—

—and the Deep would lose control—

This is what happens to Witches who never come home, she realized.

"Bayle!"

No response. Bayle had her eyes squeezed shut in concentration, tears streaming across her cheeks.

"We all need to know how to stay calm within the storm," Tembi whispered, Matindi's words from years ago taking on entirely new meanings. But meditation? That was a tiny bandage on a gushing artery (*Why did that comparison come to mind?*) and they needed—

Tembi began to sing.

It was a quiet song. A sad song, with a glad message. Most of all, it was a folk song from Atlantis that Bayle had taught her late one night as they sat by the lake and watched the stars.

It was as old as her planet, Bayle had said. Possibly older.

The water is wide and I cannot cross over
And neither have I wings to fly
Build me a boat that can carry two
And both shall row
My friend and I...

Tembi felt a little weak; she laid her head against Bayle's chest. Bayle seemed to be breathing easier, and as Tembi began the second verse, her friend joined in:

As I look out across the sea
A bright horizon beckons me
And I am called to do my best
And be the most
That I can be...

The Deep calmed. Not enough to join in the song, but enough to pull them into itself.

Their fall slowed, stopped...

...and Bayle stepped off of the Rails, taking Tembi with her.

The smell of the sea, saltwater and wind; the calling of seabirds...

"Are we dead?" Tembi asked. She had the notion that she was lying face-down on a carpeted floor, but that couldn't be right. Not unless— "Wait. Are we there? Are we on Atlantis?"

"Yeah." There was a thump as Bayle rolled herself over. "Oh gods, we're home!"

Tembi sat up and looked around. They were in a large room, a bed with four posts and a canopy on a dais to one side, with various pieces of elegant wooden furniture placed throughout the rest of the space. The far wall was nothing but windows overlooking the ocean. Nearly everything that wasn't furniture was a rich, deep blue that was very much like the color of Bayle's eyes, but there was also a distressing amount of pink among the little-girl toys scattered here and there.

"Tembi!" Bayle had managed to pull herself upright. "You're bleeding!"

"What?" Tembi tried to stand and collapsed: the fabric of her Spacers' kit had been torn to shreds, and her legs were leaking blood across the floor.

"Oh," she groaned. "Oh, Deep." It hadn't hurt until she had seen the damage; now, nothing existed except those stripes of searing pain across her flesh.

Bayle staggered to her feet and walked to the open door on wobbly legs. "Hey!" she shouted. "Hey! We need some help in here!"

"No, I'm okay," Tembi said, gingerly poking at the new holes in her legs. "It looks worse than it is."

"I can't carry you," Bayle said, as she lowered herself to the floor. "So unless you want to walk…"

"You could jump us again," Tembi said.

Her friend glared at her, then collapsed flat on her back with a nervous giggle. "Oh gods, did this really happen?!"

"Yeah, we're wearing the proof," Tembi said. Her legs hurt, but there were footsteps in the hallway and voices calling Bayle's name. Soon, this would all be over.

Bayle sat up in panic. "We're wearing the proof! Tembi, the uniforms!"

"Scheisse!" Tembi tried to fumble with the clasps on the jacket, but gave up. The only way to hide the uniforms in time— "Deep! Get rid of the uniforms!"

There was a quick twisting sensation, and then the room was rather chilly.

"Um…" Bayle began.

Tembi shook her head in resignation.

"The Deep doesn't understand underwear, then?"

"No," Tembi replied. "No, it does not."

That was how Bayle's family maid found them: both of them naked, one of them bleeding from wounds across her legs, and laughing their fool heads off.

They were, of course, rushed straight to the hospital.

The next hour was spent catching up with the world.

Oh, and lying. Lots and lots of lying.

"Bayle found out she could jump, so I begged her to take me to see Matindi," Tembi said, as a technician pieced what remained of her skin together so the medical 'bots would have something to work with. "This is all my fault."

"It is *not* your fault, and that is *not* what happened!" Bayle said, all but crying. "I was showing Tembi I had learned how to jump, and she touched my hand at the wrong time. That's all."

Then they indulged in some hysterics, which they were both badly in need of anyhow. They finally stopped when the physicians recommended some sedatives to help them calm down, but the idea of being lost again? No. Neither of them wanted that.

Bayle's father, a tall and distinguished Atlantean nobleman with Bayle's blue eyes and thick black hair, had taken a seat by his daughter's bedside and refused to leave.

"Lord Oliver?" Tembi asked, once their hospital room was relatively calm and the 'bots were knitting her legs back into a patchworked whole. "How long have we been gone?"

"Please, call me Ollie," he said to Tembi.

"Uh…sir? I don't think I can—"

"Almost two months," he said absently, his eyes fixed on his daughter. "I thought I'd lost you, Minnow."

Tembi's stomach twisted, as if the Deep had jumped her without warning. "Two months?"

Lord Oliver nodded. "No one had any idea where you'd gone until Bayle's datasig appeared early this morning. We couldn't get a lock on it, and about an hour later it disappeared again. The two of you appearing in her bedroom?" He shook his head, his face showing the exhaustion he must have felt during the last few months. "We'd given up hope."

"We're back now, Daddy," Bayle said, as she hugged him.

"Two months…" Tembi's brain was squirming under the weight of a hundred different things that demanded attention all at once. She decided to go with the most important one. "Is Matindi all right?"

"Matindi is fine," said a voice from the doorway. "Completely scraping furious, but fine."

Matindi pushed aside the privacy curtains and entered the room. The green-skinned Witch was walking with the help of a cane, but otherwise looked the same as she had before she had been poisoned.

"Matindi!" Tembi nearly leapt from the bed, but a great weight pressed her arms against the mattress. "Um, Deep?"

"Oh, you aren't moving one centimeter, young lady," Matindi said. "Matthew has gone to get your mother, and then we are going to have a very long talk about the dangers of untrained self-teleportation."

"Matthew—" Yet another thing that demanded attention squirmed to the surface. "Matthew's been released?"

Matindi nodded. "They assaults didn't stop once he was arrested, so they couldn't hold him for cause."

That wasn't the most satisfying answer. Being released without cause wasn't the same thing as being found innocent, but Tembi had been lost in space for two months so she'd take what she could get.

"Who else has been poisoned?" she asked.

"Tembi?" Matindi said, as she finally reached the side of the bed and moved within hugging range. "Hush."

They spent five days in the hospital. The first two days were used to put Tembi's skin back together—difficult to injure apparently meant difficult to repair, as it took significantly less time to fix her severe concussion than the most minor cuts on her legs—and the next three days were devoted to doctors who examined them in the attempt to learn where they had been for the past two months.

Somewhere in the middle of that, they managed to get Matindi and Matthew alone, and they finally told them what had really happened.

Calls were made for confirmation. The *Moonstone* had arrived in dock as scheduled, with all hands accounted for. There were no reports that a lockship had tried to apprehend them, although the *Moonstone* was currently off-duty for unscheduled repairs.

"You're sure you weren't kidnapped?" Matthew asked (for the eleventh time).

"Yes." Tembi flexed her feet to feel the new skin on her legs twist around the old. It was an intensely creepy sensation. The doctors promised it would fade as her new skin hardened to match the rest of her, but for the time being she felt like a broken ceramic doll that had been glued back together.

"Well, not by the Sabenta," Bayle clarified. "But somebody kidnapped us."

Matindi was sitting in one of the hospital room's oversized chairs, her chin resting on the silver head of her cane. "The Deep confirms that a Witch was involved," she said. "And that it's promised to keep the identity of that Witch a secret."

"What does that mean?" Bayle asked. "That the Witch outranks you? That's, what? Ten Witches at most?"

"Five," Matthew said. "And four of them have been poisoned themselves. Domino is still in the hospital on Found."

"Who's the last one?"

"Williamson," Matindi said.

"The Librarian outranks you?" Bayle sounded incredulous.

"Of course he does," Matindi replied. "If you're thinking he's involved, rethink that. The Tower Council already sent three Witches to question him. He laughed, answered their questions, and then made them clean a bathroom."

"Ugh," Tembi winced, then asked, "What would it take to convince the Deep to listen to a Witch who doesn't outrank you?"

"A very good reason," Matthew said. "One that it can understand and remember."

"So what do we do now?" Tembi asked.

"*You*," Matindi said, pointing her cane at Tembi and Bayle, "do nothing. If there's a mad Witch jumping around, poisoning people and kidnapping little girls, Matthew and I don't want you anywhere near Lancaster."

"But—" Tembi began at the same time Bayle lifted an eyebrow and asked, coldly: "Little girls?"

"Look at it this way," Matthew said, as he helped Matindi to her feet. "Everyone else believes you're the only Witches who've returned after being lost along the Rails. We've told them you need some time to recover, which is only natural. If you come back now, they'll be suspicious."

Thus trapped, Tembi and Bayle spent the next two weeks on Atlantis. They tried to keep busy. Yoga and meditation for the first couple of days; learning more Atlantian folk songs the next. Bayle was happy to show off her homeworld: Atlantis was beautiful. Every place Bayle had taken her looked like something from the channels, with hillside villas and small towns carved up the sides of mountains. Everything in a town was in walking distance, and everywhere you went, you overlooked the sea. Except, of course, in those towns built at sea level; when you were there, you needed boats to glide through the canals cut into the stony feet of the mountains.

Bayle told Matindi she wanted to practice jumping with another person on her own world, where she felt safe. Soon after that, Leps came out to give them private lessons; several times she brought a jump teacher to help Bayle master the finer points of moving herself and another person through the Deep.

The first time Bayle jumped after their escape from the Sabenta spaceship, she moved less than a meter away, and was pale and shaking at the end of the short trip. The second time she jumped, it was across her bedroom. Then, across the great dining hall her family used for formal gatherings. Soon, Bayle was taking the two of them across Atlantis, and then up to the docking station on its moon, then over to a nearby orbiting space station…

"I think you've got this," Tembi told her, after Bayle had jumped them to yet another shoe store on a remote corner of her planet.

"It was such a traumatic experience," Bayle said, as she tried on a pair of tall black leather boots. "Best to practice and be completely sure before we try a long jump to Lancaster, don't you think?"

"But you don't even like shoes," Tembi offered weakly.

Bayle sniffed. "I don't like wearing shoes," she said. "There's a difference."

Tembi didn't mind, much. As the friend of an Atlantean noble lady, she was learning the planet was full of pleasant experiences just waiting to be had: shopping was only a small part of it. Dancing and parties at night, long days in the sun by the water… And the food? It leaned heavily on fish and crustaceans, but Bayle had proved that the trick to enjoying all forms of seafood was a sufficient quantity of butter.

It was a nice vacation. Except, deep down? Tembi knew that neither of them could afford the time for a vacation. She tried not to dwell on what might be happening at Lancaster, or out in Sagittarius. Or how the Deep was acting like a beaten dog in their dreams. Most of her time asleep was spent assuring the Deep that it wasn't its fault that she and Bayle had nearly gone missing along the Rails.

"You asked me to teach her how to sing," Tembi said, patting its downy feathers. "I thought that meant…well, I thought you meant communication. I didn't know you meant she needed to learn how to focus. It was a misunderstanding."

Nothing worked. The Deep would sigh and mope, and beg for forgiveness until Tembi could coax it into receiving another a belly rub.

(She was working her way up to asking it the question that was now living and breathing in the front of her mind: how had the Deep known—and known for months!—that Bayle would need to learn that particular definition of singing? Any decent answer to that question would probably leave her screaming, Tembi knew, but if the Deep could see through time as well as space, then… Yes. So much screaming. And too much happening in her brain for Tembi to calm down and relax. They had been gone for *two whole months,* gods take it all!)

Tembi was starting to feel stir-crazy when, nearly three weeks to the second after Bayle had dropped them onto the floor of her childhood bedroom, she surprised Tembi by announcing it was time to leave.

"Ready?" she asked.

"For what? Lunch?" Tembi was poking at her new soundkit and didn't bother to look up. She had thrown the one Kalais had given her for Solstice into the sea; its replacement had seemed like a good investment but performed like it was full of angry sand.

"Ready to go back to Lancaster," Bayle clarified.

"Oh? *Oh!*" Tembi leapt to her feet. "Really?"

"Matindi wouldn't allow the Deep to let us make the jump," Bayle sighed. "Not until we'd been grounded for three weeks."

Tembi flew around the room, packing. "And now?"

"The Deep says it can send for Matindi if we don't want to risk it ourselves."

Tembi laughed. When she slowed down to stuff her clothing into her bag, Bayle surprised her by dropping a small box of deep ocean blue onto the top of the pile.

"What's this?" Tembi asked, as she picked up the box and settled herself on the bed beside Bayle.

"A memento. You, me, and the Deep know what happened on the Rails," Bayle replied. "And we all know that we wouldn't have gotten back home without you."

Tembi opened the box. Six golden earrings sat on a pile of soft cloth, each one set with a stone that reflected all of the colors of the Deep.

"Atlantean opal," Bayle said. She was blushing. "Native to... well. The name speaks for itself."

"They're beautiful," Tembi said. "But you don't have to—"

"I did." Bayle shut her up with a hug. "This is something I had to do—I don't think we'll ever forget what happened on that jump, but I always want you to know how grateful I am."

Tembi didn't know how to reply to something that earnest and heartfelt, so she hugged Bayle back and thanked her. And then, without any difficulty whatsoever, Bayle wrapped them in the Deep and jumped them home to Lancaster.

painted woman
knows
painted woman
cares
NO

Excerpt from "Notes from the Deep," 16 July 3616 CE

Chapter Twenty-Seven

It was maddening how quickly life got back to normal. It reminded her of that first jump with Matindi, but instead of nobody noticing she had been gone for the afternoon, nobody seemed to care that she and Bayle had been gone for months. Well, no. Not exactly. They cared, but after a few days of "Welcome back!," life resumed its usual patterns. This was utterly infuriating—surely, *something* had changed!

But no. Every single little thing rolled on as it had before.

"Why," Tembi grumbled to Bayle and Steven over their first tumbarranchos since their return, "would someone kidnap us if nothing happened?"

Steven sighed theatrically. "Maybe they wanted nothing to happen," he said. "Maybe by getting you out of the way, they made sure nothing would happen."

"Some people love the status quo," Bayle added, nodding.

"Well, who did it, then?" Tembi glared at her meal as if it contained answers; when it refused to give them up, she set upon it with a knife and fork in revenge.

"Domino, obviously," Bayle replied.

"What? Domino?" Tembi shook her head. "She's the only poisoning victim still in the hospital. Matthew said she almost died! Why her?"

"I don't like her," Bayle said simply.

"That's fair," Steven said.

"You're not taking this seriously!" Tembi said, jabbing at Steven with her fork.

He parried it easily with a hand, the tines sliding harmlessly off of his scaly skin. "Tembi?" he said, his usual layers of humor stripped away. "I'm really glad you're both back home safely, but this is a job for the law. You ever think that sticking you in stasis for two months was a warning?"

Bayle was nodding. "Seriously, Tembi, think about it: they didn't kill us, but they could have. We were at their mercy for two months—it would've been easy! This was *definitely* a warning."

Tembi had to admit that they made a good point.

Her lessons were quieter. Their jump across the galaxy meant that Bayle could no longer pretend she was a poor student, and both she and Steven had been moved up to the next class. Two other students had come in to replace them. Tembi was still the youngest, but she was no longer the newest, and that made her unreasonably happy.

Her nights were spent studying, or talking to Matindi and Matthew at the kitchen table, or dancing. Her friends were right, she told herself. It had been a warning…

…and the poisonings were definitely a matter for the law…

…and she was only sixteen—no, wait. She was seventeen now. There had been a missed birthday while she was in stasis. She still needed to wrap her head around that. But seventeen was still young enough that age was a good excuse to keep from hunting down the person who had tried to murder Matindi…

…she didn't get much studying done.

And then, one night, it rained.

It *poured!* With *thunder* and *lightning!*

Severe weather was almost unheard-of on Found, so these rare and seldom storms became reasons for small celebrations. Matindi set up a fire cage in the common room and lit a small fire. Matthew jumped to Earth and returned with marshmallows, sweet crackers, and chocolate, and they showed Tembi how to blend these together in age-old alchemy. They played card games on the floor (Matthew was trying to teach the Deep how to play poker, which wasn't going well as the Deep didn't seem to understand why it couldn't just snatch the cards it needed out of the deck), and laughed about nothing, and went to bed early to snuggle under an extra layer of blankets.

Where Tembi stared at the ceiling and listened to the rain.

After two hours of wondering if she would ever sleep again, she threw back the covers, got dressed, and slipped out the window.

She expected to get drenched to the bone within seconds, but as she padded through the puddles, she realized the rain wasn't touching her. She looked up; the rain came within a few centimeters of her body and then vanished.

"Thanks, Deep," she said.

The smell of tumbarranchos, thick and hot, brushed against the edges of her mind.

"I think the store's closed," she told it.

The smell grew stronger. Slabs of fresh tomato and avocado, buried beneath layers of carved pork...

Her stomach roared in response. "All right," she said. "Won't hurt to check."

The hopper was running. Fifteen minutes later, she was walking through the streets of Hub. The city was hers—no one else was braving the rain, not even other Witches.

"Thanks for bringing me here," Tembi told the Deep, as the two of them leapt across a flooded street. She hadn't remembered to wear shoes, and she splashed through puddles and kicked up huge waves of water like a child. "This is fun!"

The smell of tumbarranchos roared back at her, too strong to ignore.

"I know, I know!"

Four more turns and a quick run up the street, and she was standing in front of the tumbarrancho shop. It was quite firmly closed, with the lights off and the chairs stacked on top of the tables. She wondered if the Deep understood, *I told you so.*

A scraping, shuffling noise came from a sheltered alcove tucked behind a large potted plant.

Tembi turned to find a human shape in a Spacers' kit crawling out from behind the plant.

Her heart leapt in her throat. The kidnapper? No, probably not. Any Witch who was skilled enough to drop two people into a ship moving at FLT speeds wouldn't be skulking in the bushes in the rain.

Maybe a homeless person? But outside? In this weather?

Maybe they were hurt.

"Hey," she called, and moved outside of easy grabbing range, just in case an old Marumaru trick for rolling sympathetic marks had finally made its way to Found. "Are you okay?"

"Tembi—"

Kalais's voice.

Kalais!

"I'm glad you're not dead," she said, and turned to leave. She found herself floating, the soles of her feet unable to make contact with the pavement. "Deep, no! I don't want to see him!"

"Tembi, it's not what you think." Her ex-boyfriend stood. "I need help."

"And lots of it, too!" she snapped at him.

"I deserve that," he said. "I deserve everything you can throw at me, but please, hear me out.

"The Deep wants you to listen," he added, playing his trump card.

She glared at him, then at her feet hovering just above a puddle. "Fine," she said. "But not here. Somewhere with other people around us."

"I don't—"

"I want witnesses, or I'm going back to Lancaster right now."

Kalais closed his eyes, and then pushed back the hood of his jacket. He ran his thumb along his jawline, where the band of silver-blue paint in whirling wind patterns began. These ran up his right cheek, stopping just below his eyebrow.

"Gods!" Tembi burst out laughing. "You must think I'm the biggest idiot!"

He dipped the sleeve of his jacket into the nearest puddle, then scrubbed at his cheek. The curls of silver-blue paint disappeared. As soon as he was done, these reappeared.

"What are you using?" she asked. "Cosmetic 'bots?"

He threw up his hands in frustration, and stepped from the shelter of the alcove into the downpour.

The rain stopped just above his clothing; too late, Tembi realized he was dry.

"I need help," he said again, his tone close to begging. "Please. Just hear me out."

"Oh, scheisse!" Tembi swore. "Fine. What do you want?"

"I need to get back to the *Moonstone*," he said. "I woke up in Hub a few hours ago—I have to get back!"

She shook her head. "No," she said. "Sorry. If the Deep's tagged you for a Witch, you've got to go to Lancaster.

"You'll be in my class," she realized, her heart cratering through the pavement. "Oh, Deep, what were you *thinking?!*"

"That it's tired of waiting on Lancaster to help the Sabenta!" he said, too loud. His voice dropped. "Listen, Tembi, please. This solves everything. If I'm a Witch, the Sabenta won't have to go through Lancaster. They can just use me instead."

Tembi buried her head in her hands. "That's not how it works," she said. "That's… That's how you get yourself and a ship full of people lost forever on the Rails. Trust me on this, okay?"

"I do trust you," he said. "You and the Deep. That's why I knew the Deep would bring you here if I waited. But this is too important. I've got to risk it—I've got to get back to the *Moonstone.* If you can't jump me, can you get Bayle?"

"Deep?" Tembi called. "Could you please bring Matindi here?"

"Tembi!"

"Shut up," she said. "I'm helping you because the Deep wants me to, and, yes, because maybe we'll be able to use you to help the Sabenta. But if you go back to your ship without any training, you're going to accidentally murder a whole lot of people."

"But—"

"I can't let you do that," she said, poking him in the center of his chest. "That'll be on my conscience forever."

"But the Deep chose me! It wants me to help—this isn't fair!"

"Well, what's fair isn't always what's ethical!" she snapped back, then shook her head. "Gods, now I'm turning into Matindi!"

Matindi. Tembi looked around. The green-skinned Witch should have been here by now. Even if she were sleeping, the Deep could wake her and have her by Tembi's side within moments.

The seconds stretched out into minutes. Tembi ignored Kalais as best she could, even when he tried to leave and found that his feet no longer touched the pavement.

Finally, Tembi gave in to the obvious. "Matindi's not coming," she told Kalais. "We'll have to go to Lancaster."

"No," he said, shaking his head. "If you won't help me get back to my ship, just let me go. I'll buy a ticket and get there myself."

"Nope," Tembi said, and started walking. She was able to hide her satisfaction at Kalais floating along behind her, as immobile as if his arms had been chained to his sides. He argued and swore, and pleaded, and asked as politely as he could. She kept walking, not bothering to look behind her.

Then, his voice fell to a low whisper. "Tembi—"

"Shut up."

"Tembi—"

"I said, shut—"

"Tembi, there's someone following us."

"Good one," she said.

"No!" he said. "Look!"

She gave an exaggerated sigh and turned.

There, standing halfway down the block, its features lost beneath the rain and the shadows, was a figure in black.

Tembi shook her head at Kalais. "How dumb do you think I am?" she asked, then started waving. "Hi, Rabbit! Glad you're not dead, too!"

A red light began to glow in the center of the dark figure's chest.

"Down!" shouted Kalais, as the Deep let him drop. He crashed into Tembi and brought her to the ground behind a large stone planter. The planter ate the bolt of red light, then boiled away into a pile of steaming molten lava on the sidewalk, each drop of rain sizzling as it landed.

"What—" Tembi began.

"Heat gun!" Kalais grabbed her hand, pulled her to her feet, and started running. "It's got a long recharge time, but if the beam hits you, you're dead!"

"Is this a *joke?!*"

"Do you want to risk it?"

She didn't; she stopped fighting him and began to run. "Deep!" she shouted, and turned them both towards the nearest building. She leapt and kept running, moving straight up the side of the building and hauling Kalais behind her.

Another splash of hot red light hit the sidewalk directly beneath them. The ground melted and puddled into a small crater.

"Gods!" Kalais said with a gasp, as the heat from the sidewalk reached them.

"Keep running!" Tembi shouted. "We're clear once we get to the roof!"

It was an office building, almost a skyscraper. The lights were off, the building empty; that was good. But the building was a flat, featureless slab of plass, with nowhere to take shelter.

They were completely exposed. That was bad. Very, very bad.

The heat gun fired again, then once again, crashing against the building in giant waves of heat. Huge round chunks appeared in the building's face, as if a giant had taken a hot spoon and carved rounded scoops out of a sheet of frozen cream. Both times the heat gun fired, a massive burst of heat roared up the building after them: the second time it happened, Kalais cried out in pain.

"C'mon!" Tembi shouted as he faltered. When he didn't move, she grabbed his arms with both of hers and pulled as hard as she could. The momentum propelled him up the side of the building: he moved—he *soared!*—with Tembi close on his heels.

When they reached the roof, she seized him by the cuffs of his pants and threw him forward. He flew across the rooftop garden, stopping only when he crashed into the top of a carambola tree.

Tembi reached him in a single giant leap across the rooftop. "Get up," she said. "We need to put some distance between us and that gun."

"My legs…" Kalais pulled up one of the legs on his Spacers' uniform. His boots were charred; the skin poking out above their tops was badly burnt. "It hurts to move."

"Scraping wonderful," Tembi said. She noticed the hem of her own robes was shorter by a good ten centimeters, and the soles of her feet were tender. If it wasn't for her skin, she'd be worse off than Kalais. "Deep? I need help."

Kalais began to levitate in the air again. "Oh no," he groaned.

"Oh yes," Tembi replied. She grabbed him by the hood of his jacket and began to run, bounding from rooftop to rooftop, flying across streets, feeling the rain sheet away from her body as she landed—

—she wasn't enjoying it, not exactly, but it was intensely therapeutic to haul a lying manipulative ex-boyfriend across a city. She *might* have *accidentally* banged him against a cornice or two—

—to finally touch down and skid to a stop on a flat roof, nearly a kilometer away from where they had first seen the figure with the heat gun. Tembi dropped to the plass roof, gasping for breath. Running with the Deep was exhilarating but not easy; her legs felt as if she had been sprinting across soft sand for hours.

"Are we safe?" she asked, panting. "What's the range on that gun?"

"Poor." Kalais was examining his legs. The unprotected skin on his shins had been crisped black and was beginning to blister. He pulled off his boots, took out a sonic knife, and began to cut the tops off of each boot. "It's not the range that we need to worry about—it's the tracking feature. Heat guns can lock on a target."

He gingerly slipped his feet back inside the boots. Now several centimeters shorter, they no longer touched the burned skin on his legs. "There. Now I can at least walk."

"Flip back and explain the tracking feature."

"Heat guns are stupid weapons." Kalais stood and began to move around the rooftop, slowly, as if expecting sudden pain. "Used only when you want to intimidate the survivors. Small radius but massive damage, long recharge time between bursts.

"They had to add a tracking feature to make them useful," he added. "Otherwise, an opponent would just have to wait for the first burst to discharge, then run and hide."

"You mean…like we just did?" A slow gnawing terror was starting to eat away at Tembi's stomach.

Kalais laughed. "Yeah, but the way we escaped? If they wanted to catch us, they'd have to be—"

"—a Witch," Tembi finished for him. "Get up."

"What? Why?"

"We need to get somewhere public." She moved to the side of the building and peered over the edge, cautiously. Was that a dark figure in the shadows across the street? The rain made it hard to see. "A hopper station? Where is that?"

He consulted the data device on the sleeve of his Spacers' uniform. "Three blocks south, one block west," he said. "But I don't want to go to Lancast—"

A noise, small but sudden.

Tembi hissed silence at Kalais, and turned towards the familiar *whump* sound of displaced air rushing away from a human body. The dark figure was there, a few meters away.

"Move!" Tembi grabbed Kalais and threw him towards the edge of the building. The Deep caught him, and they ran.

"It's a Witch?" Kalais peered over his shoulder.

Tembi nodded, unable to spare the energy for talking. They leapt to another rooftop, and then Tembi grabbed Kalais around the waist and jumped over the side of the building.

It was a ten-story drop, and every centimeter of the fall, she wondered if this would be the time when the Deep decided to abandon her again, to leave her alone to squish open on the sidewalk below—

—her mind lit up with a feeling of laughter, a taste of sweet cream and mangos—

"This isn't a *game!*" she shouted aloud, but in this moment…

…this one long moment…

…she could hear the Deep more clearly than ever before, more clearly than those snippets of humor or sadness that sometimes cut through the noise in her brain to reach her, more clearly than she could hear herself…

…and she knew the Deep was having *fun!*

She grabbed a window ledge and stopped her fall, then sent a command to the Deep to loop around Kalais and send him spinning back up into the air.

He landed beside her with a grunt and a gasp. She pulled him into the hollow of the window, hiding their bodies from anyone looking down.

"Tembi, c'mon!" he said. "We have to keep going!"

"Quiet," she said, staring up the side of the building to the roofline.

"Tembi!"

"Quiet!" she said again. "The Deep doesn't let its Witches get hurt. Not if it knows it can stop it."

"But—"

"Do you have any idea how hard I had to fight it to let me take martial arts?" Tembi fixed her eyes on where the shadowy figure's head would appear. "It's still beating itself up over cutting my legs, even though it did that while trying to save me. And it thinks it should've kept Matindi from being poisoned—it cries every night about that!

"But it loves games," she continued. "The Deep thinks this is a game, and if a heat gun is a stupid weapon to use on a Witch… Well, maybe this is all just a game.

"So I'm going to play."

"Um—"

"Shut up," she said.

A head peeked over the edge of the roof.

Tembi lashed out with the Deep—she grabbed the figure in her mind's eye and pulled.

It was easier than sending foam balls flying towards targets in the classroom. The figure was lifted up and over the edge, then sent hurtling across the street in a great sopping wet mess of cloth and rain, their robes pulling away from their face—

No! she thought to herself as they flew past. Then, as the events of the last few months came together: *Oh!*

The heat gun appeared in Tembi's hand. It was a short, squat, hideous thing that resembled a carnivore bred for killing. She asked the Deep to break it into a thousand pieces; the gun shattered into scraps of itself in the air, and she picked out the parts that were most likely its power cells and stuffed these into her pocket.

"Now," she said, "we go home."

---

stonegirl
listen
fireboy
listen

Excerpt from "Notes from the Deep," 16 July 3616 CE

Chapter Twenty-Eight

They reached the hopper station without further incident, and made it back to Lancaster without being shot down from the air. Not that Tembi was worried about that. Not anymore.

Kalais followed her to Matindi's house, as quiet and as obedient as a puppy. There was no more talk of getting back to his ship: he was in pain, yes, but Tembi thought that disarming their assailant had gone a long way towards proving the value of formal training as a Witch.

Matindi greeted them at the door with sleep-slow eyes: the Deep had finally woken her. She broke out a fresh Medkit and propped Kalais on the couch to treat his legs, and then shooed Tembi over to the kitchen table to interrogate her.

Tembi had no reason to lie; she told Matindi everything. Almost everything: she left out the part where the mysterious figure might no longer be mysterious. It had been raining, after all, a downpour in the dead of night. She wasn't completely sure about what she had seen. But the heat gun's power cells were unmistakably military in their origins, and when Matindi flipped on the local news channels, they learned an office building in the center of town had been destroyed by lightning.

They asked the Deep about that—the Deep *laughed*.

After that, she and Matindi sat, neither one of them talking. Matindi had her chamomile tea; Tembi abstained. They both kept sneaking glances at Kalais, waiting until they were reasonably sure he was asleep.

(He's a spy, they reminded each other in low voices, so let's play it safe for now.)

"I think," Matindi said, "that this young man will be more trouble than he's worth."

"No argument here," Tembi said. "I don't know what the Deep

was thinking."

"Me neither." Matindi shook her head. "But I stand by my belief that you're proof that the Deep is looking to change Lancaster. Maybe Kalais is more of the same—maybe the Deep wants us to fully commit to helping the Sabenta, and not just shuttle refuges out of harm's way."

"Maybe," Tembi said quietly.

"What's on your mind?"

"The Deep…" Tembi chose her words carefully. "Tonight? That's proof that the Deep is working with a Witch. I thought I was in real danger until I felt how much fun it was having. The Deep must… It must really trust that Witch."

Matindi nodded. "Or it trusted the Witch wouldn't hurt you."

"Same thing."

"Almost," Matindi said. She stood and ruffled Tembi's hair on her way to the sink. "Going to tell me who it was?"

Tembi laughed in the wild lilting way of the Deep, kissed Matindi on the cheek, and went to bed.

The Deep was waiting for her in the dream, leaping and bouncing across the featureless plane like an excited child. Fiery red diamonds scattered beneath it with each step.

"I know, I know," she said, as she buried its face in its silky fur. "You've been so good at keeping this a secret. Take me to him."

The two of them flew across the plane, colors bubbling out from the Deep. It sang, swooping and soaring in time with its own music.

Tembi, in no mood to join in its song tonight, stayed silent.

The Deep pulled itself to a stop and circled a small figure standing far below.

The figure waved.

The Deep landed and wrapped itself around him, chiming in happy pink and blue clouds.

"Moto." Tembi nodded at him from the back of the Deep. "How are you going to explain the building to Domino?"

"What building?" he asked, a grin playing around the edges of his mouth. "The one that was struck by lightning?"

"Someone could have been hurt." She dismounted and slid to the ground. Moto was shorter here in the dream, and barefoot. She didn't think she had ever seen him without shoes before. Even on the sparring mat, he wore cotton wraps over his feet.

The Deep said something in orange: judging by the smell of the color, it was not polite.

"Give me time," Moto told it. "She's confused. She doesn't know how long we've been planning this."

He turned back to Tembi. "I had to know if you could keep your head when it mattered," he said. "I'm sorry if we scared you."

"If?" Tembi snapped. *"If?!"*

Moto had the good sense to look embarrassed. "We had to know."

"Did Domino drop a building on you when you started working for her?"

"What?" The grin dropped from his face. "Domino? No, she's got nothing to do with this."

The Deep huffed and tiny silver sparks appeared around its talons.

"Humans can only successfully communicate one concept at a time," Moto told it. "You know that. I need to put events in order for her."

The sparks faded as the Deep sighed and shuffled around Tembi before flumping to the ground in a pile of feathery rainbows.

"To clarify," Mako said, as he rolled his eyes at the Deep, "Domino is one of the many reasons that the Deep sought us out, but she wasn't involved with what happened tonight."

That answer seemed to mollify the Deep; it began to purr.

It didn't mollify Tembi. Not at *all*. "A test," she said. "You took down a building because of a stupid *test?!*"

"Yes," he said. "More to hide the evidence of the test, but yes."

Tembi shook her head. She was dangerously close to shouting. Or worse. She realized her ears were plastered flat against her skull, and took several deep breaths until she could move them again.

"Why?" she asked. "Don't say you needed to test me. That's not enough."

"Yes, it is," he said. "If you hadn't beaten that man to a pulp in the alley? Then you'd be right.

"But you did." Moto stared at her, his smile gone. "We had to know if you'd break when it mattered. Do you have any idea what Domino is capable of? Burning a few holes in a building is nothing. If we're going against her, then we need to—"

"Wait!" Tembi threw up her hands. "Stop. Going against Domino?"

"Tembi, don't you get it? She's responsible for all of this." Moto took her by the shoulders. "She's the one who's been pushing Lancaster away from helping the Sabenta. And..." he paused and studied her face before adding, "She's the one who poisoned Matindi."

"But—" Her thoughts smushed up against each other and formed a disgusting, confusing mess. "But Domino's in the hospital!"

"Yes, because she thought she was immune to the toxin," he said. "She's Adhamantian—all she had to do is spread it on her hands and then touch you. Since her skin is—"

"Oh gods..." Tembi cut him off. "That night... The night Matindi was poisoned... Domino's hands were so cold!"

"Turns out that even Domino couldn't fight repeated exposure forever," he said. "Bioaccumulation finally got to her."

"The Deep wouldn't let her hurt anyone! Even herself!"

The purring stopped; Moto tilted his head to listen. "The Deep isn't sure what the difference is between hand lotion and poison. It says humans are always grooming themselves," he said. "And it didn't realize what was happening before it was too late.

"I didn't, either," he said. "Domino does her own dirty work."

This was too much for Tembi. She turned away from him and slumped against the Deep. "I don't want to do this here," she said, shaping each word as carefully as she could; she was dangerously close to crying. "Somewhere else. I want to—I need to be somewhere real!"

Moto fell silent, then nodded. "Deep?"

Space twisted around them.

"Oh!" Tembi found herself fully dressed in a set of rough tan robes she knew she didn't own, and standing in the center of a street in Marumaru. The sun was setting; a woman with a cart full of shopping swerved to avoid colliding with Tembi, and said something exceptionally unkind. Tembi darted off to an empty spot on the sidewalk. A moment later, Moto appeared beside her, wearing a set of tan robes identical to hers.

"Is this still part of the dream?" she asked him.

"You tell me." He was staring at his bare feet and wiggling his toes.

Tembi shut her eyes. Voices, everywhere: happy, sad, arguing, laughing, loving... Behind these, the presence of the Deep, watching over them.

"It's not," she decided. "We're here. We're home."

"Yeah," Moto said. "Well, you're home. I grew up about seven hundred klicks to the west."

Home.

All of the sights and smells of home, all of the quarrels and the smiling faces, all of the noise, all of the music, all of the streets scoured down to their bones by storms.

But...not home. Not anymore.

The Deep bumped against the edges of her mind, trying to comfort her. She realized it was getting easier to sense its presence. In fact, all night she'd been able to feel it more clearly than ever before.

"It'll be another few years before you can hear everything it says," Moto said. "But more will start to come to you."

"How'd you know what I was thinking?"

"Because I was you," he said. "Seven or eight years ago? I was in the same place. Trying to make sense of something more powerful than I'll ever be, but it *needed* me.

"That's why you're here," he added. "It needs us."

"Because of the Sabenta?" She stepped aside to let a handful of children race by, their worn robes causing something of a twinge in her throat. "Lancaster is finally paying attention to the Sabenta, and Kalais…? I guess Kalais is right. If he's a Witch, Matindi and Matthew can use that as proof that the Deep wants us to get involved. Not just in helping the refugees, but shutting down the camps!"

Her heart lifted. Not much, but enough. She had been thinking about Kalais becoming a Witch from the wrong side of things. The selfish side of things. On the other side was a range of options—good ones—where people would be helped instead of—

Moto interrupted her train of thought. "Not the Sabenta," he said. "The Deep says something is coming. Something…"

"Something what?"

He stopped walking so he could meet her eyes. "Something dangerous," he said. "Something that makes bringing down a building…" he paused and tilted his head again. "The Deep keeps talking about ants building bridges.

"C'mon," he said, and leapt into the air.

Gasps from the crowd as Moto soared above their heads.

Tembi waved at them, and followed.

The two of them bounded across the rooftops of Marumaru. Tembi was more careful than she was when she ran the rooftops in Hub: gardens and water cisterns here were for survival, not decoration or vanity, and she wasn't about to damage them if she could avoid it.

The Deep heard her, and lifted her up. Her bare feet alighted on the buildings, a light *tap!* and she was up again, higher than ever before. It wasn't flying, but oh, so near!

From up here, there was a beauty to her city that she had never appreciated on the ground. The city was a patchwork of colored cubes, stacked into mountains. Small townships like those on Atlantis, but where those mountains were made of earth drawn from the seas, these were designed and assembled.

The sky was clear; sunset was coming, and red was working

its way into the reflections in the plass windows and on the unpainted metal. Clean clothing flapped on the lines, and the mingled smells of dinner cooking rose from a thousand kitchens.

Moto led her across Marumaru, higher and higher, moving up the shipping container mountains. Far below, children cheered and ran after them, trying to keep pace with the Witches soaring in the evening sky.

Tembi grinned.

Then, she recognized her family's old street, well-worn but clean.

Her family's old home.

So small.

Moto landed on its roof. She dropped lightly beside him and looked around. It was so small! Her entire childhood home would have fit inside Matindi's common room. Whoever had purchased it from her mother hadn't upgraded the old weather cage; she saw a dent in the cage generator where she had accidentally smacked it with a chair. But the garden seemed to be thriving, with new plants growing in the dirt she and her sisters had hoisted up with buckets and an old anti-grav sled they had stolen from the loading docks of a grocery store up in Blue.

"Any regrets?" he asked.

She touched the leaf of a pepper plant; she couldn't feel it, but the leaf bruised beneath her fingers. "Some," she said. "And none."

He sat on the edge of her old house, his legs dangling over the side. The fall down that side of the stack was sheer and probably lethal; Tembi could still hear her mother yelling at her to stay back, curse it all, don't you have any sense?!

"What's coming?" she asked.

"I don't know," he said. "But the Deep needs us to fight."

"Is it worse than what's happening to the Sabenta?"

"Yes, but it's connected to the conflict in Sagittarius…" Moto's voice was barely there, as if he was worried someone might overhear. "I think that's why the Deep has been pushing Lancaster to get involved."

The idea that the Deep could see through time wanted out! *out!* ***out!*** of her head (*Did someone hide us in the Deep for two months, or…or…were we moved forward?*) but Tembi wasn't ready to let it run free. Not yet. Instead, it was easier to ask, "How long has it known that something worse is coming?"

"I don't know," he said. "Long enough to start making plans."

"Poor Deep," Tembi sighed. "Planning is so hard for it."

"No kidding," Moto said, nodding. "It doesn't understand consequences too well, either. You're not the only one it chose as a little kid," he said. "You're just the one who got caught."

"What?" Tembi sat and gawped at him like a dying fish "Who?! You?!"

"Yup," Moto nodded. "Woke up on a starship when I was eleven. The Witch stationed there knew exactly what had happened—she's great, by the way, you'll love her—and she helped me hide until I was eighteen."

That was…

…um…

…she stared at the streets of Marumaru, unblinking.

Moto seemed to accept she needed a moment to herself, and sat silently beside her, watching the sun go down.

"Why us?" she finally managed to ask. "Why take people from Adhama?"

"The Deep probably heard that Witches were too thin-skinned and took it literally," Moto said, then cracked a smile. "I don't know. I'd guess it has something to do with Domino."

"Not everybody's like her, though," he added. He was staring at his toes as he wiggled them again. The gesture made him seem younger and quite adorable. "There're tons of Witches out there who don't like how Lancaster manages the Deep. They put in their time and retire, or get posted to remote stations where they won't be bothered. I think we have more allies than we know."

A rush of light colors and the smell of unprotected electronics flooded Tembi's mind.

"I don't know what that means," she told the Deep, and the sensations disappeared in the taste of cold metal. "I don't know what any of that means."

"It means the Deep wants us to recruit allies," Moto said. "No, wait. Warriors?"

"I must be hearing that wrong." He shook his head. "It says we'll need the princess. Is that Bayle?"

"Probably," she said. A blue the color of Bayle's eyes rested against the setting sun before it disappeared, and she felt the Deep bump against her legs. "Definitely."

"And the...rogue? Criminal-not-criminal?" Moto shook his head. "The word doesn't translate from Deep to Basic."

"Yes, it does," Tembi shook her head in resignation. "Why do we need Kalais?"

"Oh, the word is spy," Moto said. "The Deep says we'll need someone with his skills, and he was compatible as a Witch."

"Compatible? *Him?!*"

"Well, yes," Moto said, as he stared up at the sky. "The Deep says he's got a broken heart."

Tembi groaned and fell backwards to sprawl flat on the roof with a heavy *thump!*

"You don't have to like him," Moto said. "Can you trust him enough to work with him?"

"Yeah," she replied. "If our alliance helps the Sabenta? Yeah, I can trust him with that."

The stars were beginning to come out, little flecks of bright within the purple sky. Soon, there'd be bats, and wingbuds, and all the other night creatures of Adhama that were precious and familiar.

"Hey?"

A quiet voice, soft and timid. Tembi leaned to her left and peered over the roof to see a little boy's face staring up at her. He was seven, maybe eight, with wide eyes and something of a scowl.

"Hey," she replied.

As soon as the little boy was sure the noises on his rooftop weren't caused by monsters, he turned fierce. "Get off of my house!" he shouted.

"I used to live here!" Tembi said.

The little boy reached inside the door and came out with a sharp metal bar. "Get off of my house!" he said again, as he started for the ladder.

Tembi glanced over at Moto: he was laughing.

"Fine," Tembi said with a sigh, as she and Moto launched themselves into the night sky, the boy staring after them.

---

stonegirl come
translate
fight
hurry
hurry hurry hurry

Excerpt from "Notes from the Deep," 25 September 3468 CE

Chapter Twenty-Nine

On the day Domino was released from the hospital, Tembi was waiting. She had dressed in her best robes, the black ones with the gold trim, and wore the scarf which matched her golden birds to hold back her hair. She stopped at the edge of the crowd—for there was a crowd, mostly reporters for the channels, there to question Lancaster's voice to the Earth Assembly about her health and the would-be assassin who, for some odd reason, hadn't managed to kill anyone—and began to speak.

For a woman who had recently been on the brink of death, Domino appeared hale and hearty. She wore her usual prismatic robes beneath her waterfall of rainbow hair, and she had painted her lips in silver. She walked with the help of a cane; when Tembi saw this, she felt cold fury at what had happened to Matindi all over again.

Moto was here. He nodded and smiled to Tembi, exactly as he would have if she was still nothing more than a little girl from his homeworld whom he had taught to spar.

"She'll try to recruit you," Moto had said the night before in the Deep's dream. "Let her, but don't make it easy for her."

Tembi had nodded, and wrapped the Deep around her like a warm blanket.

She felt the Deep clearly today, pacing around her, wings and tail whipping back and forth. "Calm," she whispered to it. "I'm fine, Moto is fine, and I'm going to be working with this woman for a long time. She's one of your Witches, so you *know* there's something good in her. We will put things right."

The Deep settled around her legs, muttering to itself.

Domino stopped at the top of the stairs leading from the hospital to the greenway below. It was intentional—all of this was intentional—as Domino could have easily jumped herself to

Lancaster Tower without having to deal with the media.

"Good afternoon," she said. "Thank you for your concern. I feel quite well, and my physicians expect me to make a full recovery."

Questions then, shouted out by the journalists. Domino appeared to know most of them and called upon them by name. The questions ranged across all topics from trade to treaty violations, but the journalists kept returning to the matter of the Sabenta.

"I would like to make a statement on the Sabenta," Domino finally said. This was greeted by chatter among the journalists, and the refocusing of a dozen different kinds of recording devices. "Since the time of our institution's founding, it has been Lancaster's policy to stay out of all conflict scenarios. This was done at the request of the Deep, and also because we felt it was impossible to make an objective determination of which parties held the moral high ground during war.

"However," she continued, long hair floating behind her as if the Deep was on the move. "The situation with the Sabenta was severe enough to cause the Deep distress. We were taking steps to aid in the relocation of Sabenta refugees when the Deep chose a new Witch, a young soldier named Kalais.

"The Deep has never before chosen a soldier to become a Witch," Domino said. "Never. The Deep always chooses younger persons, but out of the thousands of Witches in the galaxy, not one has ever had any military experience. After lengthy discussion with the Deep, we have concluded that it found Lancaster's inaction in this matter to be the wrong course of action.

"I will be presenting these findings in person to the Earth Assembly," she said. Her gaze turned to Tembi as she spoke; Tembi felt that Domino was speaking directly to her. "And will petition the Assembly to consider immediate action to stop the conflict in Sagittarius."

Aggressive chatter from the journalists.

Domino ended the press conference, but stayed to talk with some of the reporters. Tembi was near enough to hear her quiet laughter, to hear her say, "Off the record, off the record," over and over again.

When it was over and the crowd had dispersed, Domino crooked a finger at Tembi. The girl rose from her seat on the hospital stairs, and walked over to meet the mountain-tall Witch.

"Moto?" Domino said. "I wish to walk alone with Tembi."

Moto nodded and fell back several dozen meters, out of earshot but close enough to jump to Domino's defense should the situation arise.

"You don't actually need a bodyguard, do you?" Tembi asked.

Domino gave the slightest of nods, and began to walk towards the hospital's gardens.

Tembi stepped around Domino and put herself directly in the tall Witch's path. "I know you poisoned Matindi," she said, chin and ears high.

Domino's silver lips twisted up at their corners. Not a smile, no, but perhaps a second cousin to a smile. "Are you here to challenge me, little sister?"

"No," Tembi said. "I'm here to learn why."

That answer took Domino by surprise. She cocked her head at Tembi. "Oh?"

"Matindi says you're fair," Tembi said. "No matter what, you're always fair. Which means you had a reason to try and kill her, and all the others."

"Child," Domino said, as she resumed her walk along the garden path, "I never tried to kill them."

Tembi and Moto had already guessed at this part of it, but she had thought it was important to hear it from Domino. Confirmation and diligence were their new watchwords. "What?" she asked. "Really? But—"

"They are my friends, my colleagues…" Domino paused to move an injured sun moth from a patch of shade onto the branch of a nearby tree. "…I'd never forgive myself if I truly hurt them."

"They weren't sure Matindi would be able to wake up." Off-script, but Tembi needed to know the answer.

"It was a plant-based toxin," Domino said, as she resumed her slow, precise walk along the path. "It reacted poorly with her genome. It was a consequence I should have foreseen and prevented."

"Aren't you sorry?"

Domino glanced down at her. "No," she said. "Matindi lived, and for a time it prevented Lancaster from joining the Sabenta."

"Each time there was a poisoning, it slowed down the Tower Council," Tembi realized.

The tall woman nodded. "Small delays are more effective than large ones," Domino said. "A single large delay forces those involved to make contingency plans. Small delays result in small, seemingly manageable changes. Over time, small delays become cumulative, and no one has noticed."

"That's smart," Tembi said. "Did Moto help?"

"Why would he?" Domino said. "Here is my advice to you, little sister—if something must be done that will cause pain, do it yourself, and accept the burden."

Out of the corner of her eye, Tembi stared at Domino's face. The woman's skin was flawless, and harder than stone. Maybe harder than steel.

"Did you abduct us? Me and Bayle?" she asked.

Domino twisted her lips twisted into the tiny smile of a teacher who is especially proud of a student who's figured out a difficult problem, but is nevertheless picky about the methods used to express the solution. "Yes."

It was another mystery that Tembi had figured out. Well, Bayle had figured it out—Bayle had jumped them back to Atlantis, and the two of them had walked through the streets of her hometown as Tembi told her about Moto and Kalais and the rain and the heat gun and the building and Domino and…

…and everything…

…and Bayle had gone silent, and then asked if Moto had been the one to stick them into stasis for two months, because if *he* hadn't, then…

"…you put us in stasis," Tembi said slowly, her hands pressed flat against her robes so she wouldn't do anything stupid, such as try to slap that tiny smile off of Domino's face. "For two months? How did you hide us for two months?"

Domino kept walking, and that tiny smile grew a little bigger.

Tembi tried another approach. "It was another delaying tactic, wasn't it? If we were caught on their ship and accused them of abducting us? It would slow down the Council's decision to become involved with the Sabenta."

"And it would also send a message to the Sabenta, "Domino clarified. "They kept pushing for more. They wouldn't have been satisfied with the relocation of refugees—they would have wanted our help with every aspect of their movement.

"Never do anything for one purpose, Tembi," she added. "Always be running two games at once."

Tembi heard herself gasp. "You were a spy," she realized. "Lancaster's spy—Lancaster has *spies?!*"

"Of course," Domino said. "What kind of job did you think I wanted you to do?"

Hands flat, Tembi reminded herself. *Chin up. Ears high.*

"I thought you needed someone to take Moto's place," she said, and reminded herself it was fine if her voice was a little weak. She was seventeen, and *oh!* the games this woman played were so far out of her league—

"Moto doesn't have the patience for espionage," Domino said. "He burns too strong, bless his heart. I need someone with a cool head. Someone who sees the logic in doing what must be done, even if the methods disturb her."

"You still want me to work for you?"

"Of course," Domino said again. "If it's of any consolation, this work gets easier over time." She glided over to a mossy garden bench in the shade of a bottle tree and sat, patting the bench beside her.

Tembi tucked her robes behind her legs and joined her, keeping a suspicious eye on Domino. "Why do you do this?" she asked. "This…work."

"Because someone has to," Domino said. "The galaxy isn't fair. People like me? They try to make sure there's a balance between what happens, and what needs to happen."

"Okay," Tembi said, very slowly, as if tasting the edges of the word. "But how is any of what you did fair to the Sabenta?"

"It's not," Domino said gently. "It's fair to Lancaster. What I did was to preserve our laws, not theirs. I know it's unpleasant, but I'm but merely one woman. I represent Lancaster's interests as best as I can.

"If it makes you feel better," she added, as she pushed a stray lock of rainbow hair behind her ear, "the Tower Council has now committed our resources to helping the Sabenta. So, now? I work on their behalf as well, and I will fight for them to the best of my ability."

"If you put your mind to it, you could probably end the war for them this scraping afternoon," Tembi muttered to herself.

Domino's ears twitched, and she very nearly smiled. "I know it's complicated," she said. "Look at it this way—Lancaster is an institution that must be protected, sometimes from itself. Change is necessary, but not always for the best. I don't agree with the Council's decision to help the Sabenta, but what I want doesn't matter.

"Our traditions are everything," Domino said. "The rule to keep the Deep from being used in war was valuable—a core of our institution. And now? That's gone. Each war will have to be weighed on a case-by-case basis, to see if it is worth our intervention, because…"

Domino trailed off, waiting, her eyes tracking every move of Tembi's face.

"…because they'll all be worth it," Tembi finished for her. "We'll have good reasons to get involved in all of them. At least, to some degree."

"Very good," Domino said. "Yes. You understand, then. There will always be wars."

"Yes," Tembi said, her chin and ears high. "There will."

they come
mother father
not far

Excerpt from "Notes from the Deep," 10 July 4402 CE

Acknowledgements

Thank you for coming along on Tembi's first journey into the Deep. Supply chains are one of the most important innovations in history, but we take them for granted. We can't help it: we're the kind of creatures who will, no matter how far we travel, always remember the sharks and dinosaurs, and quickly forget about the chickens. Now, Tembi has to navigate a war, where the mundane details of transportation can save (or destroy) civilizations. I hope you get the chance to come along for her journey. She'll be a little older, a little wiser, and able to hear the Deep, and none of this will prepare her for what's about to come.

Brown, you put up with my nonsense and give so much good in return. As always, know that I love you and that I'm lucky to have you as my husband.

This book couldn't have been written without help. Thanks to Seanan, Tiff, Kevin, Fuzz, Gary, Cora, Sara, and especially Sigrid. I couldn't have poked this world into shape without you.

Thanks also to John Rogers, who knows exactly why spaceships need coffee mugs on strings, and to Danny and Jes for the copy edits!

And good wishes to Iolanthe!

About the Author

K.B. Spangler lives in North Carolina with her husband and two awful yet wonderful dogs. They live in the decaying house of a famous dead poet. She is the author and artist of the webcomic *A Girl and Her Fed*, and numerous novels and short stories. All projects include themes of privacy, politics, technology, civil liberties, the human experience, and how the lines between these blur like the dickens. Additional information on Tembi's world, as well as other projects and stories, can be found at kbspangler.com, and on Twitter at @kbspangler.

Made in the USA
Columbia, SC
26 June 2021

41023365R10146